ONLY
FRIENDS

ONLY FRIENDS

⟫ A NOVEL ⟪

Lydia San Andres

PRIMERO
SUEÑO PRESS
—
ATRIA

New York Amsterdam/Antwerp London
Toronto Sydney/Melbourne New Delhi

PRIMERO
SUEÑO PRESS

ATRIA

An Imprint of Simon & Schuster, LLC
1230 Avenue of the Americas
New York, NY 10020

First Primero Sueño Press/Atria Paperback edition February 2026

PRIMERO SUEÑO PRESS / ATRIA PAPERBACK and colophon are registered trademarks of Simon & Schuster, LLC

For information about special discounts for bulk purchases, please contact Simon & Schuster Special Sales at 1-866-506-1949 or business@simonandschuster.com.

The Simon & Schuster Speakers Bureau can bring authors to your live event. For more information or to book an event, contact the Simon & Schuster Speakers Bureau at 1-866-248-3049 or visit our website at www.simonspeakers.com.

Interior design by Esther Paradelo

Manufactured in the United States of America

1   3   5   7   9   10   8   6   4   2

Library of Congress Cataloging-in-Publication Data has been applied for.

ISBN 978-1-6680-9806-6
ISBN 978-1-6680-9807-3 (ebook)

Let's stay in touch! Scan here to get book recommendations, exclusive offers, and more delivered to your inbox.

To all my fellow hot messes.
No matter how much you pivot and procrastinate,
I hope you always get your screenplays done in the end.

1

INT. A MESSY MANHATTAN APARTMENT—DAY

We SWEEP over an orange couch lit with
brightening morning light, revealing a
collection of crumpled tissues and empty
pints of ice cream, until we reach a pair of
hands scribbling LIAR in marker on the cover
of a romance novel, then melodramatically
tossing the paperback across the room. We
PULL BACK to see the owner of the hands—she's
Latina, in pajamas and a fuzzy robe, the
mascara smeared under her eyes evidence of an
all-night crying session. This is MARIA, 26.

> MARIA (into her phone)
> I'm done dating. Forever. And I'm going
> to tell you exactly why, because everyone
> loves ten minutes of exposition at the
> beginning of every romcom.

I deleted the whole thing with a groan of frustration, resisting the
urge to toss my laptop across the room like Maria had the romance
novel. Okay, so that sucked. Big deal—I could always start again. It
wasn't like this was my eleventh attempt to write the beginning of
my screenplay or anything.

I let out another groan, this one tinged with panic.

Kicking a pile of clean laundry off my bed, I stretched out my legs
and transferred my laptop from the flower-shaped cushion it had

been resting on to my lap. Big mistake, I discovered, as its underside just about burned the skin off my thighs.

Clearly, the problem wasn't my screenplay—or my inability to put together a coherent sentence. It was just that my apartment was too hot. All I had to do to get the words flowing was move somewhere with a working air conditioner. And a little treat. What had I been thinking, trying to write without a little treat to keep me going?

As if she'd heard the sizzle of searing flesh from all the way in Miami, my phone buzzed with an incoming call from my cousin Yazmin.

"I know exactly what you're going to ask," I said into the phone. "If Regency romance is so popular as a genre, how come there's no Regency porn?"

I wasn't exactly trying to distract her from asking about my screenplay again—or from last night's date, which hadn't even had a chance to crash and burn since I'd gotten ghosted before it even began. But . . . Oh, who was I kidding? I was absolutely trying to distract her. And it was working.

Yaz cackled. Softly. She may have had no compunction about being on the phone with me while at work, but she was an attorney, if a newly minted one, and it wasn't like she was dying to get dirty looks from the overworked second year associate she shared her fancy office with.

"No, really, think about it. A guy on Fling who cosplays as a duke—the Duke of Harding," I added with a burst of inspiration. "Making videos in, like, skintight buckskins and Hessian boots where he tells whoever's watching what a dirty governess they are."

This time, her laugh exploded into the receiver. "You're definitely going to get me fired today. Is Fling that app for romance readers you were telling me about before my boss cut us off?"

"Yeah. Maybe I should find someone to go into partnership with. Write them scripts or whatever."

"So this is how you're procrastinating on your screenplay today.

Why don't you try getting some words in instead of . . . whatever this is?"

Flipping my laptop closed, I blew a raspberry into the phone. "Let me stop you right there. I have no need for your sensible advice this early in the morning."

Yaz and I had been practically raised as sisters when our mothers, actual sisters, moved in together to help each other care for their respective kids. That must have been why Yaz often sounded like the harassed older sibling when talking to me. "First of all, it's almost noon. Second—you quit your job to finish writing this screenplay."

"Allegedly," I muttered, my heart thudding with guilt as it did every time I came face-to-face with the fact that I'd lied to Yaz—and everyone else—about quitting when I had actually gotten fired. Shoving my laptop aside, I hustled out of my pajama shorts and into a dress, talking mostly to keep Yaz from hearing the guilt in my voice. "No, really. Think about it. Do you know how many porn scripts I could knock out in the time it takes me to write one scene in my screenplay? It's actually not a bad idea. I wonder if it's a category on Fiverr."

"Come on, be serious. You have a real opportunity here that you can't squander with endless procrastination. Do you know how many people quit their jobs to write a screenplay and actually succeed?"

She wasn't wrong. Not about that part of it. When I ran into Grace Hong, one of my old college classmates, the last thing I'd expected was for her to remember the script I'd written for the one class we'd had together before she leveraged her award-winning short into a real job in Hollywood. Or that she'd offer to get me a meeting with a producer friend when they both returned from a few weeks in L.A., after I'd shown her a couple of scenes I had written and told her I was close to finishing the screenplay—not a lie, just an exaggeration.

The truth was, even though I did open my writing software every once in a while to add a few lines of dialogue to the romcom I had

started while still in school, I'd spent the four years since gradua-
tion elbows deep in Excel sheets, having opted at the last minute to
go the practical route and major in project management instead of
film like I'd originally intended to.

That was the one and only act of practicality I'd committed in
my entire life, and I wasn't sure I'd made the right choice.

Stifling a sigh, I scooped up my purse, my sunglasses, and . . .
And after a moment of hesitation, left my laptop on the bed. Maybe
what I really needed was a break. To get away for a couple of hours
and come back to the script with fresh eyes.

Although, let's face it—what I really needed was to keep filling
out applications. None of the two dozen jobs I'd applied for since
getting fired had led to anything concrete, but at this point I'd settle
for any solid gig that would let me make rent at the end of summer
when my savings ran out.

"I'm getting worried, Mariel," Yaz continued, her thoughts as
always eerily on par with mine. "Your savings aren't going to last
forever."

The pressure of it all filled me with so much anxiety that for a
couple of seconds, I was almost breathless with it.

There was a slight pause on Yaz's side, as if she could feel my
impending heart attack. The thing about my cousin is that she
puts up a hard front, but she's all soft and gooey inside. As soon
as she realized how far over my own head I was, she was going
to start offering everything from rent money to her couch. Her
fiancée, Amal, was already annoyed at how much Yaz had helped
me out over the years, and with their wedding fast approaching,
I couldn't ask Yaz to bail me out yet again. Not that I wanted her
to—I needed to get through this on my own, if only to prove to
myself that I could.

I'm not sure how I did it, but I managed to draw in enough
breath to force a lighter tone in my voice, shooting for casual but
ending up somewhere north of flippant. "Eh, there's always credit
card debt."

I winced.

"Not that you're not making a good point," I hurried to add as I closed the door to my studio behind me, "but porn is probably five million times more profitable than romcoms. Maybe this is the pivot I—"

"No more pivots," Yaz said firmly. "You are finishing your screenplay and reaching out to Grace by the end of August at the latest. Or I will a hundred percent stop being your friend."

I let myself out of my building and turned into Tenth Avenue, oh so elegantly using the ruffled sleeve of my sundress to wipe the droplets beading on my top lip. There wasn't much I could do about the way my hair had grown three sizes, like the Grinch's heart. New York City is as humid as a concrete rainforest in the summer, and not even the hairdresser in *The Princess Diaries* could de-frizz the tower of curls sprouting from my head. At least it made for a good backdrop for the heart-shaped earrings I had just spent far too much on, considering I was no longer employed. The purse slung over my shoulder was also heart-shaped, because if there's anything you should know about me, it's that I never shy away from committing to a theme.

"You're my cousin," I scoffed, pleased at how normal my voice sounded after a couple of deep breaths. "Being my friend is in your contract."

"I'm also a corporate lawyer with plenty of experience in breaking contracts," she countered. Which, you know. Good point.

I heaved out a sigh. "Fine, fine, I'll get some work done today. I'm literally walking into a coffee shop as we speak."

For an iced matcha and a muffin, but she didn't need to know that.

The walk to the cafe from my apartment was a short one, but I was a sweaty swamp monster when I pushed open the door and joined the line. Luckily, the tiny place was air-conditioned and there was a free table under one of the vents, right next to the speaker that was blasting the latest Lady Cerulean album.

Let me tell you, I snagged that table like it was the last Coca-Cola in the desert. I set down my drink and muffin and pulled a romance novel out of my purse, daydreaming idly about the Duke of Harding. I could practically see him in my mind. He'd be charming and courteous, but with a rakish glint in his eye that promised a wild time. He'd have the kind of smile that made your knees quiver. And forearms—he'd definitely have strong forearms.

I was still rooting in my purse—the heart shape was cute but things tended to get lost in the pointy bottom—when someone jostled my chair so hard, my book flew right off the table.

This was New York, and a crowded coffee shop to boot—getting jostled came with the territory. I wouldn't have even looked up if the person who'd bumped into me hadn't leaned over at the same time I did to pick up my book.

He got to it first, and held it out to me. I took it from him, a smile at the ready—which instantly withered when I saw his face.

Milo still wore the button-down shirts and bow ties that I'd always thought made him look adorably like a third grade math teacher. That was one of the first things I noticed. Then, as my gaze raked hungrily over him as if I hadn't seen him in years instead of just a couple months, I saw dozens of other little things that made my heart squeeze inside my chest.

Like the slightly disheveled hair that I used to love running my fingers through. And the deep tan across the bridge of his nose and the peek of gold-framed glasses in his shirt pocket. That one little freckle right where his eyes crinkled when he laughed. The ink stains on his pale blue cuffs from his collection of fountain pens.

In the months since our breakup, I had almost convinced myself that the next time I saw him, he would be looking haggard and haunted, with dark circles under his eyes and the realization that life without me was meaningless written all over his face. How was it fair that he looked exactly the same as always when I felt like I'd gone through a wringer and come out all twisted and inside out?

"Mariel." My name popped out of his mouth like he was as surprised as I was.

"Milo, hi. What . . ." I cleared my throat. "What brings you to the neighborhood?"

"I have a meeting in that building," he said, gesturing vaguely to the large pane of glass separating us from the sidewalk. Or, I guess, at one of the buildings beyond it.

I didn't exactly care, because I had just been blinded by the sunshine glinting off his *wedding ring*, a brief flash of light that felt like a knife to the guts. To my credit, I didn't hyperventilate. Mostly because I couldn't quite seem to catch my breath.

"I had a break in between classes," Milo continued.

"Classes?" I echoed, clutching the paperback for all I was worth.

"I got into the doctoral program at Columbia."

"Oh, that's—good for you, congrats." My smile could not have been more strained if I'd pulled an actual muscle on my cheek.

"I'm actually taking a summer intensive," he told me, without the slightest trace of awkwardness. "You remember that course on Byzantine aesthetics I used to talk about?"

Vividly. Milo had finished his master's in Classics the spring before. I couldn't count the number of times I had listened to him fret over his PhD applications, or geek out over that one course taught by the professor he wanted to TA for.

"Yeah, sure," I replied, aiming for enthusiastic and falling not just short, but flat on my face. "Oh wow, that's great that you got in. Love that for you."

At that point in my life, I had given up on the idea that I could ever be a cool, calm, collected ice queen. Did I have to actually babble, though?

Milo rested a hand on my table. The hand with the wedding ring, because of course it was. "Listen, Mariel, there's something I've been meaning to tell you."

That short phrase was all it took for my stomach to begin sinking. I probably would have up and run away if I hadn't been hemmed in by overly caffeinated people on all sides. I held up a hand so forcefully that if I'd been directing traffic, cars would have been screeching to a halt around me.

Not Milo. You'd think someone that smart would find it impossible to be so completely oblivious to the utter panic flashing on his ex's face. I didn't want to hear about him getting married. Or his wife. Or how they were probably living in perfect bliss.

He was earnestly pushing his hair off his forehead and leaning even closer. "I know we didn't exactly end on a good note, and I know that's entirely on me."

Understatement of the millennium, seeing as the reason we were no longer together was because the previous fall, he had pretended to move to Greece to work on a dig when all along he had been in Jersey City with another woman. Not just that—he'd gone radio silent for weeks, ignoring every single one of my texts and calls so that I spiraled so hard that Yaz had to talk me out of booking a flight to Athens because I was convinced that something terrible had happened. Mostly because I wouldn't have been able to find him if I'd gone, since I didn't have an address for him—oh, and also, he wasn't there.

I was no stranger to being ghosted, but what Milo had done was so much worse. He'd made plans for the future, knowing the whole time that he was with someone else. He'd cooked for me and bought me flowers and trekked all over the city helping me find whatever unhinged object my interior designer boss wanted for one of her clients.

He'd made me believe that what we had was real.

Apparently oblivious to all the warning signs flashing over my face, Milo continued, "I could not be more sorry about how things worked out and I've been wanting to apologize—"

"Oh, fuck off," I snapped, barely noticing the flash of motion as about half the people in line at the counter turned to look at us. "You lied to my face every day for weeks about being in Europe. Then you disappeared on me. And when I finally confronted you about it, you chose to tell me that it was my fault you lied in the first place. You kept telling me I took up too much space, just to make me feel small. I'm so done with you."

"Mariel," he began, and just the way he said my name, with that air of long-suffering patience, made something in me snap. "You have every right to—"

"No," I said, scrabbling for my things and starting to stuff them haphazardly into my purse. Even my muffin. Thankfully, I wasn't so far gone that I tried to do the same thing with my iced matcha but, you know, it was a close call. "You don't get to make yourself feel like some kind of good guy by shooting your apology all over my face when I was miserable for weeks thanks to you being the worst kind of garbage human. So, yes. Fuck you, fuck your *I'm so sorry things didn't work out*, and fuck you ever feeling anything but shitty about the way you treated me."

My words were met with a round of applause from what felt like everyone in the coffee shop.

I had daydreamed about a moment like this ever since I caught him and his girlfriend—his real girlfriend, which I clearly wasn't— kissing with their hands linked at the opening of an exhibition on art from Ancient Greece. Which I'd only gone to because I was so desperately worried about Milo that I was seeking out anything that reminded me of him. It had been months of me fantasizing about telling him off to his face the way I hadn't been able to back then.

And now that it was actually happening, I was horrified to feel the sting of tears behind my eyes.

I was still sitting down, and Milo was standing there next to me looking all solemn and brave and like he expected a medal for letting me yell at him in the middle of a crowded cafe. It was laughable and unfair that I still knew him so well—knew he wasn't going to push the apology, but he wasn't going to slink back to his seat, either. He was going to stand there and take whatever I flung at him, all the while feeling virtuous about letting me have my little tantrum.

So I finished shoving things into my bag, not caring that I was mashing the paperback into my muffin. And then I stood, intending to walk out without saying another word.

But I must have scraped back my chair too hard, because it toppled over. Right into the person who'd just started squeezing behind me with two full cup holders balanced on top of each other.

If this had happened in the romcom I was writing, all eight glasses of whipped cream-festooned iced coffee would have splashed all over the woman at the next table, setting off a chain reaction that would end with Milo getting a pie to the face.

Unfortunately, this was real life, and the only one who ended up covered in whipped cream—and coffee—was me.

"Goodbye, Milo," I said, trying not to let the icy mess dribbling down my cleavage rob me of whatever dignity I had left. "Enjoy summer school."

2

I made a graceful exit, by which I mean that I shot through the warren of tables and chairs like a misfired cannonball, colliding with a pair of kids in tie-dye T-shirts and getting tangled in someone's dog's leash at the door.

When my green jelly sandals finally touched the sidewalk, the change in temperature hit me like a gale-force wind—like I needed another punch after what had just happened in there. The desperate need to not be there when Milo came out propelled me the rest of the way down the street.

At least I'd gotten my say. I should have felt triumphant about that, but as I walked back to my apartment all I could think of was the glint of Milo's wedding ring.

Seeing it had felt like suddenly dropping into an old, forgotten well—the dual shock of what you thought was solid ground unexpectedly opening up beneath you, only for your breath to be snatched again when you hit the cold water. Or maybe it was like becoming a well yourself, one that had once been full and now held no more than a puddle.

It wasn't like I hadn't thought of what it would be like to run into him, even though I'd made a point of avoiding the places he used to frequent. I'd carved up Manhattan into little Milo-free zones. And even when I stayed firmly within those boundaries, every once in a while I had moments of feeling my heart squeeze inside my chest as my imagination chased itself over a cliff picturing him coming out of the grocery store I was about to walk into, or hanging out at the Thai restaurant around the corner from my place.

All that effort, only to be blindsided by a metal circle.

I was dripping more than coffee by the time I got back to my shoebox of a studio, conveniently located at the top of five flights of stairs. Leaving my stained dress bunched by the door, I stepped into the shower.

I should just leave the city. It wasn't like I had anything tying me to New York anymore—not a boyfriend and not a job. I could pretend to write my screenplay from anywhere. Preferably somewhere cheap. Or free, like Yaz's couch.

The last thing I wanted, though, was to be the source of another fight between Yaz and Amal, who had a lot of opinions about the way I leaned on Yaz for, well, everything. And now that they were only a few months away from getting married and had purchased a couch—not to mention a condo—together, she had a say on who got to sleep on it.

And honestly, I was also sick of the way I couldn't seem to get my shit together. Things needed to change. I needed to change.

But how, when it felt like the foundations of me were built on fault lines where everyone else got solid ground?

Sighing, I wrapped myself up in a towel and went to find my rattiest pair of pajamas.

I'd met Milo at the absolute lowest point of my dating life. I'd been single for a long time—scratch that. I'd been single *always*, too flighty to focus on a single hobby, much less one person. But then I moved to New York, and all of a sudden I was alone in a new city and full of doubts about whether I should have stayed in Miami. Tía Nena, Yaz's mom, had just moved to the DR to open her own restaurant, Yaz and Amal had just gotten engaged, and my own mother was on her sixth or seventh year of *Eat Pray Love*-ing around the world.

I guess it was no surprise that he had slid in so easily, with his promises and his plans and his bow ties and rumpled hair.

And it wasn't like things had gotten better since him. Take the date I'd gone on the previous week. This guy I'd matched with on one of the apps asks me out for coffee, right? We meet up at this cute cafe, chat about food and travel and all that fun stuff. He even walks me to the subway to give me a soft, lingering kiss goodbye. A couple of days later, I try to go onto his profile to thank him for a nice time and maybe talk about a second date . . . only to find out that it had vanished. Because he'd unmatched us. Which, let's face it, is the most cowardly form of ghosting. And then for it all to have happened again last night, with a different guy?

I was so tired.

Pretty much everyone I'd ever dated ended up ghosting me. Even my mother hopped on the trend when she barely bothered to wait until my eighteenth birthday to peace out and take to the open roads or whatever. Milo doing it too was only the cherry on top of a shitty sundae.

I'd given finding love a good try and it hadn't worked out, so it was probably time to move on to another pursuit. One that was less soul-sucking and confidence-destroying.

Like screenwriting!

Snorting at my delusional self, I reached into the laundry pile next to my bed and started rooting through scratchy T-shirts and sweatpants with stretched-out waistbands. It wasn't like I needed something fancy for another afternoon of pizza and YouTube.

I grabbed the shorts I had discarded earlier and looked down at them for a long moment.

"You know what?" I told the shorts. "Fuck this."

Flinging them aside, I yanked a fresh dress over my head instead and was halfway down the stairs before I could think twice about it. I was done crying over Milo. It was time to pull out one of my Weapons of Mass Distraction. I was going to the movies.

The way I saw it, I had two choices—I could either stay home and wallow, or I could go sit in front of a gigantic screen and consume enough popcorn and M&M's to make myself forget there was such a thing as feelings.

I could have trekked all the way downtown for the Alamo Drafthouse, but there was no way I was descending into the bowels of the subway in this weather, so the slightly greasy theater in Times Square would have to do. I made my way down to 42nd Street at a surprisingly fast clip, considering that the summer air had turned my blood into pancake syrup.

And here's the thing. As much as I pretended that I had become yet another unimpressed New Yorker, striding up and down the streets of the city like I didn't even notice all the amazing sights around me, I had to admit to feeling the teensiest bit of awe whenever I saw Times Square. Yes, it was true, the slow-moving tourists could be annoying. And I hated being stopped every few minutes by people dressed up like Marvel characters and people trying to sell me tickets to comedy shows. But this tiny section of the city was a shot of concentrated energy and color, all flashing lights and Broadway marquees reflecting on skyscraper windows and gleaming cars and sidewalks that literally shimmered.

Maybe it was just that Yaz, theater kid in denial that she was, had made me rewatch the pilot episode of the canceled-too-early series *Smash* so many times that the image of Katherine McPhee bursting out from the subway and into the glory of Times Square while the music swelled was just engraved in my brain. But more than that . . .

This was the New York City thousands of people dreamed of. The New York City that had lived in my imagination for years, that shiny place full of well-dressed people where things might go awry every once in a while, but where everything always works out.

Even in the daytime, when the lights were no match for the blazing summer sun, there was something magical about Times Square.

I know, I know. It was deeply uncool of me to be so wide-eyed, especially after having been in the city for a couple years. Especially when it came to movie theaters. The cool ones were all south of Union Square, where there were small cinemas that were managing to stay in business by playing independent films and the classics. You know, the stuff of film buffs' dreams. I was a blockbuster girlie, though, and the Times Square AMC was good enough for me.

I mean, if nothing else, it beat being parked in front of a DVD by my mom as a kid whenever it was her turn to look after Yaz and me.

Maybe that was why I'd been so quick to tell Grace Hong that I was still writing. After being dumped by Milo and getting fired a couple of months later, I'd needed the kind of comfort that only movies could give me. Just watching wasn't enough—I needed to live in them, and pull them apart, and refashion the pieces into something that spoke to me. Or spoke for me.

I swallowed back a groan. I didn't want to think about Milo, and I didn't want to think about my failed attempt to write a screenplay, either. I wanted two hours' worth of oblivion, and a lot of snacks.

But as I skirted a little kid throwing a tantrum in the middle of the sidewalk, I couldn't help but think that maybe there was a reason why I was finding it so hard to write my romcom. How could I expect myself to write convincingly about finding love when the one time I had come close to it had been an utter lie?

I used my sleeve again to wipe beads of sweat off my forehead. Times Square felt like it was more crowded than ever. I caught snatches of conversations as I trudged to the theater, weaving around groups of tourists standing in the middle of the sidewalk, gazing up at the screens, and at a couple of guys who were dancing in what looked like Disney prince costumes.

None of it registered—at least not until I walked past a couple of blonde girls in denim shorts and matching crop tops.

"OMG, that's Lady Cerulean," one of them squealed.

"Where? On a billboard?" her friend asked.

"No! There! Right there!"

"*Where?*" I blurted out, whipping my head back and forth to look around me.

A glimpse of Lady Cerulean was exactly what I needed to turn this shit sandwich of a day around. Her real name was actually Milady Sandoval. I'd read somewhere that she'd originally made up the name Lady Cerulean to post fanfic online and that she kept using it when her music career started popping off so that her fandom friends knew how to find her shows. That was easily ten years ago.

Since then, she'd reached heights of fame that Beyoncé and Taylor Swift could only dream of.

Why would someone that famous hang out in Times Square, you might ask? Well, Lady C lives in the city and she's known to come up with these elaborate disguises that allow her to roam around, getting inspiration for her songs.

I couldn't spot anyone who might be her, though. I glanced back at the girl to ask and found her staring intently at me.

"Me?" I yelped, aware that a few of the people around us had come to an abrupt stop and were openly staring. "You think I'm Lady Cerulean?"

"Everyone knows about her disguises," the girl informed me, eyeing my heart-shaped earrings. Or maybe my hair, which was neither pink nor shaped like a heart, but definitely attention worthy.

"But I'm not even the right body type," I argued, lowering my—you guessed it—on-theme heart-shaped sunglasses. I'm average height and almost-but-not-quite curvy and Lady C is tall and slim, with a neck like a graceful swan and legs that go on forever. And her butt and hips are definitely more sculpted than mine.

I kept trying to point that out, but none of the tourists seemed to be in the mood to listen to logic. A bunch of them had their phones out and pointed at me, making me wish that my sunglasses were the large, dark kind. And that I had a hat big enough for my hair to fit into.

"That's a wig, right?" someone said, and I started to back away as two pairs of hands started reaching for my curls.

It was official—today *sucked*.

Another hand landed on my shoulder. And like, I wasn't going to panic or anything. Up until then, the whole thing had seemed so funny that I was already mentally adding it to my screenplay. But then another hand brushed the strap of my dress and, well, panic suddenly seemed like a good idea.

I needed to get out of there. The only problem was, the starstruck crowd had surrounded me on all sides—and it was closing in.

If this had been happening in my screenplay, I—

Oh, fuck that.

A burst of fear-spiked adrenaline went through me. "Sorry to disappoint you," I said, raising my voice in an attempt to project confidence. "But you've got the wrong girl, babes. Granted, I'm all starlight and flair and I have talent coming out of my—"

The tourists shifted, their attention momentarily diverted from me, as a Black guy sporting a crown popped out through the crowd and sauntered to where I was standing. In his cream-and-gold suit, he was a dead ringer for Naveen from *The Princess and the Frog*. "Where are you folks from? You have plans this evening? Hey sir, you look like you appreciate humor—do you have any interest in stand-up comedy?"

A brief murmur of uncertainty rose from the crowd, though a couple of people answered him, looking interested as he began hawking free tickets to a comedy club.

I was still rooted to the spot, half-afraid to make any sudden movements in case it drew the attention of the crowd again. But then the guy tossed a look over his shoulder at me and mouthed, "Go!"

I whirled around, intending to run the hell out of there, and came face-to-face with another guy. One who was dressed in breeches that were molded to his thighs. Under his teal waistcoat, his billowing white shirt covered an appealingly broad chest and shoulders that looked like they had been made for the express purpose of resting your head on them.

My gaze skipped higher, all the way to his eyes. A rich chocolate brown, they were ringed by very dark lashes and pale skin that gleamed in the glow of the billboards around us.

It was him. The Duke of Harding.

● ● ●

My heart stuttered to a stop before restarting like an ancient car engine.

As it roared back to life, I had to take a moment to blink and tell myself that my mind hadn't conjured up a fictional duke in a moment of distress. Even if the guy standing in front of me was too perfectly handsome to be real.

He flashed a smile at me, as if he could tell what I was thinking. And then he held out his hand.

Let me tell you, I didn't even hesitate—I put my hand in his and let him pull me through the crowd, both of us bursting into a run as soon as we were clear.

His long legs ate up the sidewalk like Pac-Man eats dots. Not exactly endowed in the leg department myself, I scrambled to keep up. It was like four or five blocks before I noticed that we were still holding hands. And since it wasn't a romantic thing at all—more like a *did we just escape a raving mob and also narrowly avoid getting hit by that car* kind of thing—I didn't bother disentangling my fingers from his until another few blocks were safely behind us.

Promising myself to sign up for a gym membership as soon as I solved my cash-flow issue, I leaned against the hot brick side of a building, hands on my thighs, probably looking like a goldfish that had just made an unwise leap from its bowl as I sucked in breath after breath.

Looking much more composed—and much less sweaty—than me, the guy stood under his own power, looking mildly alarmed at my wheezing.

"You okay there? That was . . ."

"Unholy," I supplied through a hard inhale. Finally, I got my shit together enough be able to say, "I look *nothing* like Lady Cerulean."

"There *is* all the starlight and flair, though," he said, and I let out a breathless laugh.

Away from the crowd, no longer about to succumb to a panic attack, I took a moment to examine him. It wasn't just the outfit that made him look like he should be on the cover of a romance novel—it was the way his warm brown eyes caught the light, the way he held his mouth like he was on the verge of a smile.

"I know it's like a sauna out here, but can I thank you with some coffee or something? I mean, unless you have to get back to—" I waved in the general direction of Times Square. "I did interrupt your performance."

He grimaced. "Yeah, that was my buddy Chase's idea. He's the dancer and I'm just . . . humoring him. To be honest, you probably did us a favor—if it wasn't for you, I'd probably be getting arrested as we speak for accidentally assaulting someone with my flailing limbs."

The way he moved told another story. Maybe he didn't have the tightly controlled grace that had made Prince Naveen look like a panther as he strolled through the crowd, but he knew how to use his body to his advantage.

And that included his face, I noticed when he punctuated his words with a smile that should have been accompanied by a cartoon sparkle in his teeth. "My name's Dash."

"Dash and Chase? Cute," I blurted out. "I'm Mariel."

I held out my hand for a dorky handshake, and immediately realized what a mistake that was as our fingers met and electricity *zinged* through me. It wasn't just leftover panic, either; it was my body alerting me to the fact that Dash was stupid hot. Which was completely unnecessary, because I had eyes that worked. "So, uh, how about that coffee?"

A slow grin broke over his face. "I could never say no to coffee."

Which, to each his own. Not everyone has to share my opinions about hot bean juice. And I *had* offered.

I didn't think I could take another coffee shop that day—luckily, the restaurant down the street from us had a beverages window where Dash could get a Thai iced coffee. Ordering a pink lemonade for myself, I reached into my purse for my phone and came up with a handful of crumbs. Also known as the muffin from earlier, now mashed to oblivion. Just another reason for me to be mad at Milo.

Dash eyed me with obvious amusement as I wiped my hand on my dress and dug back into my cute-but-impractical purse, handing him each item as I pulled it out.

Holding assorted lip glosses and scrunchies in one hand, he shook crumbs off my emotional support paperback and glanced at the clinched couple on the cover. "You like Georgie Hart?"

The Queen of Hearts, as her fandom called her, had been writing Regency romances for, oh, about fifty-eight decades. A slight exaggeration, maybe, though she'd been so prolific that it was easy to believe that her best-selling books had been around forever.

"I like romance novels in general." My fingers finally came into contact with my phone. Brandishing it triumphantly, I turned back to the bored cashier.

"Me too," Dash said.

"Really?" I blurted out as I paid. "I don't think I've ever met a guy who was into romance. Not that guys aren't allowed to be into romance, of course."

Grabbing our drinks, we strolled away toward a little neighborhood park as Dash started waxing poetic over a Beverly Jenkins he had just finished. It was marginally less hot under the leafy canopy, so we found an empty bench near the dog play area and settled in to watch the pups.

"I haven't read any Ms. Bev in a while," I told him. "I've been making my way through every Regency ever written."

"Ambitious," he said, looking . . . well, not impressed exactly. More like he didn't have the heart to tell me just how many Regency romances were out there. "Are you on Fling?"

I had to blink, mostly to make sure that he wasn't a product of my imagination after all. An incredibly hot guy with excellent taste in books is one thing—one who reads Beverly Jenkins and is on the ultimate app for romance readers? If you'd asked me an hour ago, I'd have said it would be as impossible as encountering the Duke of Harding in person.

He pulled his phone out of a hidden pocket inside his waistcoat and enthusiastically tapped away at the screen until his Fling profile came up.

> Dash, he/him/his. Former model, current cosplayer with
> an art degree that he doesn't use and a TBR that'll take
> two centuries to get through. Powered by oat milk lattes
> and the search for his own HEA.

"Follow me?" he asked, with all the earnestness of the golden retriever nosing at the ground a few feet away from us.

"Sure thing." I went into the app and quickly shot off a friend request, which he accepted instantly. His feed was an interesting mix of pictures and videos of himself in various costumes—the one he was currently wearing included—updates on what he was reading, including mini reviews headed by Fling's signature heart rating system, and boosts of other people's bookish content.

A vague idea was taking shape in my mind. Sure, the Regency porn thing had been more of an exercise in procrastination than an actual plan. But as I eyed—but did not click on—the OnlyFans link in his profile, the idea became more of a possibility.

Never mind that I'd never written spice before. I'd never really written a screenplay, either, except for that one class in college. But every romance novel and movie I'd ever devoured had begun tumbling through my mind the moment I whirled around to find him in front of me, and as I sat there and imagined him staring earnestly at the camera as a heartfelt declaration tumbled out of those full red lips . . .

I could see it.

I didn't say anything, though, not right then. I know, I know—how very unlike me to practice so much restraint. The thing is, even I knew that Regency porn was not exactly the kind of thing you spring on someone within an hour of first meeting.

"So, you have an art degree?" I asked instead, and took a sip of my lemonade.

Dash nodded. "That I use mostly for making costumes. Cosplaying is an art, a science, and my main reason for living." His lips spread into a grin that would have made my knees quiver if I had been standing. "Well, that and my grandmothers."

Was he *trying* to give me palpitations?

"Are they romance readers, too?"

"My grandmothers?" Dash shook his head. "I don't think either of them has cracked a book since the Eisenhower administration. They're casino bunnies, actually. They have this group of senior ladies called the Slot Sluts who take a bus up to Atlantic City a couple times a month."

I cracked up. "They do *not*. The Slot Sluts?"

Dash looked pleased. "I keep telling them it'd make an excellent name for a romance book club, but alas, I'm the only literate one in the family."

"Same here. It's tragic, really—my aunt is an award-winning chef with her own restaurant, and my cousin graduated law school with honors and was instantly scooped up by a corporate firm. Neither of them reads romance novels, though, so you know. It's a heavy burden on my shoulders."

It was Dash's turn to laugh. "Is your family in the city?"

"Miami and the Dominican Republic," I told him, omitting my mother's location for the simple reason that I had no idea where she was at any given time. For a couple of weeks last spring, I'd thought that she was finally out of her *Eat Pray Love* era and was ready to settle down for a season of *Under the Tuscan Sun*, but Diane Lane she is not. By the time her postcard made its way to me, she had already left Italy and gotten a job teaching English in Seoul. That was a zip code or two ago, though. "I've actually only been in New York a little over two years. Just long enough for some light heartbreak."

I had no idea what possessed me to add that. Dash nodded, though, and extended his long legs as if settling back for a story, his long fingers loosely curled around his coffee.

"We all have at least one of those," he said. "It's a rite of passage for anyone who moves here. Finding a decent apartment and find-ing love—that's how you know you've made it in New York."

"I'm not doing too badly on the apartment front. My first year, I had four roommates and a roach infestation. Now I'm in a fifth-floor walk-up and I can touch my stove while lying in bed, but at least I don't have to share a bathroom."

I did, however, spend a nauseatingly huge chunk of my salary on rent. You know, back when I had a salary. I spent a moment trying not to hyperventilate. I mean, it's not like anyone my age has any savings anyway. And I know I'm not the only one putting groceries on her credit card.

"Not having to share a bathroom is the number one sign that you've made it in New York," Dash said solemnly. "Liza Minnelli would be proud of you."

"I might have to make that into a T-shirt."

He dipped his head an inch or two, then lifted it in a way that made his hair flip. "Let me put my art degree to good use and make it for you."

There was a curl to his smile and a sparkle in his brown eyes that made my brain want to short-circuit, the way my heart had done earlier.

Not this guy flirting with me.

The second half of his sentence was still hanging in the air, though I didn't plan on answering. Finding love . . . the closest thing I'd found was a coffee stain on my favorite dress, and I would have rather gone back to Times Square than expose my latest roman-tic disaster to someone who looked like the younger brother of a Greek god.

I cleared my throat. "As someone who wasn't brave enough to major in something creative, I'm deeply curious. What was your focus?"

"Visual Merchandising. I wanted to design retail windows and displays."

"No way, that sounds amazing."

There was an air of bashfulness to the smile he gave me. "I thought so. I never did end up working as a designer, though. I'd been modeling since middle school, and it seemed like a good way to graduate from college without too much debt, so I kept at it. And then I started going on auditions and that kind of took over my life for a while. That didn't really work out, but I found cosplaying and that's way more enjoyable than putting myself through the audition process."

I nodded. "Yeah, it seems really grueling."

"It's definitely not for everyone." He took another sip of his iced coffee. "These days, I mostly pay the bills thanks to OnlyFans. I've never fully let go of the idea of going back to design, but it's been six years now. Maybe it's too late."

"I don't believe that," I said firmly. "If it's something you really love, then it's always worth pursuing."

"I guess I just feel like I'd have that kind of thing figured out by now. I mean, I'm turning thirty in less than two years."

"Dash, you're talking to the reigning queen of Doesn't Have Anything Figured Out Yet Land. I'm twenty-six, unemployed as of three weeks ago, and desperately trying to convince myself that I can write a screenplay and sell it before my savings run out. Which, spoiler alert, will happen in a couple months if my landlord keeps insisting that I pay him rent, the unreasonable bastard."

That was kind of a lot to lay on someone I'd just met, but Dash just nodded. "Do you have a plan in case the screenplay thing takes longer than two months?"

"Kind of." I let my gaze skip from Dash's face to the schnauzer puppies chewing on their leashes as I tried to decide how much to tell him. The debate lasted all of two seconds—the only thing I have more of than starlight and flair is impulsivity. "At the risk of making you run away, screaming . . . I kind of had this idea. It's a little out there and very impractical, but it might be doable?"

"If it has anything to do with Liza Minnelli . . ."

I shook my head, smiling. And here's the thing—I may not be the smartest person in the room, or the most driven, or the most likely to succeed at, well, anything. But one thing I do have is a master's degree in smooth talking. So even though I didn't have anything prepared—and even though it had been all of a couple of hours since the Duke of Harding had popped into my head—I launched into a pitch that I was pretty sure would have gotten me a meeting with a studio if I'd been in Hollywood, modifying my original idea as I went.

"Cosplaying as a Regency duke to make videos for social media," he repeated. "It's so simple and yet so brilliant. I can't believe no one's ever thought of it."

"I'd just be writing the scripts, of course. I'd need to find someone to collaborate with to make everything happen. But I'm not wrong, right? If done properly, it could actually be pretty profitable."

"If done properly, you could have a whole phenomenon on your hands. I mean, think of the possibilities. What I eat in a day as a cynical duke who refuses to fall in love with the penniless beauty he married out of convenience."

"Get ready with me to tell the wallflower I love her," I shot back, instantly caught up in the glow of creating with someone else.

"Day in the life of a reformed rake who's starting to develop feelings for the spunky governess taking care of his ward."

"Storytime: I married an heiress in order to save my failing estate and I just realized I'm incredibly attracted to her."

I could have kept going for hours, but Dash's phone buzzed with a text. He glanced down at it, then said, "Chase is asking if we got away okay. And if we're hungry."

"Tell him I'm always hungry. And that I'm treating you guys for helping me escape with all my limbs intact."

The three of us ended up at a dive bar on Tenth where the menu was mostly limited to wings and fries, but the three-dollar beer more than made up for it. If Dash was as earnest as a golden retriever, Chase made the word *cocky* come to life as he flirted with all the bartenders and scored us free shots.

At one point, a Lady Cerulean song came on the speakers and the three of us grinned at each other like we were sharing an inside joke. The giddy fizz of it shot through me, intensifying when Dash helped me down from the barstool and tugged me to where Chase was already dancing, his body undulating to the pulsing rhythm.

Dash's gaze lingered on mine even after he had let go of my hand, and he looked so serious that I had to hip check him. For whatever reason, that cracked us both up—and then we burst out laughing again when we realized that Chase was so absorbed in making eyes at the bartender that he had no idea what had just happened.

It was one of those moments. You know, the shimmering ones that are destined to become a memory so full of light, you'll never remember how dim it really was inside that dive bar.

3

"You better be writing."

I tapped on the speakerphone icon as I tried to negotiate my wristlet, my apartment keys, bag of cookies, and the pink lemonade I was holding. "Hey, Yaz."

Kicking the door closed, I dropped everything but the drink and cookies on the kitchen counter, which was so close to the door that the latter didn't open all the way—kind of annoying the handful of times I had actually tried to cook, but a handy drop-off station for all the takeout I usually had instead of turning on the two-burner stove.

"I don't hear any typing," Yaz said. That girl was going to take the courtrooms by storm when she was finally allowed to first-chair a case. Not that corporate lawyers went to court, as far as I knew—my understanding of the profession had been shaped more by binging hours of courtroom dramas than by Yaz's infrequent explanations about what she did at work. "What else could you possibly be doing?"

"Oh, you know, just working on a little self-sabotage, no big deal."

"*Mariel.*" I would have been able to hear her groan even without the benefit of a phone connection. "What exactly is the plan here? I'm running out of encouraging pep talks and sage elder cousin advice."

Snagging the cookies, I toed off my sandals and curled up against the fringed pillow wedged in the corner between my bed and the wall. I'd spent most of that morning trying to write—then filling out job applications in a haze of panic when I realized how not productive my writing session had been. "Can you order some more? In bulk, preferably. I'm nowhere near close to being done making mistakes."

"Mistakes are one thing. Doing everything you can to *not* write your screenplay after you quit your good-paying job to—"

"I didn't," I blurted out, and immediately bit my lip.

Sure, I'd been feeling guilty about lying to Yaz about what had really gone down with work. Sure, I'd tried to assuage that guilt by promising myself that I would tell her soon. But in that context, *soon* meant when my screenplay was a reality and wildly successful and able to be used as proof that I wasn't a flighty screwup. Soon didn't mean right this second.

Miserably, I crunched on a cookie.

"Didn't what?" she asked. "Procrastinate?"

"Quit my job. I got fired." My foot started to jiggle up and down, more a product of my nerves than of all the sugar I was shoveling in. "You know I was asked to take the lead on the brownstone renovation? Which ended up being like a week before I found out that Milo was lying to me?"

"Mariel," Yaz said heavily.

Elaine, my boss and the proprietor of the interior design firm I used to work for, was always saying that in interior design, project management was less than half the job—our true objective was keeping the clients happy.

"Half of them treat me like a couples' therapist and the other half like their personal assistant," she'd told me one day as she'd taken a moment to approve a budget I had put together. "Being flexible and understanding goes with the job."

Turns out, being flexible and understanding was not exactly in my wheelhouse. Being patient, either. I might have been able to get through the project, even with Mrs. Greyson firing off one unreasonable demand after another. But then the breakup happened and two months of dealing with Mrs. Greyson took its toll on me. I wish I was one of those people who can take refuge in their work, but all I could do those days was call in sick, burrito myself in blankets, and read every Regency romance I could get my grubby little paws on. Eventually, though, I had to go back to work—and when I did, I lost it on one of our most important clients and got fired.

And then I lied to my family about it because I couldn't stand for them to see me fail at one more thing.

Getting fired had been a new low, which was kind of an achievement when you thought about how many of those I'd already reached. If things kept going the way they were, I was going to be plunging to subterranean depths soon.

"I kind of yelled at the owner of the brownstone," I told Yaz. "She asked that I be taken off the project. And Elaine was exasperated with me by then—I'd been calling out a lot, and the truth is that I'd never really been all that excited about the work."

"Because you wanted to write a screenplay. That you're currently avoiding working on." Yaz sounded like she was getting a headache. "I don't get why you couldn't just write on the side."

"Oh, you know I've always hated side hustle culture," I lied. By which I meant, I *had* tried to write on the side and my document had remained as blank as it was now. "And anyway, now I have all this time for the screenplay and . . . other projects." I broke off a piece of cookie and popped it into my mouth.

"Other . . . Mariel, you're not really going through with the whole Regency porn thing, are you?"

"Why shouldn't I?" I asked defensively.

"Because you have something else you need to be doing? It's really worrying that I have to keep reminding you of that, by the way."

"Well, you don't have to. I haven't forgotten about the screenplay. And look at it this way—at least this will give me something good to write about."

"I thought you already had something good to write about."

I waved a hand in the air even though she couldn't see it. "Something other than the trials and tribulations of an innocent interior designer being sucked into her clients' seedy world of luxury and blackmail. Look. Some women are out there girl-bossing too close to the sun. Me? I'm daydreaming my way to fame and fortune. Well, maybe just fortune—nothing I've seen of fame makes me feel like I'd like it for myself. It's all PR relationships and secretly tipping off paparazzi and—"

Yaz's sigh cut through my chatter like a warm knife slicing through butter. "Just . . . promise me you've got it all under control."

Did I, though? I was well over my head with a rent that I only got approved for because of a job I no longer had. My bank account was about to fold up into a puff of dust and I had like three scenes written on the screenplay that was supposed to get me an agent, a sale, and enough money that I wouldn't have to buy cookies with a credit card.

I was, to put it mildly, extremely fucked.

"It's gonna be fine," I said into the phone, rubbing a hand over my face. "Probably. I mean, how am I supposed to get my life together without a cute, slightly uptight, enemy turned love interest to make me want to tame my wild ways?"

I could *hear* Yaz's eye roll. I'm sure I don't have to tell you that she's never willingly read a romance novel.

"Since when are you the kind of person who sits around waiting for someone to make you shape up?" she demanded.

"It's a new thing I'm trying out." I slurped some of my lemonade, but not even the cold, tart sweetness was enough to quiet down the anxiety screaming inside me.

"This wouldn't have anything to do with you running into Milo yesterday, would it?"

Damn it. I knew I shouldn't have texted Yaz about it.

"I mean, I never had my shit together when I was with him, so probably not. I just . . . Yaz, I know I don't have the best track record when it comes to making good life decisions. But being fired from the studio . . . Honestly, I think it's taken me one step closer to the person I've always wanted to be. Not the person I was *trying* to be when I was with Milo, but the person I truly, genuinely am. And hey, if all else fails, I can always come live off you. Your fancy attorney salary can absolutely keep me in the manner to which I've grown accustomed."

"Mariel, actual billionaires couldn't afford your baked goods and sugary drinks habit." Yaz's laugh wafted out through my phone's speakers, and I felt a pleasant little tug in my chest at having made my cousin laugh.

And having distracted her from the lecture she'd been about to deliver.

"I know it all sounds a little too wild, even for me. But trust the process, okay?"

"I might have to, albeit reluctantly—for now. I believe in you and I believe in your talent. But I also believe that you need to plaster your butt to your chair and get some real work done if you want your daydreams to turn into something real. I want to be supportive, and I want you to be true to yourself, but honestly, I think that whole Milo thing knocked you off course. And instead of trying to keep your life from going off the rails, it seems like you've been doing your best to push it over."

It was easy for her to talk. Yaz had come out of the womb with a torts textbook in one hand and a wedding veil in the other. She and Amal may have just gotten engaged, but they'd been together since before they started the first grade. Yaz had never flailed the way I had my entire life.

"I know he broke your heart," she said softly, "but he doesn't get to break your life, too."

"He hasn't." I folded down the top of the paper bag the cookies had come in. "I don't think."

Hadn't he, though, if only peripherally? As much as I hated to give him that much credit, Yaz wasn't wrong about the breakup knocking me off course. But maybe that was the push I'd needed. That, and getting fired.

Yaz and I talked for almost an hour longer, catching each other up on the latest addition to the menu at her mother's restaurant and the overly complicated travel plans Amal was making for their honeymoon. There was a slight chance Yaz would spend her five days off from work lugging her carry-on from one airport to another, and there was a much bigger chance that Mami and Aunt Nena would spend at least a month telling her they should have gone to a resort in Punta Cana instead.

I even told her about this weird little movie from the nineties that I'd streamed a few days before, even though Yaz rarely had time to look at anything but contracts.

The only thing I failed to mention was the doubt that had been circling my head for weeks, as unwanted as an infestation of fruit flies. I hadn't been good enough for Milo, or for all the men I'd tried to date after him. I hadn't been good enough at my job.

What if I wasn't a good enough writer to make my biggest dream come true?

◆ ◆ ◆

Yaz didn't bother to keep lecturing me about wasting time on my Duke of Harding idea, but mostly because she predicted that I would forget about it in less than a week. You know, as I usually did. She didn't even have to remind me about my jewelry-making phase or the time I thought I could take barre classes without seriously injuring myself.

Or the summer I was *convinced* that I could get my life together if I started Bullet Journaling—not to mention, make some extra cash if I recorded my process and posted it to YouTube. So I spent a huge chunk of a paycheck on these gorgeous notebooks and an assortment of mind-bogglingly expensive pens and stickers and washi tape and . . . And somehow I spent so much that I had to ask Yaz to help me cover a bunch of my bills. It was all going to be worth it, though . . . only, getting my monthly spreads to look on paper like what I'd envisioned in my head had been so frustrating that I'd ended up quitting two weeks into my Bujo journey.

Unlike 99 percent of my impulsive ideas, though, the Regency one didn't fade away as soon as it flashed through my brain. And I *was* going to need a paying gig if I was going to keep doing stuff like eating and being housed.

No pressure, right?

So yeah, was it any wonder that I found myself on Fling the next day, following the link to Dash's OnlyFans profile? None of the stuff on there was super-explicit—it was mostly videos of him flirting with the camera while shirtless and a few pictures of him posing in underwear. Nothing you wouldn't see outside of a perfume ad on a billboard in Times Square. There was this one picture, though, of him in a pair of sweatpants, that—

A notification lit up the screen of my phone and I yelped, throwing my hands up into the air. Unfortunately, the phone went up into the air, too—but don't worry, my nose broke its fall.

Rubbing my throbbing appendage (heh), I swiped OnlyFans off my screen and went back to Fling, where I had a message waiting for me from none other than Dash himself. He'd sent me a drawing of a T-shirt with the words *Liza Minnelli would be proud of you* emblazoned across the chest.

Iconic, I texted. I might need a matching sweatshirt.

While I waited for him to reply, I tapped back to his profile. He wasn't the most frequent poster, and I suspected he would have a hell of a lot more followers than he already did if he dedicated a little more time to replying to the besotted people in his comments, though I could see why he'd want to ignore some of the more, well, intense ones. What little he'd posted was articulate and funny—a little glimpse of the man behind the face, and an assurance that his personality sparkled as hard as his smile did.

As it had each time I'd seen that smile, my heart began to do a weird fluttery dance. Not because I was into him or anything, though he was terrifyingly attractive.

It was just that every time I looked at his profile picture, possibilities started to bloom inside me like tiny butterfly-covered flowers, until I felt like a veritable fucking garden. I'd never felt this excited before—not over my screenplay, not over any of the projects I'd overseen as project manager, and definitely not over any of the dates I'd been on since Milo. Or maybe even before him.

It may have started off as an attempt to distract both Yaz and myself, but every atom in my soul was yearning to bring the Duke of Harding to life. And I wanted Dash to help me.

And Dash . . . Dash was taking his sweet time typing out a message. I watched the three dots under his name appear and reappear for an annoyingly long time before text finally flashed onto my screen. Let me tell you, it was worth the wait.

So, I was thinking about your Duke of Harding idea. Feel free to say no if it's not what you had in mind, but would you consider letting me collab with you?

I was lying on my back in bed with my feet propped up on my headboard, and I tried to sit up so fast that I rolled right off the mattress. I practically dislocated something as I hit the floor with a thump they probably felt all the way in the first floor.

I might be interested! I typed back, all cool nonchalance, and rubbed my elbow. Want to meet up tomorrow and discuss the details?

Dash agreed with gratifying enthusiasm. We spent the next few minutes working out where and when we were going to meet. I sent Dash a link to a coffee shop in Greenwich Village—it was a sweaty subway ride from my apartment in Hell's Kitchen, but I figured that in the interest of general safety, I'd better meet him in a different neighborhood.

The day of the meeting I decided at the last minute to walk there, which might have been longer and sweatier than the subway, but at least it helped me burn off some of the jitters.

"Sorry!" I told Dash breathlessly as I hurried inside. "Sorry, sorry, I know I'm late!"

"It's no big deal," he said easily.

"I, uh." I cast a glance around the coffee shop. "I know it's sauna levels of hot out here, but do you want to walk and talk? I have coffee-related trauma that I still haven't healed from."

I was mostly exaggerating for effect, as one does, but there was a grain of truth to my words. Although I was holding on to the hope that the universe wouldn't be cruel enough to put on a repeat performance of the other day. At least not where the spilled coffee was concerned—I still wasn't sure how I was going to get the stains out of my dress.

I was already wired enough that consuming a caffeinated beverage would only result in my head blowing clear off my shoulders. So I went for a watermelon lime slushy instead, pleased at how the bright color shining through the plastic tumbler went with my pink romper.

Stepping out of the aggressively air-conditioned cafe, we headed out into Washington Square Park to stroll among all the other fools who weren't smart enough to stay out of the heat.

"I just want to clarify—again—that I'm not actually affiliated with any, like, production companies. I'm just a little guy with a laptop who wants to write you some scripts," I said, knowing I was rambling and yet utterly helpless to stop. "Potentially, I mean. If you found the stuff I sent you not horrible and wanted me to keep doing it."

Okay, so I was nervous.

"I do, yeah. To be honest, I've been trying to find a good niche for a while—I've mostly retired from trying to model, and right now I'm mostly focusing on my content creation." He caught my gaze and held it with such disarming sincerity that I almost forgot to draw in my next breath. "Which leads me to the question. Would this idea be something I could explore with some, uh, spicier content? The thing is, I've had a hard time getting any visibility on OnlyFans lately, and I'm kind of worried about audience retention. Chase has been telling me for weeks that I need a gimmick."

Well, that took care of that. I let out a sigh of relief that must not have translated, because Dash's shoulders rose noticeably.

"My content isn't the most explicit, but I'd understand if you'd rather not be involved in it at all," he said, shoving a lock of hair off his forehead and looking kind of like I do when I wish I would've kept my big mouth shut. "It's just that OnlyFans is how I'm making the bulk of my income right now and—"

"Actually, that would be amazing," I blurted out, and some of the tension left Dash's shoulders. "There's like no Regency-themed spice out there—not a single naked duke to be found in the whole internet. And trust me, I looked. You'd corner the market, or whatever. Corporate-speak is clearly not my forte."

"Until you reached out to me, I'd never really considered taking cosplay to the next level." Dash took a sip of coffee. "Which is actually kind of weird, given how much Regency I read."

"Oh yeah?"

"My mother named me Dashwood." Grimacing, he led us to an empty bench. "It would have been Marianne or Elinor if I'd been a girl, but to her huge disappointment, she only had me. And let's not even talk about the fact that my dad's last name is Bennet—though maybe she would've stayed married to him if it had been Darcy."

I cocked my head as I sat down. "So does that make you sense or sensibility?"

"A little bit of both, I guess," he said. And then he did this leading-man hair flip that might have been an unconscious gesture, but from the tiny smile on the corner of his lips it was obvious that he knew what an effect it had on other people.

And it was. Having an effect on me, I mean. My knees didn't shake and I didn't feel sparks or electricity or whatever it is you're supposed to feel, but there was definitely . . . something.

A little catch in my breath. So tiny it was almost imperceptible. But perceive it I did, and it was probably what made me pop out with "Too bad she didn't name you Hardwood—that would've been even more on theme."

He roared out a laugh so loud, it scared off the squirrel that had been stealthily scurrying down the tree trunk behind us. A few feet away, an older couple on another bench smiled in our direction. Part of me wanted to go up to them and explain that no, this wasn't a date, and no, we weren't two young people in the golden haze of a summer romance, just a potential working relationship that involved social media and dicks. Well, dick, singular. Potentially.

"I mean, you're not wrong," Dash said when he recovered. There was an easiness to his grin that felt like . . . well, like beers and hot dogs on a summer Saturday. Like a picnic blanket that's just been unfurled over fresh grass and—

Ah, fuck.

I had no choice but to keep digging myself in even deeper, if only to keep that last thought from showing on my too expressive face. "I mean, it's not like Dashwood isn't on brand either."

His groan was threaded through with laughter. "I know, right? I'd have used it as a stage name, if it weren't so on the nose."

"And *the dashing Duke of Harding* isn't?" I said, snickering.

"It's kind of unfair that your name is so normal."

"Oh, there's plenty of stuff about me worth poking fun at," I told him. "You'll find out eventually."

"I hope I do."

Honestly, it was pretty rude that a man who looked like he should be cast in bronze had the charisma to say something like that, as he gave me a warm, sparkly-eyed smile, and somehow come off as charming instead of like a total fuckboy.

Banishing away thoughts of beer, hot dogs, picnic blankets, and other summery treats, I pushed a stray curl behind my ear and dug into my bag for the notebook and pen I had stashed inside. "So I think I gave you a pretty thorough overview of the whole thing by email. Not that there's all that much to it—basically, I write the scripts and you, uh, dress up as the Duke and perform them. I have a lot of free time right now, what with being funemployed and all, so I would love to be involved in sourcing the costumes and arranging the set or whatever it takes to, you know, pull the vision together."

He nodded. "Sure. I'd appreciate the help. I usually make content in my apartment, so helping me put together a set would involve going all the way up to Hell's Kit—"

"*Shut up*," I blurted out before he had a chance to finish his sentence. "I live in Hell's Kitchen. Fifty-second and Ninth."

Dash cracked up again. "Then why'd you have me come all the way down here?"

"I needed to make sure you weren't a serial killer first," I replied, shrugging.

"You have no way of knowing I'm not."

"True, but now I have a strand of your hair in case the police have to comb my corpse for DNA evidence and uh, that got way dark way fast so let's pretend I didn't say that." I waved a hand in the air, as if to clear the subject from between us. "So anyway, yes, I will make the huge sacrifice of trekking all the way to your apartment in the same neighborhood as mine. I probably have a couple of things we could use—if you like them, we can plan the rest around that."

"Sure. The set doesn't have to be anything fancy; we basically just need a corner and, like, a chair."

"A nice upholstered chair. And maybe some drapery and a vase of flowers or two," I added, making a note on my notebook. "We want these videos to be eye-catching and aesthetically appealing."

He tilted his head like a nineteenth-century coquette. "Are you saying my face isn't aesthetically appealing enough on its own?"

"Aren't you a little too beautiful to be fishing for compliments?"

"Let me tell you something, Mariel." Dash shifted closer, and if I'd been writing a scene for the Duke, I would have described that glint in his eye as *wicked*. And the little shiver that went through my body when he dropped his voice to speak in my ear? Definitely a *frisson*. "Dukes? We're just people. We need adulation and flattery just like anyone else. We need . . . attention."

He hadn't laid a single finger on me, but I felt like I'd just been caressed.

I stared at him in astonishment. "I'm so jealous. If I could do that as well as you can, I would never have to pay for my own drinks again. Maybe not even my rent."

He grinned, clearly delighted with himself. "I'd be more than happy to buy you a drink or two."

"Aw, look at you being all gallant in real life." I gave my watermelon slushy a shake. "I'm definitely up for celebrating this partnership with some frosé. If I've managed to convince you that you *should* go into partnership with me and not run away screaming."

"I'll hold off on the running for when it's less hot." Dash took a last swig of his coffee and set the cup down on the few inches of park bench between us. "There is one other thing I wanted to talk to you about, though. I think that Chase would be a great addition to the project. He's been wanting to get into content creation for a while. I haven't told him about your idea, but if you wanted more people to write scripts for, I know he'll be into it."

"I can see it. You're the gentleman, he's the rake. He can be Lord Loving," I added gleefully.

"Hah! He'll like that. He's going to be away for the next few weeks, doing some research for his dissertation, but I'll shoot him an email."

I tried to nod in a way that conveyed my enthusiasm but not my desperation. "Please, feel free. I have more than enough ideas for the two of you." Not to mention, I could really use the money.

We talked through the financials, and even that came together pretty painlessly when Dash agreed that I would get a percentage of all the income generated by the videos, instead of a flat fee for each script.

"There's just one final thing," I said, capping my pen as I finished taking notes for the contract I was going to ask Yaz to draw up for us even though I knew exactly how she was going to react when I told her I was doing this for real. "Can you do a British accent?"

He paused for a second, looking thoughtful. Then he said, "You'll pardon me for being so bold, but I should very much like to be your duke, Lady Mariel," in a crisp, upper-crust accent that wouldn't have sounded out of place in a Jane Austen adaptation.

Somehow—who the hell knows how—I managed not to swoon, faint, or scream. I merely grinned at him and held out my hand for him to shake. "A pleasure to meet you, Your Grace."

4

An overly caffeinated Dash and I met up at the 50th Street subway station and made our way into Williamsburg for a day of armchair thrifting. A quick email to one of my old coworkers had provided me with a list of the consignment stores used to source antique furniture for the studio's clients. It was all bound to be expensive and my personal budget didn't extend far enough to afford so much as a matchstick from Brooklyn's pricey thrift stores, but Dash had come up with a decent production budget for our first batch of videos.

Anyway, we'd be able to hit all the flea markets that Sunday if it turned out nothing in the stores was within our reach.

That late in the morning, the L train was empty enough that we were free to spread out on the hard plastic seats. In theory. In reality, we ended up huddled together when Dash pulled out his tablet and started showing me some of the graphics he'd been working on.

We'd gone back and forth texting on the color palette the night before, and we'd settled on bubblegum pink, cornflower blue, and the loveliest shade of lavender. Dash had translated that into this floral motif curled around a coat of arms that managed to look simultaneously regal—dukely?—and modern.

"Eye-catching and aesthetic, right?" Dash asked, passing me the iPad so I could scroll through all the versions.

"Like your face," I replied, earning myself a smile and one of those patented hair flips that made parts of my anatomy follow suit.

I mean, the L train was making my stomach flip, too, if in a slightly different way.

We made it to the Bedford Ave stop without any more acrobatics, and from there it was a brisk walk to the first store on my list. I kept catching sight of our reflections in storefronts—me in pink and red, curls spiraling every which way, and a much taller Dash in a graphic T-shirt and black shorts that made him look like the model that he was.

And I wasn't the only one who thought so. It wasn't like his face made anyone stop in their tracks or anything, but pretty much everyone we passed gave him a once-over. He must have been used to it, because he barely seemed to notice the glances being thrown his way, even though they weren't at all subtle.

Somehow, we got to Thrifty without anyone throwing themselves at Dash's feet and either proclaiming their undying love or begging to have his babies. If you ask me, though, it was a close call.

As the door chimed behind us, I made a beeline for the clothes and accessories section at the back. He already had the breeches, and we'd commissioned shirts, a coat, and a cravat from someone we'd found on Etsy, but he still needed tall leather boots. And if we found a riding crop, I definitely wasn't going to complain.

Or ask that he use it on me.

Disappointingly, I didn't find any equestrian implements among the designer dresses and vintage band T-shirts. What I did rustle up from the crowded racks was a cape—a slim camel hair one, more runway-ready than Regency. Still, I couldn't resist slipping it around my shoulders and going over to pose in the mirror. Dash followed with a pair of large, round Jackie O sunglasses and a cream-colored beret.

He took one look at himself and made a face, plopping the beret on top of my curls. "Looks better on you."

I squinted at myself. "This outfit makes me look like one of those girls who has enough of her shit together to have a morning routine that doesn't involve listening to boyfriend audios."

Dash glanced down at me. "Boyfriend audios?"

"Like micro audiobooks where a very talented voice actor goes through different scenarios as if he's talking directly to the listener.

Kind of like what we're going to do, actually. I may or may not have fallen asleep to one of those channels every day for, uh, an undisclosed length of time after my last breakup. Hugging a pillow. While he went to bed with someone else."

Dash winced. "Ouch."

"It's not as bad as it sounds," I told him, shrugging. "I could still be with Bruno."

"Bruno?"

"The man we don't talk about." I flashed Dash a smile.

He snorted and put his sunglasses back onto the tray they'd come from. "I can see how a fictional boyfriend would be preferable to most of the men in this city. A fictional boyfriend never drops his wet towels on the bathroom floor."

"Or leaves the seat up."

"Or hogs the covers," Dash said.

All of a sudden, my mind clicked over into an idea. "Dude, we should record videos."

Dash blinked, glancing away from the mirror he was checking himself out in. "I thought that was the plan?"

"No, like, non-spicy ones for regular social media." Excitement made me fling my arms out. "Like boyfriend audios, only as the Duke of Harding. All the ones I used to listen to are sound only, but since you've got the looks and the costume and everything and I happen to believe that wastefulness is a sin . . ."

"Your boyfriend the duke," he said slowly. "Who reads you poetry and cuddles you to sleep."

"And comforts you after a nightmare," I chimed in.

"And gets a little naughty in the carriage on your way to a ball."

"And strokes your hair in bed on Sunday mornings, listing all the reasons why he wants to make you his duchess."

Unconsciously, we'd drifted together until we were standing toe to toe, me with my face turned up to look into Dash's as he said, "And convinces you to sneak into the stables for a midnight kiss."

Of all the things, that was what made a little shiver run through me.

"A man after my own heart," I declared, thumping my chest—partly in illustration, and partly to get rid of the uncomfortable tingling sensation radiating from it. "You know, it kind of reminds me of these second-person POV fics that used to be a big thing on Tumblr back in the day."

"Don't tell me—X Reader fics?" His patented hair flip didn't quite hide the glint of laughter in his eyes at my surprised expression. "I had a lot of free time in high school, okay? And a lot of feelings about Sherlock Holmes and John Watson."

"Oh yeah? Care to share any of those with me?"

"Maybe let's wait until we know each other better before I bare my entire soul to you," he said, laughing. "And my OTPs. All you have to know is that I have spent the past twelve or so years exploring the dark, shadowy corners of online fandom, so there's really not much you can throw at me that'll surprise me."

"I noticed that."

"And yet, you look surprised."

I spread my hands. "It's just that I wouldn't have taken you for the sensitive, artsy type who reads Sherlock/Watson fanfic on Tumblr. You strike me as the kind of person who was popular in high school—and middle school." I looked him up and down. "Maybe even elementary school."

There was a flicker in his eyes, as if he was startled that I'd read him so easily. But come on. The grin and the hair flip alone were a dead giveaway.

"Well, I was, I guess," he said slowly. "But it wasn't always great. All of that came with a lot of pressure, and I had enough of that at home. I was modeling at the time, so there was that, too. There was something really appealing about disappearing into anonymity for a few hours every day and fandom was that for me."

"As someone who has lived in blissful anonymity for most of her life, I agree." Still wearing the cape and beret, I turned to go through the menswear rack. "So how come you ended up literally baring everything for a living?"

Dash flung an arm over the rack, his head hanging down just enough that I was staring full into his eyes when he said, "I don't mind being looked at. I just want to be seen sometimes."

Ohh. Oh, no. The *crushing* earnestness in his eyes. It was too much. Way too much for me to cope with.

Who the hell walks around just *saying* stuff like that?

If this had been happening in my screenplay, he would have gotten the reply he deserved—a soulful gaze into his eyes, followed by an intense "I see you" and an epic kiss.

And, like, even outside of a romcom, a decent friend would have replied with something equally as thoughtful.

This being me, what he got was . . . a flail.

"I can't imagine a more terrifying thing than being seen, unless it's ultra low-rise jeans," I said. "Wait, is that stool shaped like a *strawberry*? I need it."

My cherry earrings swung as I whirled around and marched toward the housewares and furniture section. Dash trailed after me, looking faintly amused when I bypassed the stool and snatched a vase off a shelf instead, cradling it in my arms like it was my long-lost son.

"This will be perfect for our set," I said.

"Uh, Mariel? Not to be rude or anything, but that is the ugliest fucking vase I've ever seen."

"You're not wrong," I admitted. "But the shape is great. I figure we can paint over the—oh lord, are those ba—"

Dash stepped in so close, my curls must have been brushing his jaw. "Grapes," he said after a moment's inspection. "I think."

"That's a relief." I couldn't quite bring myself to look at him yet.

"I don't think any of the chairs here are right for the Duke's parlor," Dash said, sticking his hands in his pockets. If he was annoyed or upset at my brushing off his attempt to get all real and vulnerable, he wasn't showing it. "Maybe we should pay for the vase and head for the next place?"

"It's a plan." I started for the cash register—and stopped suddenly when I felt myself being tugged backward. I twisted around. "Wha—"

"You might want to leave the cape and beret, unless you're planning on doing a little cosplaying yourself."

"As what, an ice cream cone with a scoop of vanilla? I've never worn beige in my life."

Shrugging off the cape, I folded it over my arm and put it back where it came from. By the time I caught up with Dash at the cash register, he was already paying for the vase.

I stuffed it into my tote and we strolled back out into the grimy street. I was going to need some sugar if I was going to make it through today. "Speaking of ice cream—want to go have a cone at the waterfront?"

"A cone? It's not even eleven in the morning."

"So? Haven't you ever heard of a breakfast banana split? Made with three scoops of coffee-flavored ice cream?"

Dash looked scandalized. "*What?*"

"And whipped cream, and a little cereal sprinkled on top for crunch," I added, laughing at Dash's shudder. "Oh, don't be so conventional. Breakfast is a societal construct."

"So are pants, but you don't see me walking around in my boxers."

"Honestly, I doubt you'd stand out that much in this city. Then again," I added, without thinking, "with that ass you might just start a riot."

Luckily for me, Dash just laughed. "Wouldn't be the first time," he said, winking.

There was a sharp intake of breath, and I turned my head just in time to see a gray-haired man almost walk into a pole, utterly distracted by Dash's wink.

I bit my lip to hide my smile. As an oblivious Dash walked on, I made a mental note to have business cards made to hand out to any other passersby who found themselves too awestruck by his face to keep from colliding against obstacles in their path.

◆ ◆ ◆

We settled for a bakery, where Dash got a croissant and yet another latte and I opted for a loaded to-go waffle that was breakfast-adjacent if you squinted. From the bakery, it wasn't too far a walk to the long path that bordered the East River. Under the brilliant blue sky, the Manhattan skyline shone like a tiara made out of steel and glass.

"Come on," I said. "There's a bench up there."

"Tired already?"

"Never. But I do have to write down all the stuff we were talking about before I forget it."

Even before reaching the bench, I was already scrabbling in my tote for my notebook and pen—so intently that I would've walked into a trash can had Dash not gently seized me by the shoulders and steered me away.

"Thanks," I said, plopping down on the hot metal seat. "I turn into a menace whenever I try to walk and literally do anything else. Okay, so."

I bent over my notebook, scribbling down furiously all the things we'd just said plus a couple of fresh ideas. I must have gone into a little bit of a hyperfocus spiral, because when I resurfaced, it was to find Dash kind of . . . gazing at me. Like he liked what he saw. Which couldn't have been the case because I was pretty sure I had a smear of syrup on my chin.

And maybe it was the sun beaming down behind him, but I felt so dazzled I had to blink a couple of times. The stroll in the sun had brushed glowing pink over the bridge of his nose and the top of his cheekbones, and even his eyes looked more golden than the dark brown they actually were.

It took me an embarrassingly long moment to realize he was talking. "Got it all down?"

I gave him a brisk nod. "All of it and more. I'll work on turning a couple of these into scripts tonight. I think we should shoot for minute-long videos to start with, and then we can adjust depending on viewer feedback. That sound good?"

"It does, yeah." Dash ran his fingers through his hair.

I squinted at him. "You okay?"

"Yeah," he said again. "I just . . . this just . . ." There was a richness to the breath he let out, as if he were laughing at himself under his breath. "I haven't been this excited about a project in a long time, and that's probably thanks to you. Your enthusiasm is . . ."

"Concerning?" I supplied.

Dash gave me a sidelong look. "I was gonna say inspiring. And contagious. I honestly can't wait to start shooting—and I can't wait to see what else you come up with."

"Careful what you wish for. Things can get pretty wild in here." Jamming my pen into the notebook's spiral freed up my hand so that I could tap my temple in illustration. "I've been told I have a dangerous imagination."

"Oh yeah?" Dash got up and offered me his hand. "Luckily for you, I happen to like a little danger now and then."

The second store on my list looked a lot more promising than the first one, and not just because of all the sugar swirling inside me. For starters, the place was crammed with furniture. Literally. Through the open garage-style doors, I could see piles of spindly legged tables and chairs, and sofas that looked like venerable old dowagers swathed in faded chintz.

"This is it—I can feel it," I declared as I dragged Dash inside. "This is where we're going to find the Duke's chair. And maybe a cute little table for the vase."

And drapes and a snuffbox and I still hadn't given up on the riding crop.

I plunged into the precariously stacked mounds of furniture like I was Indiana Jones scouting for a mythical treasure.

There were quite a few sleek mid-century modern pieces, some clunkers that could only have come from the nineties shabby chic, let's-hide-TVs-in-distressed-armoires era, but so far nothing that resembled the image in my head.

"I want an armchair," I said over my shoulder to Dash. "High-backed, so that it'll frame your head and torso. Upholstered, though the fabric doesn't matter as we'll probably have to redo that anyway."

"Noted."

Hunting for treasure among piles of junk is always hard work. I spotted a gold candlestick and set it aside, but all my energy was focused on finding The Chair.

I thought Dash was similarly engrossed, but it turned out his silence was due to something else. "So, hey," he said, clearing his throat. "I hope I didn't make you uncomfortable earlier with all that . . ."

Letting go of the rocking chair I'd been wrestling with, I glanced at him. "Unbridled honesty and painful earnestness?" I'd intended to be funny, but at Dash's wince, I rushed to add, "You're fine. I'm the one who should apologize for basically running away when you were trying to open up."

"No, no. I mean, we haven't known each other that long. I shouldn't be laying all that stuff on you."

I waved a hand in the air. "Oh, it's not your fault that I'm incapable of facing genuine human emotion without feeling the urge to bolt. I think I might be part android."

Dash's naturally upturned lips twitched. "Then I'm sorry for disturbing your android sensibilities. I just . . . want you to know that it's totally okay to run away or simply tell me to shut up if I'm getting too emotional."

"In all honesty, I will probably do both of those things at once. And maybe let out a scream or two." I came to a sudden stop as my roaming gaze caught a glimpse of someone familiar. Something halfway between a whimper and a groan escaped my lips. "Ohhh. Oh no."

"What?" Dash whispered, following me as I dove behind a massive gumball machine. "It's not Bruno, is it?"

"Bru— Milo? No. *No*," I added, breathing hard. "It's just . . . someone I used to know from work."

"And I take it you don't want to say hello?" he asked dryly.

"I don't even want to exist in the same universe as her." I snuck a peek around the spheric glass of the machine, which was thankfully clouded from years of disuse. "Shit, I think they're coming this way."

Before I could explain to Dash that I had the emotional maturity of a potato and that I would do pretty much anything to avoid my former boss and her client, he was seizing me by the wrist.

"What are you doing?" I asked as I stumbled and caught myself against his chest. Or maybe he caught me—his arm was suddenly around my waist and the contact was making my brain short out.

For a second, Dash looked like he'd had the wind knocked out of him. Then he flashed me one of his grins and lowered his face to mine, as if he were seconds away from kissing me. "What every romantic hero does when the leading lady needs to hide from the bad guys."

I was too aware of my chest rising and falling with each breath, the ruffles on my pleated top brushing his T-shirt. "Saved by the Duke," I murmured.

Except for the slight curling of his lips, Dash didn't move. But the warm, coffee-scented breath that trailed over my lips was as good as a caress. I inhaled—in preparation for what, I couldn't tell you, because it wasn't like we were actually going to kiss or anything. Try telling that to my body, though. His hand was light on my waist, but it felt like the only thing preventing me from floating right up to the store's high ceiling. Because just the thought, just the possibility of getting to kiss Dash was enough to send me soaring.

I couldn't even remember how we'd come to stand like this in the first place. All I knew was that it felt so right that I was prepared to risk *everything* just for one tiny brush of—

"Mariel?"

I *knew* I should have straightened my hair and dyed it purple. Mentally cursing myself out for letting Yaz convince me otherwise, I disentangled myself from Dash and turned around to face my former boss. "Elaine. Hi. It's nice to see you." I shifted my gaze behind her, to the woman in the pearly gray shift dress who looked like she didn't want to exist in the same universe as me, either. "And Mrs. Greyson. I hope you're well."

Both women answered my greeting with pleasant smiles and murmured greetings, though I was sure I saw a wary glint in Elaine's eyes. And who could blame her? The last time I was face-to-face with Mrs. Greyson, I was screaming at her.

In the process of installing a built-in that had been added to the family room on a whim, after most of the room had already been finished, one of the younger members of the contractor's crew had accidentally scratched the expensive wallpaper. In the interest of saving both time and money, because we were already behind schedule and over budget, I'd asked our wallpaper guy to replace the damaged segment with a remnant. Mrs. Greyson had scrutinized the entire process, fretting over whether the pattern was matching up perfectly and pointing out smears of paste that would become invisible when it dried.

It shouldn't have been a big deal, especially since she'd been acting that way for the entire length of the renovation. But that day, in my emotionally charged post-breakup state, her entitlement fell on me like dynamite sticks in a bonfire.

And I exploded. "What the hell is wrong with you?" I raged at her. "Can't you see he's doing his best? Can't you see we're all doing our best?"

Not my finest moment. Or my most professional either. Especially considering it had happened in front of the crew . . . and the Greysons' nanny . . . and their ten- and eight-year-olds . . . and a friend of the children's who'd come over for a playdate.

Had my frustration been justified? Well, maybe. Mrs. Greyson was the most demanding client I'd ever been tasked with appeasing, and the way she nitpicked everything the contractors did made for a tense and toxic work environment. But I still shouldn't have raised my voice. And even though I'd apologized, the fact that I'd exploded now hung over the three of us.

"How's the renovation going?" I asked, just to cut into the awkward silence.

"We're almost done," Elaine answered. "Just working on the final details."

Her gaze skipped to Dash, and the expectant pause that followed reminded me that I hadn't introduced them. Silly of me not to use him as a human buffer.

"Oh! This is my friend Dash. We're looking for an armchair."

He leaned forward slightly, offering his hand first to Elaine and then to Mrs. Greyson, who slid her slim fingers into his palm for the briefest shake I'd ever seen. His smile didn't falter as he let his hand fall to his side and made easy small talk with Elaine, diverting the women's attention away from me as if I had come right out and asked him to.

Not even Dash's warmth could melt the frostiness in Mrs. Greyson's excruciatingly polite smile. An ice queen like her would never have lost control the way I had. As Dash and Elaine discussed . . . I don't know, something about armchairs maybe, I found myself examining Mrs. Greyson—her sleek, pulled-back hair, the discreet studs in her ears, the way her expression was as smooth and blank as a fresh piece of paper. She hadn't even blinked while I yelled at her, just stood there in frosty silence until my voice was ragged. Only then had she said, "Was that all?"—and turned around to glide out of the room in her noiseless Chanel flats.

I've always been loud and I've always taken up more than my share of space, but I had never felt so bad about it.

Luckily for me, Elaine and Mrs. Greyson seemed as eager as I was to put some distance between us, and at the timely intervention of a salesperson, Dash and I made our escape.

"So, that was kind of awkward," he said once we were clear across the room. "What happened?"

I kept my gaze straight ahead, all the better to ignore the sympathy in his warm brown eyes. "The redhead, Elaine, used to be my boss at the interior design firm I was working at up until about three weeks ago. The other lady was—still is, I guess—a client."

"Sounds like something big went down there."

"If by that you mean a catastrophe of apocalyptic proportions, then yes. Something did go down." My fingers twitched restlessly, but even with emotions roiling inside my chest like a ship in a storm, I knew better than to run my hand through my well-defined curls. I settled for curling up my hand into a fist and shoving it into my pocket. "I know right now it looks like I have people-shaped land mines all around the city, but I promise, I'm actually pretty easy to get along with. You just happened to have met me at a pretty weird time in my life."

"I believe you," he said easily, loping along on his ridiculously long legs. "You don't really strike me as the sort of person who leaves a trail of enemies wherever she goes."

"I mean, I wouldn't mind calling Elaine and Mrs. Greyson my enemies. Sounds a hell of a lot better than *the lady who fired me* and *the lady who got me fired*." I came to a halt next to a pinball machine. "Actually, that's not fair to Mrs. Greyson. I got myself fired. She was just . . . the catalyst. And I was incredibly unprofessional and deserved to lose my job. It all worked out for the best, though," I added lightly. "Because employed people don't hang around Times Square in broad daylight and get mistaken for pop stars and chased by a pitchfork-wielding mob."

"I think they were wielding smartphones, not pitchforks," Dash remarked. "But I'm happy the stars aligned and we ended up meeting."

I paused, partly to debate with myself whether or not I should add anything more, and partly to stare at a section of the store that seemed to be made mostly of chairs. Turns out, taking the time to actually look at the piles of furniture meant that I was able to see something interesting lurking underneath a very obviously fake Eames lounge chair.

Looking—what a concept.

"I think I see something. Can you help me get these tables off? Actually, hold on."

I pulled out my phone and cued up a song, then asked Dash to hold it, which he did, looking faintly amused. I turned back to the pile, and as the first strains of the Indiana Jones theme filled the air, I dug out a shapely armchair. Her curved back was crowned with roses and vines carved out of wood, and her legs and arms undulated with sinuous, languorous grace.

She was the sexiest chair I'd ever seen.

"That's it, all right," Dash remarked.

Her upholstery was pretty tattered, but like I'd told Dash earlier, I was planning to re-cover whatever we found anyway. "Pink velvet," I said, circling my precious. "Bubblegum pink—it'll pop on camera and it'll look amazing against your skin."

"Which means the draperies will have to be the paler blue we picked out, right? And my coat is that deep ultramarine, so we'll have three values for the foreground, background, and middle ground . . ." Dash looked thoughtful.

I nodded, grateful for the opportunity to change the subject back to our project. "The drapes should be light and plain enough that they'll add texture without being too distracting. The chair will frame your body and the coat and shirt will frame your . . ." I gestured in the general direction of his chest. "Torso."

"Sounds like you've been thinking a lot about my . . . torso," he said teasingly, the twinkle in his eyes taking the edge off his smirk.

I kept my tone light. "Sorry to break it to you, buddy, but thinking about your torso is my literal job now."

"You're a total heartbreaker, Mariel, did you know that?" He literally winked at me as he stepped close enough to slip my phone into my pocket. And though he turned away almost immediately to wave down the salesperson, I had the impression that he could tell just how badly that wink had weakened my knees.

It wasn't my imagination, right? He'd been flirty with me from the moment we'd met. But was it flirt*ing*—Oprah emphasis on the last syllable—or was it just a mixture of his natural charisma and my flighty imagination?

Either way . . . I had no intention of acting on it.

5

So it turned out that Dash lived less than four blocks away from me. You'd think I'd have noticed him around the neighborhood before, but it hadn't been that long since he'd moved uptown from Crown Heights. At least, that was what he told me when I ran into him at the laundromat a few days later.

I'd procrastinated so much on laundry that I didn't even have beat-up sweats to wear and had to settle for one of the poufy pink dresses hanging in the back corner of my closet. I toned it down by putting on a green striped T-shirt underneath and pairing the whole thing with a pair of sneakers and a New Yorker tote that had seen better days.

You know, and an eight-hundred-pound bag of dirty laundry that I could barely drag down the stairs of my walk-up.

Wearing a light blue T-shirt that brought out his tan, Dash looked like someone who had cartoon birds and mice laying out fresh clothes for him every day.

Running into him at the laundromat didn't surprise me, and not just because it was bound to happen sooner or later, with us living within a ten-block radius of each other. He'd flashed into my mind so often in the days after our trip out to Williamsburg that like any good Dominican, I felt as though I'd called him with my thoughts.

"Hey there," I said, a little jolt twanging through me as I hauled my bag closer to one of the two machines that were free.

"Mariel!" Looking truly delighted to see me, he slammed the door of his washer shut and came over to give me a hug. A real one, too, the kind where both his arms came around me and I found myself with my nose buried in his collarbone.

Thinking about how romance novelists always described the hero's scent, I took an experimental sniff and tried to decide what Dash smelled like. A little like detergent, but that was a given in our current location. Sun-soaked skin, with faint whiffs of coffee. Notes of something citrusy, probably his soap or shampoo.

"Mariel, are you . . . sniffing me?"

His voice rumbled over my skin in a way that made me want to burrow closer. Reluctantly, I pulled away and gave him a bright smile. "Just doing some research!"

Ignoring his confused look, I dragged my laundry bag over the grimy floor. Of course, I had to try to shove my entire load (heh) at once into one of the sleek silver machines so that he didn't notice the huge discrepancy in my ratio of ratty panties versus pretty, lacy ones, and of course, that only resulted in my spilling everything onto the dirty tiles. A—cute and extremely ladylike—grunt of frustration escaped my lips as I hunkered down and started picking up sweaty shorts and crumpled dresses and flinging them into the open washer.

"You got anything good planned for today?" I asked, craning my neck up to see him lounging against the machines, his long, elegant fingers curled around his phone.

The machine Dash had claimed was already humming its way through a wash cycle. "Not really. I usually call my grandmas on Saturdays, so they'll be waiting by their phone and probably bickering over it as per usual, but that's about it."

I grinned up at him. "That's adorable."

"*They* are," he said, a smile crinkling the corners of his eyes. "It was the best thing to come out of my parents' blink-and-you'll-miss-it relationship—Nana and Grandma fell in love when everything between my parents was imploding, right around the time I was born. Now they live together, and more importantly, they and the other Slot Sluts roll into Atlantic City every month together. They're in Vegas now, though, and Nana tells me they're dominating the blackjack table."

Glancing down at his phone, he said, "I should call now, actually, if I want to catch them before they head out to the breakfast buffet."

Dash strolled out and I busied myself trying to find my detergent. If I peeked out the window, though, I could see him running a hand through his thick hair as he paced up and down the sidewalk, dazzling passersby with smiles they didn't realize were meant for his grandmas.

By the time he came back inside and plopped down next to me, I was studiously reading a Regency novel—okay, skimming, but only because the seats were next to the window and it was distracting how so many people kept slowing down to check out Dash.

"Whatcha reading?" he asked, his fingers loosely curled around a to-go cup.

"One of the Regencies from my pile. I'm making a list of all the tropes and all the hot stuff dukes do."

Dash grinned. "I started a spreadsheet. You know, there's this tiny little bookstore a few blocks away that sells used paperbacks, mostly romance. I'm talking Mills & Boon from the seventies type stuff. We should go check it out."

"Right now?"

He checked his phone. "I have eighteen minutes left on my machine. Doesn't give us a lot of time to browse, so maybe while we're drying?"

There really was no need for my heart to get all acrobatic again over his casual use of the word *we* in relation to himself, me, and the kind of domestic task that I saw couples performing on lazy weekend mornings. "Sounds like the perfect way to spend a Saturday."

I meant it, too. Not just because I would get to spend a little more time going weak-kneed at the sight of Dash flipping his hair, but because it had been a while since I'd had actual plans with an actual person on a weekend morning. If by any chance I made it through a couple of dates with someone without getting ghosted, none of those guys were willing to commit to more than the occasional after-work and pre-hookup drink. I'd made exactly zero friends in the city outside of my job, and the awkwardness over having been fired meant that I hadn't really hung out with anyone other than Dash in weeks.

It had gotten so bad that I had almost—almost being the operative word—considered joining a gym or taking some sort of class, just to have the occasional conversation with anyone other than the bodega guy, who I was pretty sure was getting sick of hearing about my screenplay.

A woman with two kids and even more laundry than me squeezed past, forcing Dash to inch closer to me to avoid being crushed between the window and her bags. I fumbled with my book, almost dropping it as his arm pressed against mine and I became reacquainted with his fresh, crisp scent.

Even after the woman passed, he didn't shift back right away—he stayed close, almost leaning on me, as if he was comfortable there. And I . . . I didn't move, either.

I mean, I didn't want him to think that I was weirded out by such a casual touch. Or that his arm brushing mine made me so tingly that I felt like I'd been dipped into a bathtub full of stars.

Dash didn't even seem like he was aware that we were still all pressed together. "At the risk of sounding like we're on a job interview or a first date," he was asking, "who would you be if you were a character in a Regency romance?"

Well, that was an unfair thing to do to my poor, overworked heart.

"Uh, the eccentric great aunt who makes inappropriate jokes and can't stop meddling in the main characters' love lives?" I shrugged, and gestured at my pink dress and striped T-shirt. "I don't think they've come up with a trope yet that encompasses all of this."

"What about the hellion?" he suggested, and I found myself leaning forward as the wicked twist in his smile sent a rush of heat washing over me. "The willful, bold, scandalous heiress that drives the hero to distraction. Who makes him want to tear off his hair—and her clothes—as she gallops around, being sassy to highwaymen and shocking everyone with her delightful impropriety."

"That does sound like me," I said, laughing as I thought about how much better it was being called a hellion than *chaotic.* "Now, if only I knew where to find a highwayman . . ."

Dash made a gun out of his thumb and forefinger and pressed it to the sliver of bare skin above the collar of my T-shirt. "Your money or your life."

I cocked an eyebrow. "Is there a third option?"

"For you?" Dash inclined his head an inch closer to mine, lowering his voice and adopting the British accent he'd laid on me the other day. "My lady, I would give you as many options as you needed. As many as it takes to satisfy you. As many as it takes until you're spent and quivering in my arms."

This time, I really did drop my paperback. "Remind me why you need a scriptwriter again?"

He sat back in his chair, looking smug, and took a casual swig of coffee. "You liked that, huh?"

I garbled something unintelligible.

Dash winked at me. "That's why they call me the talent."

I had a list of other things I could call him, including *daddy,* but in the interest of being professional—or as professional as I could be when he had just almost made me ruin my panties—I refrained.

"Yep," I said. "Talented is a thing you definitely are."

It was a sad excuse for a compliment, but it made Dash look absurdly pleased. He beamed at me, all light and sparkles and cartoon hearts, and went to fish my book from where it had skidded under a pair of rolling laundry carts.

If I didn't change the subject to something safe, I was going to do more than be unprofessional.

"How are your grandmas doing?" I asked when he rejoined me. "On their way to becoming billionaires?"

"Or broke, or outlaws," he said cheerfully. "Or reenacting the plot of all three *Hangover* movies—I wouldn't put it past those two to steal a tiger and keep it in their hotel bathroom."

"It's so nice how close you are to them," I told him, tucking *The Wallflower's Bargain* back into my bag.

"They babysat me a lot growing up, and I lived with them for a couple years before college."

"Your parents weren't around?" I asked.

"Oh, they were. A little too much. It's like they were in a competition as to who helped me with more of my homework or drove me to the most auditions."

He gave a pause, like he was expecting me to commiserate. "Parents, right?" I said after a moment.

"Truly annoying," he agreed. "The grandmas didn't let me get away with much, but they were much more chilled."

I never got to meet my abuela, who passed away years before I was born. For the first time, it occurred to me to wonder about my other grandparents, on my dad's side. A momentary longing to know them bloomed in my chest, but it died down quickly—I'd already been left by enough family members.

Besides, as far as I knew, they hadn't made much of an effort to see me over the years. Just like their son.

Realizing that I had wandered down yet another dangerous path, I tried to steer us back to a safe subject. "By the way, did you have a chance to check out the scene I sent you last night?"

When I had hunkered down with my laptop, I had truly intended to make some more progress on my screenplay. But as soon as I opened my writing software, I found myself daydreaming about the Duke of Harding. As I wrote with an ease I hadn't felt in years, a knot I hadn't realized lived inside my chest began to unravel.

Next to me, Dash was nodding. "That one might be my favorite yet. I'm thinking that maybe I'll film that one first." He unlocked his phone and pulled up the document I had emailed him. "What do you think about shifting this paragraph to the hurt/comfort video and adding this here instead?"

My gaze followed the movements of his fingers as he tapped out some edits. Even if he hadn't told me about his past in fandom, I would have guessed from the way he had grasped the basics of the Duke of Harding character and built on it.

Something else struck me as we hunched over the small screen, one suggestion following quick on the heels of another until we had most of another scene written—Dash and I worked well together. Maybe it was the project or the lack of pressure or just the way he seemed so attuned to my thoughts that it was as if we were passing a single brain cell back and forth. But writing with Dash was a goddamn delight.

"We should do this together all the time," I said when Dash's machine came to the end of its cycle. "Write together, I mean."

He glanced at me from over the door of his machine. "Yeah?" he asked happily. From the way he was looking at me, you'd think I'd offered him an afternoon full of dessert and sex. God, why did he have to be so *endearing*?

"Sure," I said, and got up to pretend to check on my clothes, which were still drenched in suds.

And why did I have to be so *charmed* by him?

◆ ◆ ◆

Our clothes safely locked into a drying cycle, we ventured out toward the used bookstore. The sun had grown in heat and intensity—I took one look at a row of flowers wilting in their buckets outside a grocery store and instantly felt like one of them.

I was twisting my curls into a knot to free my sweaty neck when I felt a faint buzzing at my side. I dove into my tote for my phone, checking the name on the display before guiltily declining the call.

"It's okay if you have to take that," Dash said, slowing down.

"Nah, it's just my cousin Yaz." I tapped out a quick text to tell her that I'd call her back later. "She's just calling to check up on me—or, rather, to check that I'm working on my screenplay. And since I'm not, I'd just as soon avoid another lecture."

"Why does your cousin have to lecture you about it?"

Tossing my phone back into my bag, I shrugged. "I'm kind of terrible at getting things done, even things I want to do, and Yaz is pretty good at keeping me on track. We're both only children but

our mothers—they're sisters—lived together for most of our child-
hood, so Yaz is the closest thing to an older sister I'll ever have. And
she doesn't let me forget it for a *minute*."

"You're lucky," Dash said. "I've never been close to my cousins."

"And you're an only child, too, right?" I asked, remembering
something he'd mentioned the other day.

"I have two much younger half siblings, but for all intents and
purposes, yeah, I grew up as an only child. But I do have two kickass
grandmas, so I guess it evens out. Though neither of them are much
for lecturing."

"If it's lecturing you want," I said before I could think better of
it, "I'd be more than happy to help you out. I may be more Chaos
Muppet than Stern Brunch Daddy, but I know a thing or two about
keeping people in line."

He raised an eyebrow. "You think you can keep me in line?"

"Oh, I know I can," I shot back as we paused and Dash swiveled
to face me. "You think you're big and tough? I hate to break it to
you, Dashwood—you're nothing but a cinnamon roll."

"Does that mean you want to take a bite out of me?" he asked,
dropping his voice into a sexy drawl.

I shoved him lightly before I got the tingles again. "You wish."

Okay, so fine, we were definitely flirting. Both of us. But it was
not a problem, because neither of us was going to take it further than
that. There was too much at stake, at least for me, to put our working
relationship in jeopardy over something as ill-advised as a hookup.

Not that I wasn't used to doing six ill-advised things before
breakfast. Not that my pulse wasn't racing in anticipation of the expanding rush of heat that had begun sweeping over me the moment
I thought of the words *hooking up* in relation to Dash.

Not that—

Belatedly, I noticed that Dash was pushing open the door to the
storefront we'd stopped in front of. I had a brief moment to notice
the yellow awning and the words *Second Chance* in rolling script on
the window before Dash was gesturing me inside. He did that tall

guy thing, where he held open the door with a hand placed high overhead while I ducked under him.

"Holy shit," I breathed as I came to a stop in front of a pile of books. "This is—"

Words failed me, but Dash seemed to understand my meaning.

"Right?"

His face had lit up at my amazement, as if he hadn't really believed that I would be this entranced with what was essentially an Aladdin's cave full of worn paperbacks. Pastel and jewel-toned spines peeked out among the mottled beige of old paper, the cracked and sometimes flaking cardboard almost gleaming in the lamps suspended from the decorative tin ceiling.

The shelves were plain wood, bowing slightly under the weight of the paperbacks, and even the counter was piled with books, high enough that I could only see a glint of brown skin and close-cropped dark hair as the person standing behind them waved at Dash in response to his greeting. Strewn around the room were a few battered wooden step stools, perfect for reaching some of the higher stacks. The only thing missing was a plush armchair to cuddle up on.

Or a loveseat that fit two, my brain supplied.

"I feel like Belle in *Beauty and the Beast*," I declared as I made my way around a wobbly pile of Harlequins. "When the Beast showed her his library. Only this is better because I doubt they had romance novels in whatever-century France."

I stopped to run a finger over the glossy embossed letters of a purple-and-pink cover and, impulsively, cracked the book open and brought it to my nose.

"Oh, man. This reminds me of Mrs. Perez. This older Cuban lady who lived down the street from us growing up," I explained to Dash, taking another heady sniff. "She died when I was fourteen or so, and when her daughter came to clean out the house, she found hundreds of romance novels stacked on every surface. She didn't want to deal with all that, so she gave them to Yaz and me in exchange for us helping her pack up her mother's things. Yaz had zero interest in romance novels, but she saw how much I wanted them and busted her ass for an entire weekend."

Dash smiled. "No wonder you let her lecture you."

"I owe her a lot," I said, shrugging as I put down the book.

I hadn't realized until I said it that I did owe Yaz. I owed her peace of mind. If nothing else, I needed to make her see that she didn't need to spend another twenty-six years putting her life on hold to worry about me every time I got myself into one of my flails.

We lapsed into a comfortable silence as we browsed. I could have cheerfully left with half the store, but even a couple of dollars per paperback would be a strain on my limited resources. The two books I did get were mostly for the covers, gorgeous 1980s illustrations that depicted heroines with big dresses and bigger hair, and sinuously curving fonts.

Dash, I noticed, had a whole stack of Candlelight romances. "I'm a sucker for these," he said, handing over a twenty-dollar bill to the person behind the counter. "Hey, Shy. Mariel, this is Shiloh. They own the bookstore."

"Nice to meet you, Shy. You have a great place here."

"And you haven't seen half of it," Dash said happily, before asking Shy, "Mind if we go in the back?"

Shy nodded, their pizza-shaped earrings catching the light from the window behind them. "Sure thing, Dash. Watch out for Kitty Marlowe, though—she's not in the best mood today."

"Kitty Marlowe?" I asked.

"Shy's cat," Dash explained.

"Kitty Marlowe belongs to no one but herself," Shy said, looking amused as they finished bagging up our books. "Want me to keep your bags here until you're ready to go?"

"Sure, thanks. Come on, Mariel."

Dash led to me a green door I hadn't noticed before, mostly because it was obscured by a table piled high with pirate romances.

We stepped through, and it was like walking into a Frances Hodgson Burnett novel.

"What *is* this place?" I asked, mouth hanging open as I whirled around to take in Mary Lennox's wildest dream. Unlike most of Manhattan's green spaces, which looked like they had been manicured to within an inch of their lives, this patch of ground was properly lush. It was about the size of my apartment, which was to say not huge, but it held a few benches set along the walls and a small stage nestled underneath a second-story balcony that bloomed with pale purple flowers.

Wearing the same expression as when we'd first walked into the store, Dash perched on—I'm not shitting you—an actual wooden swing. He was tall enough that his feet dragged on the ground as he attempted to move. "I spent a lot of time here when I first moved to New York. I didn't know anyone, so I would put on my headphones and roam around the city for hours and hours, just looking at everything. When I stumbled across the store, it felt like coming home a little bit. I got into the habit of dropping in a few times a week, often enough that I got to know Shy pretty well. They hold readings back here sometimes—and burlesque performances once a month. That's where I met Chase."

"Right, I remember you said Chase was a dancer. He does burlesque, too?"

Dash nodded. "We should come see him sometime—I think he'll get back from his research trip in time to be on this month's lineup."

For once, it was my brain that was going a mile a minute, instead of my mouth. "Do you think he'd ever want to dance as Lord Loving?"

"We'll have to ask him, but I think he'd be into that, yeah."

Dash ran a hand through his hair, and for once I wasn't captivated by its gentle glide. Mostly because my mind was too busy parsing out what he'd said a few moments before.

I went behind him on the pretext of giving him a push, but it was really so that he wouldn't see my face when I asked, "Are you still lonely?"

"Sometimes. Less now than I used to be."

"I've been wondering if I should stay in the city," I said, trying to keep my tone casual. "Especially now that I don't have a job keeping me here."

Or friends. Or . . .

Or Milo, but I didn't want to even think his name here.

Dash seemed to have no problem following the direction of my thoughts, though. He dug the tips of his sneakers into the moss-edged paving stones and twisted around to look at me, making the swing's chains rattle slightly. "How long has it been since your breakup?"

I shrugged. "Long enough. I just . . . didn't think it would be this hard."

"Getting over him?"

"Dating in general." I leaned against the trunk of the tree the swing was suspended from, feeling the rough bark tug at the fabric of my dress. "I keep thinking that I'm never going to find someone to click with as thoroughly and instantly as I clicked with him."

"That may not be a bad thing," he said, toeing a different patch of moss. "It's not always about that instant click, you know. Sometimes taking the time to get to know someone can make for a deeper connection."

It sounded like he really meant what he said, but . . . "I just . . . I've never met anyone that has made me feel like he did."

"Maybe there's someone out there who will make you feel even better."

"Just one?" I said, with a raise of my eyebrow and a half-hearted leer.

He didn't take my bait, but continued to look at me with that slightly troubled crease between his brows.

I could have flailed again, I guess. Changed the subject or barreled out of the secret garden with some excuse about checking on our soon-to-be-dry laundry. But there was something about this place, so quiet and hidden and lush in the middle of so much bustle, that invited, I don't know, whispered confidences like the kind you'd share in a darkened bedroom.

Or maybe it was just Dash's expression, expectant and somehow concerned, like he was genuinely upset at the thought of me never meeting someone again. My breath snagged on its way into my lungs. Was he really that much of a hopeless romantic? Or . . .

Crossing my arms over my chest, I leaned back against the tree trunk and quickly told him the basics of what happened with Milo—also known as the reason why I had no intention of trusting another guy anytime soon. "I thought everything was going well. And then he told me he got an offer to work at a dig site in Greece. That it was an incredible opportunity, one he couldn't pass up." I shook my head. "Of course it was a lie."

"He never went?"

"Oh, he went all right," I said grimly. "All the way to fucking Jersey City. Into the apartment of his actual girlfriend."

He squinted. "Wasn't that a plotline on *Friends*? Where Chandler pretends to move to Yemen?"

"That's what kills me. It wasn't even original. And I didn't find out until a couple of weeks later when I went to an exhibit at the Met that I knew he'd been looking forward to, just to send him pictures so that he wouldn't feel like he'd missed out, and there he was. With her." I wrapped my arms around myself. "The whole thing was such a joke. I can't believe I fell for it."

"I know you're not blaming yourself for someone else's assholery," Dash said, disentangling himself from the swing as he stood up. "And I know you're not contemplating abandoning this new life you've made for yourself just because it didn't work out like you thought it would. It takes time to find your niche and your people in this city, but when you finally do, it's like magic. If you want to leave because you'd rather be somewhere else, do it. But for what it's worth, I've been lonely everywhere I've ever lived. I've been lonely in crowds and around friends."

It was hard to imagine. Dash had such an easy way around other people. I had seen with my own eyes how perfect strangers fell over themselves to catch his eye.

But maybe that just made someone feel all the more alone.

I opened my mouth to say something to that effect, but Dash wasn't finished talking.

"And also . . . I'd miss you if you go."

In this summer wonderland, sunlight was filtered through leaves and branches so that it was less harsh by the time it reached his face. His eyes were brown, and warm, and flickering with reflected green and the pink of my dress.

As if he'd read my mind, he reached over to flick one of the gauzy layers with his finger. "You look like a fairy princess in that dress. A fairy princess, and this garden is your realm."

"Does that mean you'll call me Your Highness?" I asked, trying and not fully succeeding in recapturing the bantering tone from earlier.

"I'll call you anything you want, Mariel," he said softly.

Maybe it was the seriousness of his smile, or the way his breath curled around the syllables of my name, but I felt myself drawing closer, unable to help the way my gaze skipped down to his lips.

I might have been holding my breath. Dash looked like he was, too, the dark lashes that ringed his eyes gone as still as the leaves suspended above us. I had never felt so in the moment—like all that existed was this instant, this space between one breath and the next, so full of possibility and yearning. So full of Dash and me.

And then, in the space of a second, the stillness between us was broken as a large, hulking, furry shape detached itself from a branch and landed on my shoulder, knocking me into Dash and dragging a startled scream from me.

Dash caught me, again, like the romance hero he clearly was destined to be. He held me against him with one arm as the creature leapt off my shoulder and onto the paving stones, meowing dramatically.

Dash leaned back, looking half resigned and half regretful. "Mariel, meet Kitty Marlowe."

6

After hours of serious deliberation—or, you know, a conversation that lasted all of two minutes—we decided that while Fling and OnlyFans were going to be our main platforms, we'd still create brand-new Duke of Harding profiles everywhere else, even if the only things we uploaded were teasers directing people to our other accounts.

And like sure, we didn't *strictly* need to be in the same room to do it. Thanks to the wonders of modern technology, we didn't even need to be on the same continent. But when Dash suggested getting together, who was I to say no?

And when it turned out that the suggestion involved coming over to his apartment so that we could get started on putting together the set, well . . .

Look, I was a proud member of the nosy brigade, okay? I wanted to see Dash's apartment. It was better than sitting around at home, dwelling over the almost kiss in Second Chance. There was no hiding the fact that I was uncomfortably into Dash, and in my experience, there was nothing like seeing a boy's gross bathroom and sink full of dishes to dampen the flames of a crush.

When he opened the door, he was in this crisp button down that made his tan look deeper, his smile brighter, and his eyes . . . Well, the less said about Dash's eyes, the better. Mostly because they were currently twinkling at me as if he was so thrilled that I'd accepted his invitation to come poking around his apartment—excuse me, get some work done on our project—and it had been such a long time since anybody had looked at me like they were happy to see me and . . .

And we had too much to do for me to waste time standing there in the doorway, grinning foolishly back at him.

"Let's get to it, Dashwood," I told him as I made my way inside, wielding my phone like it was some kind of shield that could protect me from his charm.

Dash didn't have a lot of furniture other than a dining table, a sunny yellow couch covered in printed throw pillows, and the bed—complete with a striped duvet and actual pillowcases—I could just about glimpse through the half-open door to his bedroom. He did, however, have a Great Wall of China made out of stacked paperbacks, which made me suspect that he was single-handedly keeping Second Chance in business.

I headed toward the couch, then thought better of it and sat at his dining table instead, still holding on to my phone in what I hoped was a businesslike manner.

Stopping first by the fridge for a couple cans of something pink and orange, he came and sat across from me. He placed the cans on a couple of coasters that were already on the table—not a good sign that Dash's apartment was going to gross me out enough to make me stop liking him—and slid one of them toward me. "I remembered that you're not into coffee, so I got you sparkling water instead."

"To match my personality?" I batted my eyelashes at him as I pulled the tab.

"Did you get something in your eye?" he asked mildly.

"I'm being sparkling, Dashwood. I'm extremely disappointed at your failure to recognize sparkle."

"I'll try to do better next time," he assured me, beaming so much earnestness at me from across the table that I could feel myself getting all shimmery and floaty.

Then I remembered that there were no felines here to interrupt another close call.

"Anyway," I said loudly, "back to business. What should our passwords be?"

Since we hadn't gotten his Duke of Harding costume yet and couldn't take pictures for our profile, we settled on using the coat of arms as a placeholder. The whole thing took maybe ten minutes, which underscored how silly it had been to get together.

Then I remembered that we still had to upholster the armchair. Both it and the fabric were in Dash's spare room—if I'd needed anything to convince me that getting into OnlyFans was the right idea, the fact that he could afford a two-bedroom apartment in Manhattan without a roommate would have done it in a second flat. The room was nice and bright, with two windows that supplemented the professional-looking lamps he had set up behind his tripod.

"Whoa, this is a nice setup. I'd been picturing a ring light and a phone stand."

"You were picturing me?"

There was only one possible response to Dash's teasing grin, and it was to place my palm directly in the middle of his face.

"Not unless ring light is a euphemism for something. Did you get the staple gun and the pliers?"

The denim miniskirt I was wearing was extremely cute, with these little teddy bear charms sewn all over it, but it turned out to be not exactly comfortable for kneeling on the floor as we cut and ripped the old fabric away. I was also hyperaware of my legs for some reason, and the goose bumps that rippled over them whenever Dash accidentally grazed them.

Okay, I admit it. Coming over to Dash's apartment had not been the smartest move.

Once we'd stripped off all the old fabric, I got Dash to carefully go over the chair and remove any stray staples that had been left behind, while I used the pieces of fabric we'd removed as templates to start cutting into the cheerful pink velvet. Then I showed Dash how to hold the fabric taut while I went at it with a staple gun. Dash foolishly didn't look the slightest bit worried about the proximity of the staple gun in relation to his hands.

"How do you know how to do all this?"

I shrugged. "We never had that much money growing up, but my mom and my aunt Nena never let that get in the way of having a stylish home. And wardrobes—you should've seen the outfits they put together with five dollars, a visit to the thrift store, and some needle and thread."

It was mostly clothes, in the beginning. Then I spilled an entire bottle of grape juice on the couch and they figured out how to upholster fairly quickly after that.

"There were a couple of years when Yaz and I were in high school when we'd wake to find that they'd stayed up all night painting the kitchen chairs or putting wallpaper remnants on the ceiling. You'd think one of them would've ended up in interior design or something."

"Right, you mentioned that you all lived together."

I nodded, absolutely not checking out the way his forearm muscles tautened as he pulled a length of pink fabric over the armchair's back. "My mom and Tía Nena figured out it'd be easier, since they were both single. They could split the bills and share the childcare duties. Plus, Yaz and I became inseparable pretty much from the start."

"Sounds nice," he said, "having all your family together under one roof."

I folded a piece of fabric and asked him to hold it in place while I secured it to the backing. "I take it you don't see your parents as often as your grandmothers?"

Dash shook his head. "Not really. My dad got remarried like ten years ago and they have two kids. I visit maybe once or twice a year. My mom and her husband are always asking me to their beach house, but I don't make it there as often as I'd like."

He hesitated, like he wanted to say more, then thought better of it, probably scared I would flail again. It was probably for the best, but I had to admit to being the teensiest bit disappointed. Just out of plain curiosity, you know? Growing up in such a nontraditional family unit meant that I always perked up whenever I met someone in a similarly uncommon situation.

"Here, let me." Shifting on his knees, he smoothed the fabric over the chair's rolled arms and waited for me to staple it down. I couldn't quite reach the spot, though, so I ended up having to Twister my way inside Dash's arms and . . . and yeah. I squeezed the staple gun a few times, trying to pretend for both Dash's and my own benefit that I wasn't putting in way more staples than were strictly required.

That I wasn't lingering because being enclosed by a pair of muscular arms was making my entire midsection feel all floaty and shimmery and really, that wasn't exactly what you wanted to feel while holding a power tool.

"That was some quality stapling," Dash said after a moment.

He had released the fabric, but he hadn't moved, so our bodies were still touching lightly from shoulder to knee. I could have perished right then and there from the *zings* of electricity working their way through my body. Then I felt his breath caressing the side of my neck and it was like something shorted out in my brain—slowly, deliberately, I leaned against him so that we weren't just touching, we were pressing against each other.

His hand landed on my hip, his thumb grazing the half an inch of exposed skin above the waistband of my skirt. "Mariel . . ."

What were we doing? There was flirting, and then there was . . . this. This suspension, not of disbelief, but of the reality of our situation. Which was that we were working together. And that I couldn't afford any more mistakes. And that Kitty Marlowe wasn't around to save me from myself.

I guess I should count myself lucky that his phone rang just then. Definitely lucky and not disappointed. As he reached into his pocket, I scooted away from him and began fiddling with the pink piping we'd bought to use as trimming.

"Hey, Dad," Dash was saying. He'd tucked the phone into the crook of his shoulder and was idly stroking the velvet with his fingertip. "What's up?"

Through the window of the laundromat, I'd noticed that he had this way of growing brighter and more animated when he spoke with his grandmothers. Talking with his dad, the difference was subtle but I couldn't help noticing it—how his voice changed to project extra excitement and how his gestures grew a little more expansive and he turned the act of upholstering a chair into a whole event. Like he felt like he had to put on this performance for his dad's benefit.

It made me ache for him a little bit. I could just about see him as a little kid, trying his hardest to distract his parents from their trying to one-up each other.

"Sorry about that," Dash told me as he hung up a couple of minutes later. I watched him take in all the space I had put between us—though he didn't comment on it, he did stay in his side of the room. "We don't talk all that often, so I always try to be there when he calls."

"Don't sweat it. It's nice that you have a relationship with your dad." I myself had a blurry photo and a nose whose provenance was unaccounted for, so a phone call, however occasional, sounded like something out of a 1950s sitcom.

"You don't?"

I shrugged. "Never met the guy. Never wanted to, either." Pulling a glue gun out of my tote, I held it up in one hand and the pink edging in the other. "Ready to attach the trim?"

I made sure to keep my distance this time—at least, as much distance as could be kept when we were working on the same chair. But I guess it wasn't enough, because the tingles had, if anything, intensified. And they were distracting enough that the glue gun got away from me a little and I came this close to hot gluing my finger to the chair.

The next thing I knew, bright, searing pain was shooting through me.

I jerked my hand away, yelping. Dash was at my side a half second later, carefully setting the glue gun on a low table and inspecting my reddening fingertip.

"That's my typing finger. I mean, they're all my typing fingers, but that one's my favorite."

"Don't worry, I think the chances of you losing it are pretty slim." The slight curl at the corners of his lips went straight to the softest parts of me. "Come on, let's get you an ice pack."

He got some burn ointment, too, which he applied with a delicate touch as we stood in his kitchen. I gotta say, the old *being nursed back to health after a terrible accident* had never been my favorite romance novel trope, but I was starting to see the appeal.

"Here I was, hoping to dazzle you with my upholstery skills, but all I've done is make you pull out the first aid kit." I gave an exaggerated sigh, which was followed by a very real wince.

"Honestly, I'd been expecting to need it from the moment you pulled out the staple gun."

I shoved him with my good hand. "Why would you doubt my competence with power tools?"

"I would never doubt your competence at anything," he protested, raising his hands. "But you have to admit, some of those staples came pretty close to my fingertips. I have trauma now."

"Hey, if the only damage I've inflicted on you is emotional, I'd say you got off easy." I held up my finger in illustration. The sharp pain had turned into a dull throb, but the redness was already beginning to fade.

Dash's laugh wafted over me. "I don't know if I could take any more damage, emotional or otherwise. What do you say we go get some dinner instead?"

"Make it a burger and I won't sue you for workplace injury compensation."

There it was again, the smile that was full of unbridled delight. "Well then, I'd better add some ice cream, too."

And I knew I hadn't done anything to deserve that smile, and that he probably wouldn't be directing it at me if he knew how affected I was by it, but all I could do was smile back.

7

It took us another few days to finish putting together the set. For once, my long list of failed hobbies had come in useful, as least where dyeing the curtains and painting the vase were concerned. The white damask curtains were now a pale blue, which looked amazing behind the chair, and the ugly vase had been transformed with a little white paint and some blue and pink painted flowers. And I'd even had a couple of tapers left over from the two minutes I'd convinced myself I could make and sell artisanal candles.

The set looked almost as good as Dash himself.

I admit it—when he buzzed me into his building and opened the door to his apartment, I had almost passed out right then and there. His light tan breeches were *molded* to his muscular thighs, and his billowy white shirt showed just enough of his chest that the first words that popped out of my mouth were, "Are you *sure* you're shooting the non-spicy ones today?"

But that was indeed the plan.

I curled up on a regular old office chair in the corner of his spare room, my laptop out in case we needed to make any last-minute changes to the script. After our little work session at the laundromat, we'd started full-out cowriting the scripts—Dash's spreadsheet of tropes and vast knowledge of the romance genre had been a huge help in figuring out what would be the most swoon worthy.

He had placed his tripod on the windowsill, which allowed him to brace himself against the wall in a way that was probably making his biceps bulge under his shirt. Watching the image playing back on the monitor next to my chair, I felt excitement like Pop Rocks in my stomach.

"You dropped your fan outside the stables earlier," Dash said into the camera in an English accent. A slight smile was playing over his lips, as if he—or rather, the Duke—was aware of how flimsy a pretext it was. "I thought you would want me to return it."

He flipped open the fan, showing off the landscape that had been painted on the delicate silk. "In all sincerity, I was hoping for a quiet moment with you. I know it's terribly ungentlemanly of me to mention what transpired between us at your aunt's ball. That night in the rose gardens, however . . . every time I close my eyes, I see you shimmering in the moonlight. I see the stars in your eyes. And most of all, my darling, if you can forgive the impertinence of my calling you by such an intimate endearment, most of all I see the way my world has shifted to place you at its center. You are my sun, incandescent and vibrant and so beautiful you dazzle me."

He did that thing where he dropped his voice and made it just a touch gravelly. "Look at me, darling. Tell me you feel the truth of it as strongly as I do. Tell me you want to steal away with me again, and find a darkened corner to share a kiss like that last one. Did you know that your mouth looks like a rosebud? And your skin . . . your skin is velvet and silk, so soft I want to bury my face in your neck and trace the lines of your neck with my lips."

His lips curled and a sudden wicked sparkle came into his eyes. "Does that shock you? We did all that and more in the rose gardens, and I don't recall seeing you blush then. What would you say if I told you I *want* to make you blush? And sigh and gasp . . . and pant. I want to shatter you the way you've shattered me, and then I want us to remake each other."

I held my breath as Dash reached out to touch the underside of the lens, as lightly as if it were his imaginary lover's chin. "I love your smile," he said softly. "And darling, I love you."

My arms were rippling with goose bumps, and it wasn't just because Dash seemed to have that effect on me. For the first time since we'd started this thing, I knew for a fact that our videos were going to go viral. And it was all down to him.

Yes, he was brimming over with charisma, and yes, he was so intensely beautiful it was almost hard to look at him. But the truly captivating thing about Dash was that he understood the female gaze in a way few cis men seemed to. He wasn't relying on his body or even his beautiful, full lips to capture the viewer's attention, he was blazing with sincerity and barely restrained desire and just enough vulnerability to win over the most hardened of hearts.

The protective shell around mine must have started to crack, because when Dash finished his speech and clicked off the camera, I didn't just feel won over—I felt breathless with how badly I wanted to knock the filming equipment aside and beg him to say all those things to *me*.

"I think I have time do another take before we lose the light," he was saying, reaching for his tumbler and rattling the quickly melting ice cubes in his coffee before taking a swig. "Do you have any notes?"

"None, other than . . . holy crap, you're amazing." I shoved a handful of hair away from my face, grinning at him from across the room. "Amazing isn't even the right word for it, but I'll be damned if I can think of any better ones."

"And here I thought you had a really good vocabulary." Dash beamed back at me, and I couldn't help but think that in this case, *beam* was certainly the right word, because happiness was radiating out of him like moonbeams. And yeah, that was mostly because he was bathed in light from the open window, his pale skin practically gilded in it, but also because his enthusiasm was just that bright.

But before I could gather myself enough to say so out loud, Dash accidentally dribbled a few drops of iced coffee onto his shirt. "Ah, fuck," he said, his smile dimming by like half a watt. "Let me run this under cold water before it sets."

If my brain hadn't been at its prime a moment before, it fully shorted out the moment he peeled off his shirt and turned to head to the bathroom.

"Oh!" I blurted out. "You have a tattoo!"

He craned his neck to glance at his upper back in the large mirror on the wall behind me, as if he'd forgotten the arc of words sweeping under his sharply defined shoulder blade.

"What does it say?" I asked, avoiding the impulse to trace the finely molded words with my fingertips, and the gleaming skin beneath them.

"*Happy endings, they never bored me.* It's a line from 'Fuck Forever,' this song I used to be obsessed with."

"Does it have anything to do with your love of romance novels?"

"Kind of," Dash said. He was still looking backward into the mirror. "It's more of a reminder, I guess. I'm old enough to know that my parents are never getting that happily ever after I always wanted for them. But I still have time to find one for myself."

He smiled at me over his shoulder, and this time there was no flirtatious hair flip, just a half-shy, half-earnest little quirk of his lips that turned my knees into jelly. And not just because my legs were primed to run away in another flail.

"Yeah," I said softly, then cleared my throat.

We hadn't talked about the moment we'd had in the garden of Second Chance and maybe that was a good thing, because I would have rather licked a subway seat than confront the fact that Dash and I had . . . what? Almost kissed? Almost kept sharing highly personal stuff without my even coming close to breaking out into hives?

I had gone from cursing Kitty Marlowe for the interruption to being grateful for the cranky cat. I mean, who knew where we might have ended up if she hadn't broken the tension by diving directly onto my head, like it was a landing pad and she a crashing helicopter?

"If anyone's getting a happily ever after, it's you," I said, trying to sound matter of fact.

He breathed out a laugh. "I mean, I hope so. But it's not like I'm doing much about it at the moment. I'm . . . not really doing the whole dating thing right now."

"What, dating is as hard for you as it is for us mere mortals?"

Lucky for me, Dash didn't seem offended by my sarcastic remark.

"It's partly because some people get kind of weird when I tell them what I do for a living. Not always in a shame-y way, but . . . I don't know, just weird. And partly . . ." The monitor trembled when he leaned against the desk and crossed his long legs, which were as bare as his feet below the hem of his breeches. "I think I've been putting too much pressure on myself, and on all of my relationships. For a while there, I was so obsessed with finding my own happy ending that I basically kept trying to force it with everyone I was dating."

"And if there's one way to keep from getting a happy ending, it's forcing a happy ending," I said.

"Pretty much. So yeah, right now I'm just giving myself some time and space to figure out how to date without getting too . . . intense."

"I don't get why that's such a bad thing," I said before I could think better of it. "Being intense, I mean. If nothing else, it's a welcome change to all the guys who act like they have a deathly allergy to being even the slightest bit thoughtful toward the people they're hooking up with. Forget baseball—ghosting is the national pastime!"

I'd meant to make him laugh, but of course Dash took one look at me and went straight for the feels. "You've been hurt a lot, huh?"

"More like severely annoyed," I said, glancing away. "If I let myself get hurt every time someone flaked out on me, I'd be a walking wound."

"So instead you bury your head in the sand and pretend it doesn't bother you?"

He wasn't wrong, but I was in no mood to be analyzed. "Ouch, Dashwood. Way to stick a knife right in my chest." Untwisting my legs, I clambered out of the chair and snatched the shirt from his hand. "Come on, we gotta go do laundry."

Dash trailed after me. "Are you going to run away every time I try to talk about your feelings?"

"It's worked for me so far," I called from the bathroom, which was as pristine as the rest of his apartment, even if he did have more skin care products than I did. "I don't do introspection, Dash. I flit through life as light as a butterfly."

From the corner of my eye, I saw when he had reached the bathroom doorway. "And that makes you happy?"

"It makes me not unhappy," I said, knowing that if I looked up from the soap I was daubing on his shirt, my eyes would meet his in the mirror and all kinds of disaster would ensue. "That's good enough for now."

"For how long?"

"You're relentless, you know that?" I sputtered out a laugh. "You and Yaz both."

Dash stepped into the bathroom and leaned against the tiles next to the sink. "Look, I don't want to overstep," he said. "I know we haven't known each other all that long and I have no right to demand anything from you, much less a heavy conversation about your emotional life. I just . . . I can't stand to see anyone hurting, and I think you might be." I caught a flash of motion in the mirror as he shoved his hair back. "I'll back off."

The cold water trickling over my knuckles made me want to splash my face. "No, I . . . I appreciate your concern. I'd just rather not dwell on stuff"—I waved a hand in illustration, accidentally flicking droplets at his bare chest—"right now. I gotta move forward, and focus on our videos and . . ." I took a deep breath. "I just want it to mean something, you know? Moving all the way here."

It may not have worked out, but at least I could make one last effort before I had to admit defeat and let Yaz buy me a ticket back to Miami.

"Yeah," Dash said softly. "I can understand that."

I forced myself to smile. "I'm like two seconds away from wearing holes into this shirt. Do you have a hair dryer? Or an iron?"

We managed to get his wardrobe back in order without being waylaid by any more emotional detours and without losing the last of the sunlight. Watching Dash rerecord the speech, as well as a couple of short teasers for social media, I felt myself sinking into the sound of his voice, my earlier irritable panic ebbing slowly.

It wasn't often that I felt like I'd done something right. In fact, I couldn't remember the last time that had happened. Which just made it all the more important that I didn't ruin the one good thing in my life—no matter how curious I still was about what it would've been like to kiss Dash.

◆ ◆ ◆

I was on a high when I left Dash's. Some would argue that I might have *been* high, because instead of walking home, I decided to draw inspiration from what he had said that day at the bookstore and take myself on a long, twilight walk around the city.

The scent of hot piss and garbage collected together in a—shall we call it interesting?—bouquet as I wound my way out of Hell's Kitchen and into the Upper West Side. A block east would take me into Central Park, but for the moment I was content to stroll among the outdoor tables littering the sidewalk and peek into store windows that were beginning to light up.

I wasn't wearing a dress that day for once, but a shorts and shirt set that looked like pajamas, with colorful flowers printed on the soft, black, satiny material. It was light, cool, and allowed for ease of movement—which came in handy when I found myself having to dodge a bike messenger as he almost careened into me.

I yelled something rude at his back, feeling like a real New Yorker.

In the spirit of the occasion, I veered left onto Broadway, intent on treating myself to a hot dog at Gray's Papaya. And then maybe a dollar slice, because all I'd achieved with all that walking was to work up an appetite.

I was well on my way to feeling like a character in a Nora Ephron movie when my phone started doing its best impression of a demented bumblebee. I lifted it to my ear, feeling my acetate hoops clank against the screen.

"What would you say if I took a couple of days off to go visit you?" Yaz said, with no prelude.

"I'd probably pee my pants from the excitement," I said promptly. "Or do something equally as gross. Are you really thinking about it?"

"More than thinking, actually—I just booked a flight for late August. That okay with you?"

"Of course!" I exclaimed, then bit my lip. I was all for a visit, if that was all it was. But for her to book a flight so last-minute, when she should be focusing on wedding prep . . . Did she actually want to see me, or was she coming out of a sense of obligation, to make sure I hadn't flailed again? I mean, it would be understandable if she was, given my track record. It just . . . didn't feel great. "You don't have to come check up on me, you know. I really am doing fine."

"That's debatable," she said wryly. "And highly dependent on your definition of *fine*, which I don't think matches mine."

"In this case, it means doing my gremlin best."

Yaz ignored me. "But I'm not checking up on you. I just want to see you. I miss your weirdo little face."

I leaned against the bright yellow column at the entrance to Gray's. "Okay, good, because I want to see *you*. I have so many places to show you and only three-quarters of them involve food. Dash took me to a literal secret garden a couple of days ago—"

"Dash?"

"The guy I'm working with on the videos. We recorded one today, and Yaz? I really think we might have something here. He's . . ."

Magnetic. Mesmerizing.

"Really talented," I said into the phone. "Maybe you'll be able to meet him when you come."

"I definitely have to, if he's going to be your—what? Coworker? Business partner?"

I wasn't all that enthusiastic at Yaz acting like she had to vet Dash, but I tried not to show my irritation. "Let's call it partner in crime for now," I said airily. "So hey, I was just about to get dinner. Text me later with your flight info?"

"I already forwarded it all to your email," Yaz said, because of course she had. "Hope you're having something other than cookies and a sugary drink."

"For your information," I said with great dignity, "I am about to embark on one of Manhattan's most emblematic gastronomical experiences."

"Pizza, huh?"

I grinned. "Hot dogs. Call you later!"

Forty minutes later, the taste of sauerkraut still lingering in my mouth, I headed out of Gray's and into the cobalt-blue twilight. It was only marginally cooler than it had been in the daytime—the perfect evening for wandering around the block with a cone of something sweet and cold and swirly.

I wasn't the only one who thought so. Broadway was bustling with people bearing frozen treats. I stopped to pet one friendly black Labrador in a forest-green collar who seemed intent on getting in on the action.

"Sorry, buddy," I told him. "I have a strict policy against sharing food."

"Kalam, stop!" His mortified owner apologized and tugged him away, though not before his muscular tail gave my calf a hard thump goodbye.

I should have been working on my screenplay. I knew that, and not just because I'd just glimpsed another text from Yaz saying something to that effect. The truth was, every time I had tried to make progress on my romcom, all I could do was rehash all the heartbreak from the last few months. Every word of fiction I had tried to craft had turned into a thinly veiled memoir.

Maybe that was why writing the Duke of Harding's exploits had been so freeing. Putting words into his mouth—the kind of words I wished someone would say to me—was not an exercise in memory, but in hope. Hope that someday the dating app gods would smile on me and produce someone who wouldn't find it a hardship to wake up next to me two mornings in a row. Or run errands with me on a busy Saturday morning or spend Sundays lazing in bed with pancakes and a good book.

Hope that someday someone would decide I was worth sticking around for.

8

> THE DUKE OF HARDING (wickedly)
> I've already kissed you, my darling. What
> other liberties will you allow me? Might
> I trace the edge of your neckline with my
> fingertips?

D: The Duke's getting sassy!

M: **Girls don't want flowers. They want dukes to touch their necklines.**

D: I'll keep that in mind.

M: **Oh yeah? Anyone out there whose neckline you want to touch?**

D: Maybe yours. You know, for research.

M: **I'm telling HR.**

D: What? How badly you want me to touch your jshasldh

M: **Say neckline one more time and I'm coming over just to flick you on the forehead.**

D: Maybe you should.

M: **Come over? Or flick you in tender places?**

D: Stop trying to seduce me, Mariel.

M: **Then get back to work, Dashwood.**

That Friday night found me hunkered in bed with my laptop and an open bag of chips. Dash and I had quickly fallen into a routine of opening Google Docs at the same time and working together on our scripts, though sometimes our productivity devolved into conversations that were half role-play—though not the sexy variety—

and half fan fiction of our own creation. There was some very mild flirting, too, but honestly I don't think anyone would count writing each other notes on Google Docs as anything other than friendly banter.

So anyway, I was sprawled in bed with a couple of paperbacks shoved under my laptop to prevent my thighs from burning, putting together the finishing touches on the script for the next video, when the cursor blinked and new text appeared on the blank bottom of the page. *Script number five is ready to go. Safe to say we have earned ourselves a break,* Dash wrote. *Agreed.* I hesitated for like two seconds before adding, *Wanna go out for a drink?*

I regretted it as soon as I saw the words, black against the whiteness of the screen. It was Friday night—Dash probably had plans, and that was probably what he meant by taking a break. And anyway, I had plenty of ice cream in the fridge and no money to spend on overpriced—

His reply came a second later. *Hell yes. Meet me in 15?*

Manhattan closets not being exactly spacious, I kept most of my clothes in a highly curated heap on the corner of my mattress. It took me a few minutes to sort through the pile, but I finally emerged with a sleek lavender crop top and a pair of vintage shorts with a fluttery hem that hugged my hips and made my butt look even more round than usual.

It was too hot for more than a slick of gloss and a quick swipe of mascara. And even though I couldn't resist adding a little electric-blue eyeliner to make my eyes pop, my makeup was done in record time. I slung a cross-body over my shoulder, a tiny thing shaped like a strawberry that was only big enough to hold the gloss and my keys, and ran down to meet up with Dash.

He was already coming my way, and yeah, my heart skipped when I saw the slow smile that slid over his face as he spotted me, almost halfway down the block. He opened his arms as he walked toward me, as if he was that eager to see me even though we'd just spent the past several hours working together. I walked right into his hug, my cheek pressed against his button-down shirt as he clasped me loosely, just long enough for me to catch a whiff of laundry detergent and citrus aftershave. It was still enough for butterflies to invade my midsection and my knees to go a little bit weak.

I was in serious trouble.

Not that I showed it, though. I kept up a steady stream of chatter as we took off toward one of the bars on Ninth Ave. It wasn't all that busy yet, but the music was so loud that Dash had to shout our order at the bartender.

Snatching my shot from the bar practically before the bartender set it down, I knocked it back and slammed the glass back down, gasping, "It's Leo season, baby!"

Dash downed his own shot. "That hasn't technically started yet, I think."

"Spoken like a true Virgo," I scoffed.

". . . I'm not a Virgo."

"And I have no idea what I'm talking about."

I threw him a grin as I hopped up onto a stool. My knee grazed his jeans, and I'd be lying if I said that electricity didn't travel all the way up my leg and into the seam of my panties. I almost fell off, but Dash reacted quickly, stabilizing me by gripping my thighs, just below the hem of my shorts.

And get this—he apologized for grabbing me. Considering that I wanted to rub my leg all over his, he truly had nothing to worry about.

So there I sat, perched on a barstool while he stood next to me reaching for the beers the bartender had placed next to our shots, my thighs tingling. And I swear, my brain must have stopped working for a few minutes, because the next thing I knew, Dash was telling me about why he'd decided to move to Hell's Kitchen.

"I thought about staying in Brooklyn after ending things with my ex," he said. "But I wanted to put as much distance as possible between me and . . . maybe not the relationship, but the person I was in it."

I nodded my understanding. "Reinvention by relocation."

"Right. I stayed in that relationship much longer than I should have. And when I finally saw that I needed to break away, I wanted as clean a break from her as possible."

"Did it work? The reinvention?"

"Wouldn't be here if it hadn't."

He gave me a disarming little smile, and come on. There was no way he didn't know the effect he had on people. Or, like, on me specifically.

To distract myself, I started telling Dash about the time I'd gone down to Brooklyn for an errand and gotten lost. Within the span of like half an hour, I had walked through the hypermodern high rises of downtown Brooklyn and into the movie-set brownstones of Park Slope, and ended up in industrial-looking Gowanus. "It's one of the things that bowls me over about this city, how it feels like it holds a bunch of cities—or even countries," I added, thinking of Little Italy and Chinatown.

Reddish-pink light fell on his cinematic profile, molding to his lips as he said, "It's true what they say about this city having a little bit of all you could ever want."

"No palm trees—that I know of—but I feel like it's just a matter of time before they take one of the satellite islands, like Governors or Roosevelt, and turn it into a mini Miami. Then New York City will truly have *everything*."

"Speaking of Roosevelt, have you been?"

I shook my head. "I went to Governors last month and tried to have a picnic, but it started raining and I ended up leaving like ten minutes after I got there."

Dash checked the time on his phone. "It's only ten—we can make it there and back before the last tram if we hurry."

I swallowed the last of my beer and slammed down the glass. "Let's go."

Dash gestured to the bartender, telling him that we wanted to close out our tab, which he had put on his credit card. Then he turned to me and said, "Maybe next time we'll plan ahead."

Next time.

I'm not gonna lie. The tingles of excitement summoned up by those two little words followed me all the way to the closest subway station. We made it to the tramway at 60th and Second, humidity blasting over us as soon as we left the air-conditioned subway car. And then we were getting into the tram and it was swinging out over the East River, which was sparkling in the moonlight.

On the track next to us, another little red tram with the words *Roosevelt Island* printed on it in white was making its way back to the station. I watched it go by, Dash's and my reflections superimposed on the glass of our tram, and I felt oddly weightless, as if we weren't suspended in a complicated network of steel cables, but floating in the air.

Like the ground had been pulled out from under me, but in a good way.

Once we reached the island, we strolled along Main Street, which looked disappointingly like every other street in the city. Then Dash motioned me around a grassy area. "Through here."

The thing about New York is that as beautiful as it can be during the daytime, night is when it really shines.

There it was, the New York City skyline, almost more beautiful in person than it was on the screen. The buildings looked like they were made up of millions of tiny squares of light, each one of them reflected on the gently lapping water of the East River. I picked out the buildings I recognized—the Empire State bathed in violet light, the Chrysler glittering and sharp as it thrust into the darkened sky.

I folded my arms against the railing, letting the sight wash over me. "Does it ever get old?"

"Not for me," Dash said, leaning next to me. A few faint whiffs of his aftershave wafted into the air, discernible even over the miscellaneous scents of the city and the river, and so delicious that I felt my entire body tilting toward him.

"I hope it never does. That no matter how long either of us live here, we never get so used to the sights that we stop noticing them, or appreciating them, or feeling this . . . this . . ."

"Wonder," Dash supplied, his voice not quiet so much as reverent.

I glanced up at him only to realize that he was looking down at me. And it was one of those moments when everything goes still and quiet and the world fades around you and you hardly dare breathe for fear of falling back into reality.

I could have let it carry me away. Maybe, in the movie version of my life, I would have. Dash's gaze was soft, and he was so close, and there was a little smile hiding in the corner of his lips that was just begging to be kissed.

My heart was racing in complete contradiction to my pulse, which was fizzing inside my veins. I felt like I was made up of lights—not the steady ones beaming down from the buildings, but the shimmery reflections they cast on the rippling water.

And maybe I was kidding myself, but I would have bet anything that Dash felt the same way.

Only he was probably sensible enough not to act on it.

I swallowed, and took a faltering step backward.

"Wonder," I said, and even I didn't know if I was agreeing with what he'd said or simply echoing his word back at him because I was too full of this wild longing to ever come up with a suitable one of my own.

I turned around, putting the skyline at my back and gazing instead at the leafy dark of Roosevelt Island. "I hadn't realized that people actually lived here. Can you imagine the commute? Getting to work by tram or ferry?"

Dash said something in reply, but honestly, I barely heard it. I was already moving down the path, eager to leave the disappointment of not kissing him behind.

"Hold on," Dash called from behind me. "Your shoelace is untied."

Before I could do much more than glance down and confirm with my own two eyes that yes, that was my shoelace flapping in the grime, he had crouched down and was tugging my foot onto his thigh. More out of reflex than anything, I grabbed his shoulder to keep from stumbling.

He tied my shoelace for me, quickly and without fanfare, without doing anything weird or overly flirty like grazing my bare ankle or running his fingers up my leg. Honestly, I wasn't altogether sure whether or not I wanted him to. I mean, I obviously wanted him to, but I didn't really need anything testing my resolve. I had already done the responsible thing once tonight—there was no way I had the strength of will to do it again.

I'm only human, you know?

When he had pulled the knot tight, Dash glanced up at me and offered me a smile. It wasn't even a hair flip, or one of his patented dazzlers, but I could feel my stomach turning somersaults at the sight of the perfect curve made by his upper lip as it curled.

And *ugh*.

He had no business being this gorgeous. And sweet.

If you asked me, Dash didn't need yet another person drooling over him. Although, from what I'd seen, he was so used to people staring at him that he was kind of oblivious to it. That didn't mean, however, that I wanted to make him uncomfortable with my inability to keep my eyes off his plush mouth. Even if he didn't notice the staring, I'd still feel like a creep.

So I made myself glance away. And I must have done the right thing, because the universe rewarded me by making my phone buzz with an incoming text from Tía Nena. She didn't check in as often as Yaz did, but she never let more than a week go by without at least texting.

I opened WhatsApp to see a picture of a bowl filled with my favorite rice and chicken stew. *Made asopao and thought about you, Chiquita.*

"Look at what my aunt is cooking," I said as Dash straightened up and resumed walking next to me. I passed him my phone and let out a noisy sigh. "Sometimes I wonder why exactly I thought it would be a good idea to live away from my family and their magnificent cooking skills."

"Chiquita?" he said, his mouth dancing over the syllables. "What does that mean?"

"It means little. A very original nickname," I added sarcastically, "due to the fact that I've always been shorter than Yaz by like a foot. I'm also technically the youngest, by a little over four months."

"Chiquita but mighty," Dash observed, and I had to laugh.

"That's my superhero name."

I tucked my phone away as we continued strolling along the path, not talking all that much, just taking in the view. Roosevelt Island was much longer than I'd thought, and it took a while to get within view of the small stone lighthouse on the northern tip. There were still quite a few people out and about, though the park itself was closed at that hour. We spent a few minutes looking at the brass sculptures shaped like gigantic disembodied heads, then Dash happened to glance at the time.

"Shit—the last tram leaves in less than ten minutes," he said. "We'll have to make a run for it."

We took off at what was probably a slow jog for Dash, but for me felt like whatever Olympic category Usain Bolt competes in. Starlight and flair is all well and good, except when you're suddenly in the need to run the equivalent of twenty city blocks in the sultry air of midsummer.

But then the tramway came into view and Dash put on a burst of speed. And I swear it was mostly because his legs were so much longer than mine that I was terrified of being left behind, but I kinda . . . slipped my hand into his. Like I'd done when we ran out of Times Square the day we met.

His closed around mine and he didn't just hold my hand, he threaded his fingers through mine as if to make extra sure that we didn't get separated. And he didn't let go, even when we reached the station. Suddenly we were walking hand in hand and I was alternating between trying not to hyperventilate and telling myself that this meant nothing. It was just . . . convenient.

Not to mention, far less annoying than having to camp out on Roosevelt Island overnight.

I can tell you one thing, though—the feel of Dash's palm pressed against mine, grazing lightly as we walked, our fingers firmly twined together? I was soaring again.

◆ ◆ ◆

Hear me out. There is such a thing as platonic hand holding. What Dash and I were doing as we switched from the tramway to the subway, though? Yeah, it wasn't that.

We were doing that thing where we were pretending not to realize that we were still holding hands, even though it was more than obvious that we were both hyperaware of it, especially because we had to kind of edge around people as the crowd inside the subway car ebbed and flowed and we were jostled around.

I wish I had the excuse of having had too much to drink, but it had been a couple of hours since the bar and I was as clear-eyed and sober as I've ever been in my life, which was actually kind of unfortunate because the subway is all kinds of harrowing when you're sober.

"Are you hungry?"

I pounced on the distraction. "*Starving*. What did you have in mind?"

"Three words—Prince Street Pizza." He said it like it was a headline, bolded and in a bigger font than the rest of his words.

With my free hand, I checked the time on my phone, then slid it back into the pocket of my shorts. "Would it be open this late?"

"They're open until three."

"And you know that, why?" I asked, laughing. "How often are you going downtown after midnight just to grab a slice of pizza?"

"First of all, Prince Street isn't *just* pizza. It's an experience. And just so you know—someone who has as much caffeine as I do is by necessity a connoisseur of late-night snacks." His eyes sparkled as he tilted his head down to look me in the eye, and, um, yeah, I did actually feel my knees quiver. "Is that a yes?"

"I mean, I would never say no to midnight pizza. So yeah, sure, you have my enthusiastic consent."

He studied my expression. "You have no idea what Prince Street Pizza is, do you?"

"I'm assuming it involves dough and cheese and tomato sauce," I told him.

"That's the general concept, yeah. But—you know what, just wait till we get there. I won't spoil it for you."

And that was pretty much all I got out of him. I truly didn't understand why he was getting all mysterious over it, but then we got there—and by there I mean all the way to Nolita, a good sixty blocks south from where we'd started off—and I saw the line unfurling out from a fairly nondescript storefront and halfway down the street.

"This isn't some cronut type situation, is it?" I wrinkled my nose as we attached ourselves to the end of the line. If it hadn't been for the turnstile you had to go through to exit the subway, I had a feeling that we would still be holding hands. The memory of his touch still clung to my fingers, even as I pushed my hair back. "I like weird combinations as much as the next guy, but I'll have you know that I'm a pizza purist."

"Come on, Mariel. Do you really think I'd lead you astray? Especially when it comes to pizza?"

A pink neon sign advertising cupcakes blinked at us from the bakery across the street as I pretended to give Dash the side-eye.

"I don't know," I said musingly. "If anyone could lead me down the wrong path, it'd probably be you."

The corners of Dash's eyes crinkled. "I don't know whether to be flattered or offended."

"Maybe a little bit of both?" I suggested, inching forward as the line advanced. "Everyone should strive to be a little bit of a bad influence, at least sometimes."

"I'll keep that in mind. In the meantime, let me work on influencing your pizza order."

"He's right, you know." This came from one of the people in line in front of us, a brown-skinned woman with a dusting of freckles on her nose, pale green eye shadow on her lids, and fuzzy barrettes speared through her middle-parted hair. She finished taking a selfie and twisted around to face us. As she glanced Dash over, her face took on an expression I was starting to recognize—like she couldn't quite believe that the man in front of her was indeed real and not some cartoon prince. "Prince Street Pizza defies description. You just have to experience it."

"Somehow, I'm not reassured," I answered.

The brunette she was standing with hooked her finger through Barrette's belt loops and pulled her forward as the line shuffled a few inches closer to the door. "Do you eat meat?"

I nodded.

"Then just wait till you try the pepperoni. It's a religious experience."

Someone behind them snorted. "None of you are from here, are you? You have to check out Joe's Pizza before you go around saying stuff like that."

Before I could quite figure out what had happened, half the line was bonding over a friendly argument about where to find the city's best pizza. I was too new to New York to contribute much to the conversation, so I just stood back and basked in the moment.

Maybe I was just really absorbed in what everyone was saying—and making mental notes about all the places I wanted to try—but the line moved surprisingly quickly. It felt like no time had passed before Dash and I were exiting the restaurant with our paper plates.

The slices were rectangular, the dough as chunky as a good paperback. And the pepperoni—oh my god, the pepperoni. Cut thickly and curled up slightly at the edges so that each piece became a fat little cup for all the grease from the cheese. And if you don't think that sounds like the most delicious thing in the world, don't you ever talk to me or my son again.

My mouth was watering for a bite, but I felt bad about eating in front of people who were still waiting, so I resisted. As soon as we had cleared the line, I held up one of the two square slices on my plate. Looking amused, Dash followed suit.

"A toast. To the Duke of Harding. And to you, and to me, and to the city, and to tonight."

"May there be many more," Dash said, touching a corner of his pizza to a corner of mine.

Okay, so it wasn't a kiss. But it was *something*. We might not have locked lips, but the way our gazes met and held felt deliciously—or maybe disconcertingly—intimate.

I'm not actually sure what would have happened next. Like, we'd already established that there wasn't going to be any kissing that night, at least not between Dash and myself. So I wasn't really sure why my stomach sank a little when we peeled our slices apart and broke eye contact to take our first bites.

"I *have* to ask," Barrettes said, motioning to her companion to set their drinks down on a nearby window ledge. "Who's the Duke of Harding?"

"I am," Dash replied.

Barrettes tilted her head, infusing her voice with just the slightest hint of skepticism. "You're a duke?"

"Not a real one—I just play one on TV," Dash said, and gave her a little wink that left her looking faintly stunned.

"And by TV, he means social media," I added.

I think we both held our breath a little as Dash interjected with an explanation of what we were doing. But Barrettes didn't say anything out of pocket about our silly goofy project, or more importantly, about Dash being on OnlyFans.

Letting myself exhale, I chimed in with "We haven't actually gone live yet, but we'll be ready to upload our first video in a few days."

"I'll be on the lookout for it," Barrettes said, and let her companion tug her away by the belt loops.

Paper plates in hand, Dash and I ambled slowly down the crowded streets until we reached the Bowery. The Lower East Side felt kind of gritty, especially at night, one of the few remaining parts of the old, graffiti-covered Manhattan that I hadn't realized still existed. There must have been at least a handful of art galleries in every block, and Dash and I slowed down even more to peer through their windows.

It felt like one of those nights when anything could happen, when the world flung open its arms to you as if to say, *I'm yours.* And maybe it was. The world was ours, and so was the night, and so was Manhattan.

By the time we had finished our slices, we had walked several blocks down East Houston. Dash pointed out a green awning with the words Punjabi Deli printed on it, making me hungry all over again as he described his usual order. Right next to it was a bar called The Library. Neither of us were quite ready to go home, so we went past the crowd that had spilled out onto the sidewalk and headed inside.

If it was hot outside, it was sweltering in the packed bar. The Lady Cerulean song that was throbbing through the neon-tinted air was a little too loud for easy conversation, and we had to drift close together to be able to hear each other without having to shout. You'd think that after all the hand-holding Dash and I had done earlier I wouldn't be fazed by the occasional bump and graze, but every time we accidentally brushed against each other, it felt like we were striking sparks off the places where our bodies met.

My gaze kept straying to his hand. His fingers were curled loosely around his glass, his thumb slowly stroking away the condensation beading on its smooth surface. For the first time, I understood what it meant to burn with desire. Prickles of awareness danced over my skin, so scalding that I almost convinced myself Dash could feel the heat radiating from me.

By some miracle, I kept it together. And kind of disappointingly, so did he. But it wasn't *that* disappointing, because we spent the next few hours deep in conversation, resurfacing only when the music cut out and we realized that the bar was closing.

We made our way outside, and I didn't know about Dash, but I felt like I had gotten the one thing I'd been craving ever since I had moved to New York—a real connection.

The sky was starting to get that translucent quality that means that it's about to lighten, but I was still wide awake. So when Dash said we might as well go watch the sun rise over the Brooklyn Bridge, I pulled out my phone and ordered us a Lyft. We made it there right in time to catch the sun as it started to peek out from behind the buildings, suffusing the pale sky with its orange glow.

If there's one thing about this city, it's that there are always other people around, even at sunrise on a Saturday morning. Laughing, Dash and I pressed ourselves into a corner to get out of the way of joggers and of the couple shooting their engagement pictures, and we watched the night turn into a new day.

◆ ◆ ◆

```
INT. THE DUKE'S DRAWING ROOM—DAY

In the FOREGROUND, THE DUKE OF HARDING sits
on his pink armchair, reading a large tome
bound in leather. He glances up at the sound
of footsteps, and the book lies forgotten on
his lap as he spies his bluestocking.


          THE DUKE OF HARDING
    (with a wicked little curl to his lips)
    This? Yes, it is the book you were
    reading earlier. I thought I'd see what
    you found so captivating about it. Why
    you keep your gaze so firmly on its pages
    when I happen to walk past. Why it brings
    such a blush to your cheeks.
```

The Duke picks up the book and turns it
over in his hands as he studies it.

                THE DUKE OF HARDING
                  (gazing at the camera)
     I'm beginning to think it's not the book
     at all. It's much too dry to warrant such
     a response. I think perhaps it's the
     sight of my sweet butt cheeks that gets
     you all hot and jsdlkad

M: Dashwood, get off the doc. You're in my way.

D: Impossible. I'm being very helpful and productive.

M: Kinda like this morning when you asked if you
   should get us on the next flight to London so that
   we could shoot our videos in a more authentic
   location??? (I'm not saying no, btw.)

D: Hey, that was a serious offer.

M: You're in a weird mood today. I think you're spending
   too much time around me.

D: Not possible. Speaking of, though, you wanna go grab a
   coffee (or sugary drink of your choice) and help me run
   lines?

M: Nope, I'm very busy and important. (See you in front
   of the laundromat in five.)

9

I had written seven scripts and was working on an eighth when my phone buzzed with a text from Dash. I will never admit to lunging for the phone, but I will say that I reached for it a tad too aggressively, and found myself reading the text while on my back, my shaggy rug tickling the back of my neck and the remains of my cookie crushed under my elbow.

I finished editing and was just about to upload the first couple of videos (one spicy, one mild). But then I thought ... an occasion this momentous has to be celebrated, right? Or commemorated in some way?

I tapped out my reply a moment later. Hit pause on the uploading for like ten minutes. I'm coming over.

To the surprise of absolutely no one who's ever met me, I had two shoeboxes and a shopping bag's worth of party supplies in my closet. Rooting through them, I extracted a bag of confetti, two paper noisemakers, a sparkling plastic tiara, and a party hat shaped like a pineapple. It took me approximately two minutes flat to sweep them into a grocery tote, exchange my shorts and cropped tee for a blue tulle dress that wouldn't have looked out of place on a Disney princess, and make my way to the bodega at the end of my street, where I bought a couple cans of LaCroix in lieu of champagne and a few packages of powdered donuts.

Another few minutes and I was bursting through Dash's door as he pulled it open. "You have no one to blame but yourself," I told him, wielding the sparkling water like I was presenting him with the finest vintage. "You could have told me to stay home."

"I wasn't aware that was an option," he said, but he was smiling when he reached for a pair of long-stemmed wineglasses from the shelf above his sink.

"I mean, I probably wouldn't have listened."

"You look beautiful, by the way," Dash said, still facing away from me, so casually that for a second it didn't register as a compliment. He turned around right as it hit me, so he saw me go suddenly and uncharacteristically still, less deer in the headlights and more *I want to live in this moment forever.* "Should I change?"

He was in jogger shorts and an intensely blue T-shirt that made his eyes look deliciously brown. Was it the amber glow of his kitchen pendants making his cheekbones look flushed, or was Dashwood blushing?

Feeling a little hot under the collar myself, I shook my head and tried to sound as casual as he had.

"Nah, you're fine. I just wanted to look festive." I dumped my bodega purchases onto his fancy quartz countertop, trying not to think about how soft his T-shirt looked or wonder what it would feel like against my cheek. "Sorry about the crappy snacks. I can bake, but I don't have an oven."

"You can use my oven anytime you want," he offered as he set the glasses on the counter.

As gorgeous as his kitchen was, it was still Manhattan-apartment small, with so little space to maneuver that we were standing way too close for comfort. Maybe that was why my voice came out a little breathless when I repeated something I'd only said over text. "Stop trying to seduce me, Dashwood."

Blushing even harder, he eyed the powdered donuts, which had gotten slightly—okay, severely—crushed in my tote. "I think we can do better than those."

I raised my eyebrows. "Excuse me, are you dissing my bodega-shopping skills?"

"I'm just saying that I'm marinating two pieces of salmon and I have an arugula, goat cheese, and grilled nectarine salad to go with them. Have you had dinner yet?"

"Not unless you count the two donuts I had on the way here," I said, showing him where the package was open.

He uncovered the wooden bowl on the counter. Had it been in my apartment, it would've been filled with hair ties and stray earrings. This being Dash, the salad bowl held an actual salad, the arugula glistening with dressing and dusted with crumbled white cheese.

It wasn't covered in sugar, but it looked *good.*

"Did you seriously whip that up in the ten minutes it took me to get here?" I asked as he got a glass container from the fridge.

He shrugged. "It's not really that complicated, especially when you meal prep. I try to always have something ready to toss on the stove."

"Your grandmas taught you well." I snagged half a crushed donut from the open package, adding, as an explanation, "Appetizer."

"My grandmas don't cook," he said, swirling oil around a grill pan. "Hence the senior buffets at the casinos they're always in. They don't get many home-cooked meals unless I come over and bully them into eating their vegetables. According to Nana, she's rebelling from the tyranny of the kitchen and something about patriarchal expectations. Grandma just can't be bothered."

I licked powdered sugar off my finger and said, "God, I love your grandmas. Any chance they'd want to adopt a moderately talented sugar fiend who could do some serious damage at a senior buffet?"

As Dash flicked on the range hood and eased both salmon fillets into the sizzling pan, I busied myself with putting out the party supplies. The noisemakers and confetti joined the two round white plates and gleaming cutlery on the dining table, and the hats I held out to Dash so that he could have first pick because I am nothing if not gentlemanly. "Pineapple or princess?"

Dash took the tiara. "I mean, I *am* the nobleman."

"What does that make me?" I asked, adjusting the green elastic under my chin.

"Cute." There went his fingers again, raking through his hair, just before he swiveled slightly to flash that smile at full strength, right into my face.

Another small piece of my resistance crumbled away, like dirt on a cliff wall that I was hanging on to by my fingertips. The compliments and the flirting and the brief touches that were casual enough that they had plausible deniability built right into them were all great, amazing even, but they were making it so hard to keep holding on.

I couldn't let myself fall—not off the metaphorical cliff and not for Dash.

"Oh no you don't," I said, pointing at him as he looked at his reflection on the microwave to make sure his tiara was on straight.

Dash looked confused. "Don't what?"

"Try to charm me. I'm instating a firm no compliment policy for this partnership." I pretended to think about it for a second. "Unless it's about my earrings, my outfits, or my powdered donuts."

He raised an eyebrow. "Do you tend to get a lot of compliments on your powdered donuts?"

"Nope, and it's about time that changed."

I had taken my shoes off at the door, per Dash's instructions, and now I roamed barefoot on his perfectly clean hardwood, sipping my sparkling water.

Since my last visit to his apartment, he had taken the time to put up a bunch of stuff on the white walls. In actual frames, too, all neatly arranged and very unlike the haphazard collection of stuff held together by scraps of washi tape and free stickers that was on my wall. Dash had framed postcards scrawled with messages, artsy prints, and pages that looked like they'd been ripped from vintage design magazines, as well as pictures of two older ladies I assumed were his Grandma and Nana.

I was studying one of the pictures when I felt Dash walking up behind me. "Your grandmas are beautiful," I told him. "Those cheekbones!"

"Nana was a beauty queen in the late sixties," he said, pointing at one black-and-white snapshot that depicted a young White woman with a beehive hairdo and a satiny dress bisected by a sash. "And my Grandma was the prettiest debutante in her year, at least according to my aunt."

"No wonder you're so gorgeous," I blurted out. "It's bursting out of every branch of your family tree. I'm guessing that at some point in the past, one of your ancestors was responsible for a thousand ships being launched into war."

Dash looked amused. "How come you're allowed to compliment *me*?"

"I'm not," I shot back. "I'm complimenting your ancestors. And I'm really looking forward to complimenting your salmon if it's ever ready."

"It's almost done."

Dash lived in a prewar apartment. Where a more modern building might have had floor-to-ceiling windows that offered a sweeping view of Manhattan, his looked out over red brick, black iron fire escapes, and lush ivy. One of the fire escapes on the building across the street had been swagged with fairy lights, and music wafted faintly from the person sitting cross-legged below the glowing string, holding a guitar like a lover as he strummed it softly. I recognized the song he was playing from Lady Cerulean's newest album, a ballad that was really a political manifesto wrapped in poetry.

"Romantic view," I commented.

"Why do you think I bring all my dates here?" he quipped in a way that made me suspect that he hadn't brought up anyone at all.

Except for me.

"I'd do actual crimes for a view like this—my apartment looks out into the back alley where they keep the dumpsters." I glanced at him, smiling slightly to try to conceal the awareness zipping up and down my spine. "Just wait until our videos take off. I'll be out of there so fast, my landlord will think he'd been renting to a cartoon superhero."

"On that note." A sizzle from the pan on the stove punctuated Dash's sentence. "It's time to move on to the main event."

He plated the salmon and I carried the salad to the table, which had already been set with cobalt-blue place mats that matched the wineglasses, as well as rolled linen napkins in wooden rings.

"All that and you're a domestic god, too?" I asked as I slipped into a seat.

He pretended to ponder it. "Not a god, no, but the Domestic Duke has a nice ring to it. Think there might be something in that? A side channel for sharing recipes and tips for spring cleaning my castle?"

"Maybe, and also you just gave me an idea about a plotline involving a maid who's actually a countess in disguise." I flaked off a piece of salmon with my fork and felt my eyes popping open at the first juicy bite. It tasted delicately of soy, ginger, and something else I couldn't quite put my finger on. "Holy crap, if the rest of your recipes are anything like this, you might have to give up OnlyFans and become a full-time Domestic Duke. You'd make bank."

The nectarines were crisp and juicy, the chèvre just the right amount of creamy, and the arugula . . . Well, there's only so much that can be said about edible leaves, and none of it's too complimentary. But the whole thing was amazing.

Dash couldn't hide how pleased he was. "What are the odds of us convincing the Barefoot Contessa to do a collab with us? Something about nobility in the kitchen?"

"Send her a plate of this and she'll be begging you to let her cook your recipes."

"Us," Dash corrected me, and I almost let out another *holy crap*. "We're in this together, remember?"

"If by together you mean you develop the recipes, cook them, and plate them." I shrugged, sinking the tines of my fork into a firm slice of nectarine. "I can do the eating part just fine. Everything else, though . . ."

"Don't tell me you can't cook."

"It's my deepest shame. I got a little too used to having Yaz's mother around." At Dash's raised eyebrow, I elaborated. "You know, Tía Nena, the award-winning chef. Growing up, Yaz and I were part guinea pigs, part vacuum cleaners. You'd be surprised at how many things taste good with a little sprinkle of brown sugar. And bacon."

"Remind me to buy you candied bacon from Morgan's Barbecue the next time we're in Brooklyn," he said. "Do she and your mother still live together?"

"Nope. Not for a while. Tía got married a while ago, and they moved to the DR to open a restaurant."

If Dash noticed that I didn't elaborate on what my mother was up to, he was too polite to comment on it. Or maybe I was just too good at distraction. I swung into a story about the restaurant's opening week, then smoothly segued into asking Dash about the videos he was planning on uploading.

"The thumbnails and metadata are all ready to go—I literally just have to click the upload button." Holding his fork between his lips, he flipped open the laptop resting on one of the unoccupied place mats and poked at the keyboard to reveal his OnlyFans profile.

"Do you need a drumroll?" I asked, banging my palms on the table in something that could, maybe, if you were super tone deaf, be called a rhythm.

One of Dash's hands descended on mine, pressing down firmly, and at the warm touch I had to remind myself again about not swooning. Or hyperventilating, or jumping into his lap.

"I would really like to not give my neighbors an excuse to call in a noise complaint about us," he said, his eyes crinkling with humor.

His fingers were graceful and strong, and I was having a hard time figuring out why romance novel heroes always had calloused fingers, because his felt like *actual silk* against my hand and that was clearly the hottest thing ever.

Until he did a little stroke-y thing with his middle finger and I almost spontaneously combusted.

On the pretense of taking a sip of my water, I slipped my hand out from under his.

"Do you want to do the honors?" he asked after a few moments, gesturing at the upload button on the screen.

"Let's do it together," I said, and made sure to place my fingertip a respectable distance from his on the trackpad. "One . . . two . . . and . . . let's goooo!"

We were off.

◆ ◆ ◆

Dinner was forgotten as Dash quickly uploaded the second, non-spicy video into Fling, plus the teasers that he'd made directing people to our main profile from our other social media channels.

"Aaaand I just let out a breath I definitely realized I was holding," I said once that was done.

"I know what you mean. I don't think I've ever been this nervous to post a video before. I know how important this is to you. And I mean, it is to me, too, but I know you have so much riding on this. If it's any consolation, I happen to think that we're the best partnership since Ben and Jerry and our videos are going to do amazing." Dash started to do a hair flip, then remembered the tiara and settled for smiling.

I was all for immediately refreshing the handy stats counter to see how many views we'd gotten, but Dash gently closed the laptop and we went back to our meal.

"Oh, and Mariel. There's something I've been meaning to tell you."

The way my heart quickened at that harmless sentence, it was a struggle to keep my face blank. "Yeah?"

"Have you heard about the new series that's being developed based on Georgie Hart's books?"

I almost did a spit take. "*What?* That is extremely my shit. How have I not heard about it?"

"Maybe you've been a little busy with your own Regency duke,"

Dash said, laughing. "I think it's mostly based on *The Wallflower's Bargain*, but I think they're taking couples and plots from other books and sort of threading them together. They've only released a couple of stills, but the whole thing looks like a Regency novel come to life."

"Shut up, really? That's like incredible timing. If it gets popular, our videos are going to *explode*."

Dash nodded. "That's not all, though. A bunch of influencers got invited to this costume ball they're throwing to celebrate the series premiere. Some poor, misguided PR person got me confused for one of them and put my name on the invite list."

Neither one of us should have been surprised. Dash had spent all week posting the short teasers he'd filmed in his Duke of Harding getup, and the response he had gotten was staggering. The last time I'd checked, the Duke of Harding account had almost twenty thousand subscribers, almost half as much as his personal one.

I didn't exactly leap out of my chair and squeal, but I didn't not do that. "Dash, that's perfect for you. You *have* to go. I mean, you already have the costume."

"Well, yeah. I was planning to. But I was actually wondering if you would go with me."

"Sure, why not? I mean, every duke needs his entourage. Should I be your valet or your groom?"

Dash smiled. "I was thinking more along the lines of my willful, feisty heiress."

I could feel it in the air, the growing awareness—not just of the short distance separating us from each other, and how close our knees were to brushing under the table, but of the attraction between us, too insistent and obvious to deny.

I made one last-ditch attempt to break the tension with a joke. "And settle for a pretty dress instead of a fake mustache?"

"Wear the mustache if you want. Just as long as there's also petticoats," he murmured, and yes, I would definitely have described his voice as husky.

My knees were tingling. My *knees* were *tingling*. Bare below the poufy skirt of my dress, inches away from Dash's, which were also left uncovered by his jogger shorts.

Then he shifted, and his foot bumped into mine and—

I didn't combust. But some kind of chemical reaction was going through my body as I scraped back my chair, saying something about needing a glass of water even though there was a half-full one right in front of me.

Dash stood up, too, probably out of desire to be a good host and fetch me said water. All he did, though, was put himself in my path so that I brushed against him on my way to the fridge. Hesitation made me pause long enough to catch the faint scent of coffee and laundry detergent emanating from his clothes.

What was left of my resolve melted away as my skin became suffused with tiny little tingles that popped and fizzed like my blood had been replaced with champagne.

If there was still a minuscule, rational part of me listing out all the reasons why I shouldn't give in to what was clearly about to happen, it was small enough that I was able to silence it as I stepped closer to Dash.

"There'll be petticoats," I assured him. "Probably a corset, too."

He huffed out a low laugh, and it trailed over my lips like a promise as he cradled my face between his hands. The plastic tiara nestled in his curls caught the light and sparkled. "There better be a corset."

I wasn't touching him. The only point of contact between us was his hands on my face. And yet, as he looked down at me with heat in his eyes and tenderness softening his mouth, he might as well have been holding all of me.

"You want this as much as I do," he said, a little stunned, as if he'd only just realized what should've been obvious five seconds into our first meeting.

"I do." I wasn't sure if by *this* he meant just the kiss or something more, and I didn't care. I wanted it, all of it. I wanted as much of Dash as I could possibly have. As he was willing to give me.

He hadn't taken his eyes off me. I pushed lightly against the cradle of his hands, hungry to finally feel his lips on mine. Maybe it was just my usual impatience, but the moment felt like was stretching on and on, and I was probably going to ruin it by making some sort of inappropriate comment and—

His lips brushed mine.

They were just as silky as his fingertips and they tasted of summer. That was as far as I got.

It wasn't so much that my brain shut down, but that the sensation of Dash's lips against mine took over and overwhelmed every potential thought before it had a chance to coalesce.

Which was fine. The last thing you wanted when you were kissing a man who could make your heart flutter with a mere smile was to get all intellectual about it. Especially since he was currently stroking my lower lip with the tip of his tongue. If my knees had been tingling earlier, now they were going weak at the feathery touch. Lucky for me and my failing appendages, I was able to brace myself against the hard planes of his chest.

The tension was building, twining around us like tongues of smoke or the sparkles that circled Cinderella when the fairy godmother magicked her up a gown.

I was the one who deepened the kiss, grabbing handfuls of his T-shirt as I rose higher on my tiptoes to better reach the tantalizing warmth of his mouth. He pulled away slightly, but only to tease me, laying a soft kiss on the corner of my lips that made my heart flutter, before letting me reclaim his lips.

There was a sweetness to the way he kissed me, tempered with the rougher edge of his uneven breaths. It was as if he was pouring all his joy into the kiss, and every spun-sugar dream he'd ever had.

Dash's large, warm hand moved down to my neck, his thumb making little circles just below my ear. And I . . .

I was spiraling.

I'd had more than my fair share of first kisses, enough to know without a shred of uncertainty that this thing that was building between Dash and me was like nothing I'd ever felt before. It was more than mere attraction, brighter than a blaze of summer sunshine and more inevitable than fate.

This thing with Dash . . . it felt real.

Or like it had a potential to be. Which only meant that it would hurt all the more when he inevitably ghosted me.

The thought slammed into me with the force of the asteroid that killed the dinosaurs. I broke off the kiss, panting as hard as if I'd just run across the Brooklyn Bridge—at noon, on the hottest day of the year.

"You okay?" Dash murmured, sweeping back a stray curl and tucking it behind my ear. Below his furrowed brow, his velvety brown eyes were wide with mingled concern and surprise.

I stared at him for a long moment, willing myself to come up with a coherent explanation for why I was suddenly enveloped in a haze of panic.

The thing was, whatever reason I offered him, he would have understood. He would have nodded and stepped back and done the gentlemanly thing, even if it meant sitting back down to our quickly cooling salmon and pretending that the past few minutes hadn't happened.

I didn't want that. But neither could I step back into his arms as if the sparkles and magic pulsing through my veins hadn't been replaced with hot, sour panic. So instead, I just . . .

I bolted.

Literally. Without pausing to offer some sort of excuse or even grab my bag, I ran out of Dash's apartment, bursting out into the street and barely making it around the corner before I doubled over, gasping.

Yaz was wrong.

Milo hadn't just broken my heart, or my life. There was a good chance that he'd broken me, too.

10

It was a calculated retreat, not fleeing in craven cowardice. At least, that's what I told myself as I defied the swampy atmosphere and speed walked all the way to ... where the hell was I even going? Did I have a destination in mind, or was I just trying to put as much distance as humanly possible between Dash's place and me?

I couldn't call Yaz. I mean, I could, because she always made time for me, and if I was genuinely upset, she would never dream of sighing or saying I told you so, no matter how much I deserved it. But I *had* promised myself that I would stop coming to her with every single flail, especially of the romantic variety.

It was late enough that when I hesitated right in the middle of the sidewalk, I wasn't immediately barraged with half a dozen New Yorkers being vocal about this vile offense to their sensibilities. I did get stopped by a very drunk girl sweetly asking if I was all right, seconds before she told me I was cute and asked her partner if I could go home with them. Somehow, I managed to smile and thank her because hello, I wasn't so far gone that I couldn't appreciate this boost to my vanity.

Then they wandered back into the bar they had stumbled out of and I was left stranded at the drive-in like John Travolta in that musical that Yaz makes me watch over and over again, only this was an abandonment of my own making.

The panic was, if anything, stronger. It had turned into a roar in my ears, loud enough to drown out the uncomfortably hard thump of my heart. And along with it had come this sickening wave of ... familiarity.

I knew you'd overreact. That was what Milo had said to me when

I first confronted him about his lie. That the reason he'd never told me about being with other women and wanting to break up was because I was too loud, too dramatic . . . too much.

And I *know*. I'm a woman of the twenty-first century with access to the internet and decades' worth of "Am I the Asshole" scenarios. I wasn't naive enough to think that Milo trying to shift the blame onto me was anything more than a shitty excuse for his bad behavior, not to mention his cowardice. And I'd told him as much.

Still. That was the kind of thing that left a mark on you. I knew better, of course I did, but a small part of me couldn't help believing him. The truth is, I *am* too much sometimes. I can be overwhelming, even. And if there was even the slightest chance that it was the reason why I kept getting ghosted . . . Why even my own mom had exited stage left the second I was legally an adult . . .

My hands felt shaky as I rubbed my palms on the skirt of my dress. Which had a pocket. Inside of which was my phone. I skipped the part where I gave a second's worth of thought to what I was about to do and instead went immediately for my phone.

A moment later, I had scrolled past my pinned conversations from contacts I had saved as *Yazzified*, *Tía Nena*, and *Duke Dashwood*, and found a text thread that hadn't been opened in a few weeks. The name at the top had been replaced with a string of emojis—a bowl of soup, a plane, the little hat with the green bow, and an apple. Randomly chosen, kind of impersonal emojis that did a pretty decent job of conveying my relationship with her.

My mom.

I let the phone ring three times before I panicked and tapped out of the call.

I'd probably get more comfort and better advice by going into any of the bars littering Ninth Avenue and spilling my guts to a random bartender than by calling *her*.

I probably didn't have the right number for her, anyway. She changed it as often as she changed locations, and in the eight years since she'd started traveling the world, that averaged out to once every couple of months. Sometimes less.

So yeah, whatever. I kept my phone in my hand, because when you're a single girl wandering the streets of any city after midnight, it's always good to have something you can chuck at the head of a potential murderer before screaming and running. And I put my mother out of my mind, where she belonged.

It wasn't until I caught sight of myself in the glass storefront set into the basement of a brownstone that I realized I was still wearing the pineapple hat. And it didn't even go with my poufy party dress. The gods must have been watching out for me that night, because the hat's skinny green elastic had miraculously not gotten tangled in my curls and I was able to pull off the hat without breaking any strands.

As I threw it inside the garbage can outside the store, I saw the neon sign blinking at me from a corner of the window—*Twenty-Four-Hour Psychic Readings, $10*.

And look, I'm not going to say that I didn't have my doubts about Midtown Manhattan psychics and whether or not this was some sort of tourist scam or the kind of fraud perpetrated on people going through a hard time, making them believe they were in the grip of some curse that could be broken for the low, low price of their entire life savings. But I wasn't about to haul my ass uptown in search of an actual bruja this time of night.

Anyway, it wasn't like I was expecting some earth-shattering revelation about how my life line and my rising sign both indicated that I was doomed to eternal heartbreak. All I wanted, really, was someone to talk to for a beat. And maybe kill some time before going back to my apartment and facing up to the fact that I had just done exactly what I had promised myself I wouldn't and now working with Dash was going to be uncomfortable at best and no longer possible at worst and I was so close to going completely broke and having to move back to Miami and become a couch troll in Yaz and Amal's fancy Brickell condo while they got married and had babies and jobs and a life.

Spiraling, me? Never.

See, this was why it was safer to keep my emotions bottled up all nice and tight—less danger of me bursting a blood vessel in the middle of Hell's Kitchen.

Whatever. I was going in.

I may have been a perennial screwup, but at least I was smart enough to keep a couple of twenties and a MetroCard tucked into the little pocket on the back of my phone case. You know, for emergencies. And if this didn't count as one, I wasn't sure what would.

The steps down to the store were lined with flowerpots, the iron rail twined with multicolored Christmas lights. I pushed the door open to the sound of wind chimes—real ones, not the electronic kind. The place looked like something straight out of that old TV show *Charmed*, with long shelves full of crystals, packages of tarot cards, bundles of sage, and plants in handmade pots. I took a look at a price sticker, and the words popped out before I could keep them back. "Holy bougie occult shop, Batman."

A loud peal of laughter from one side of the room drew my attention to the pale-skinned woman behind the register. Her hair was blue in streaks and piled up in a messy bun, all the better to show off her earrings, which were shaped like dangling swords. "It kind of is, isn't it?"

I'm usually pretty immune to embarrassment, but even my shameless self had the grace to feel a little abashed. "Sorry. By bougie, I really meant awesome."

"Sure," the woman said dryly, pushing up the sleeves of her black mesh top. "My name's Aria and I use she/her pronouns. How can I help you?"

I went over to the register and folded my arms on the counter as I told her my name and pronouns. "I know it's kind of late, but is the psychic still in? I'm in dire need of a spiritual consultation and possibly having my soul saged."

"That would be me, and I'm sure your soul is fine. Why don't you come with me to the back?"

Motioning to the other sales associate to take over the register, she led me down a short hallway. There was a little bit of a stomp to her step, not quite like she was mad, more like she liked how the clunk of her Doc Martens sounded on the wood.

At the end of the hallway was a private room that was mostly lit by a squiggle of blue neon that matched the sign out front. The only other light was a small round lamp that looked like a crystal ball, resting on the table where a deck of tarot cards had been laid out.

"Why *are* you open twenty-four hours?" I asked as I slipped into one of the chairs. "You get a lot of tarot emergencies?"

"You'd be surprised at the amount of people who need spiritual consultations at three in the morning," Aria said, adding with a quirked eyebrow, "and how many of them come from the bar next door." She shrugged. "I live upstairs, and I've been woken up enough times by drunk strangers pounding on the door that it's just easier to hang out down here until things quiet down. And I share the space with a couple other people, so there's always someone around to cover the daytime shifts. It's kind of like a little occult collective. Will this be a love, career, or general life reading?"

"I have to choose?" I asked wryly. Then I flashed back to the hurt, confusion, and embarrassment that had crashed over Dash's face in the split second between my pulling away from him and running out. "I guess we can start with love."

I almost wanted to laugh—that was probably the hysteria at work, though, because the whole thing was deeply unfunny. Because when this evening started out, my love life had been the only thing that was under control, if only because I'd been ignoring it so aggressively. Kissing Dash was the one thing guaranteed to mess up everything else even more than it already was.

Aria started to shuffle the deck, and I noticed a slight easing in her shoulders as she handled the well-worn cards, as if she felt more in her element here than out front. "I'll be doing a three-card spread for you tonight. Roughly, the first one represents the past, the second one the present, and the third the future."

The cards she laid down on the tabletop were way less dramatic than I'd expected. Like, I'd fully imagined a horned devil crowned with pentagrams and a crumbling tower about to be struck by lightning, or maybe an ominous-looking skull blooming with red roses or pierced with swords. Instead, the three cards, each laid beside the others in a straight line, showed elegant figures on a metallic gold background, all dressed in sumptuous medieval garments.

"All right, so here we have the four of swords, the chariot, and the ace of cups." Aria studied the cards for a moment, and I also gazed down at them, as if I could glean some meaning from the rich, warm yellows and the vivid scarlets. "From the four of swords, it looks like you've been trying to take a breather after going through some turbulent times. Maybe you haven't been dating around as much as you used to, or maybe you're just hesitant to jump back into that scene after a potentially messy breakup. With the chariot in your present, though, it's clear that you're starting to move forward."

Maybe it was the mom friend vibes Aria was giving off, or maybe it was just that the seal I had slapped on my emotions was no longer enough to contain them all, but before she could move on to the next card, I found myself blurting out, "He was wearing a wedding ring. My ex, who I ran into a couple weeks ago. A *wedding ring*." The room was so still and quiet I could hear the faint thumping beat coming from the bar next door—and how pain and rage made my voice sound ragged. "And I—I—"

Aria took my outburst in stride, gazing steadily at me from across the small table as she asked, "How long has it been since you broke up?"

"Not that long. Or long enough, I guess—for him, anyway."

"Not for you?"

I shrugged. "It's not like I've been pining over him or anything. The breakup was kind of rough for me, but I pulled through and moved on. Then tonight, I kissed someone else and I—" Flipped out and ran away without saying a word. I squeezed my eyes shut. "I don't want my ex back. I know that. But he got into my head, and now I feel like I need a love exorcism. Is that a thing?"

"If it's not, it definitely should be," Aria said, her lips lifting into a brief smile that didn't erase the concern in her flawlessly outlined eyes. "Was he your first love?"

"No," I said. "Just . . . the first relationship I thought might last. Like, I'd done a pretty good job to keep things light and superficial with everyone who came before him. But he got under my skin, taking me out on these marathon dates and casually making plans for the future and not behaving like someone who had a whole other girlfriend he was keeping a secret."

"That sounds cruel," Aria said, her eyes flashing. "To promise so much when he had so little to give."

"I guess it was. And then, when I found out the truth, he just . . . cut me out of his life. Pretended I had never been a part of it. And it's not like I think Dash—the guy I kissed tonight—will do the same thing. I think I'm mostly just scared that I can't trust myself not to mess everything up. Ugh, maybe I already did." I buried my face in my hands, groaning. "I can't believe I ran away from him."

"Why did you run away?" Aria nudged the middle card toward me. I looked down at the woman swathed in yellow and red, her hair streaming behind her as her chariot gained speed. "Was it to avoid getting hurt, or to avoid feeling at all?"

"Damn," I said in a low voice. "You really are psychic."

The thing about bottling up your emotions is that there inevitably comes a moment when the pressure gets to be too much and the cork pops and however deep down you have stuffed everything, it all comes shooting messily out.

You know, like champagne. Only less fun.

I must have spent half an hour pouring my heart out to Aria, saying things I hadn't even thought I'd know how to articulate. And I had to give her props, because she didn't seem all that put out about it—she listened to me, interjecting here and there with comments that I found surprisingly insightful for someone who'd only just met me, but that probably weren't all that surprising coming from a self-professed psychic.

By the time I finally made my way back out into the street, I was feeling much steadier than when I'd come in. Aria hadn't tried to sell me anything, and when I'd finally calmed down enough for her to finish reading my cards, everything she had to say was gentle and reassuring.

Most importantly, though, Aria had helped me see that what in the moment had felt like self-preservation was probably closer to self-sabotage. "From what you've told me," she'd said, tapping on the chariot card with a black-painted fingernail, "I think you owe it to yourself to move past your fear and see what new beginnings are in store for you. It sounds easier said than done, right? It's about trusting yourself, and that kind of trust doesn't come easy to everyone. But Mariel . . . I think you're capable of it."

Without even hesitating, she'd separated the future card from the other two in the spread and handed it to me. "I want you to keep this as a reminder."

I'd tried to protest. "But—won't your deck be incomplete?"

"I have other decks," she replied seriously, holding out the card until I took it.

The ace of cups, the card that represented my future and the fresh start that was supposed to come with it, was a visual representation of *my cup runneth over*. The gold goblet in its center was overflowing with streams of metallic blue water, a gold-and-yellow sunburst behind it.

"What if he hurts me?" I'd whispered.

"What if he doesn't?" Aria countered.

I was aware, somewhere not so deep inside my consciousness, that I couldn't throw this thing entirely at Milo's feet. He'd done a shitty thing, yes, but he was merely the latest person to have that particular honor. If I was so broken that I was on the edge of hyperventilating just because I had shared a kiss with someone and it ended up meaning more to me than I had expected, well . . .

That was on me.

Which made it harder to face. Because then I'd be forced to confront the fact that maybe everyone who had ghosted me hadn't done so because they were soulless bastards, but because I drove them to it.

See, this was why I tried to limit the extent of my self-awareness. It was *blistering*.

And the thing was, I kept thinking that maybe Milo hadn't broken me, but that not taking a chance on Dash probably would. Never mind that after my little roadrunner moment, it was doubtful that he would want to take a chance on *me*.

Even if that was the case, though, and even if it turned out that I'd ruined my last shot, I knew that if nothing else, I had to stop running.

◆ ◆ ◆

It was late, and I was so emotionally wrung out by my impromptu therapy session with Aria that it was tempting to go to my apartment and wait until the next day to face Dash. But with the ace of cups in my pocket and the words *I have to stop running* ringing in my head, I made the conscious choice to go back to Dash's to apologize and explain.

As I turned onto the still-busy Ninth Avenue, my gaze snagged on a late-night vendor whose blanket was spread with jewelry. Or, more specifically, on the silver H dangling from the heavy silver links of a necklace.

Get this—it turned out that the vendor had necklaces with every letter, but he'd sold out of all but the H. Call it a sign, or the universe rewarding me for letting Aria read me for filth. Whatever it was, I tapped my phone to the vendor's card reader so fast, sparks should have shot out of the screen.

Now armed with an apology *and* a gift, I shot Dash a text saying I was on my way over and began walking without waiting for an answer.

Which proved to be a mistake, I realized the second time I hit the buzzer and got no answer.

Okay, so Dash didn't want to talk to me. Fair enough. Pretending not to be home was a little much, but I couldn't blame him for being fed up with my antics. Or maybe he'd gone out and found himself someone with less issues to hook up with. Understandable, really.

Defiantly swallowing down the lump that rose to my throat, I shoved the necklace into my pocket and walked away. This was it. I'd messed up, again, and I'd ruined everything, again. Honestly, maybe it was just as well that I'd kept getting ghosted before I had a chance to get this far.

I'd find a way to smooth things over in the morning so that it wasn't too awkward going forward. With my track record, you'd think I'd have more practice in that kind of thing, but the truth was, Yaz was often the one doing the smoothing for me. The thought made me cringe—I'd relied on her way too much in the past.

I made it all the way back to my street before I realized that my keys were in the bag I had left at Dash's.

"Cool, cool," I said out loud, trying not to panic. An emergency locksmith was probably more expensive than what I could afford. Maybe Aria would let me hang out in the shop until morning?

I started to turn, then swiveled back as I spotted someone leaning against the outside of my building. His face was in shadows, but as he peeled himself off the wall and stepped into the circle of light cast by a streetlamp, I saw a T-shirt the color of the summer sky, a pair of gray joggers, and a bright orange tote bag emblazoned in pink letters reading *More Books That I Don't Need.*

My breath caught inside my chest, which suddenly felt so tight that only one word managed to squeeze past. "Dash."

11

It was possible I may have breathed out his name, for all the world like a sheltered wallflower encountering the handsome duke as he rose from a pond with his white shirt plastered to his abs. I was almost too surprised by the sight of him to make a mental note about pushing Dash into the Turtle Pond at Central Park—you know, for science.

"I saw your text," he said, fiddling with his phone. "I figured we should probably talk in person."

I won't lie. My stomach sank at the seriousness in his tone. At least Dash had the courtesy to break things off in person, unlike pretty much everyone I'd ever dated.

"You don't mind coming upstairs, do you?" I asked him, squaring my shoulders. If there was one thing I didn't aspire to, it was to be a New York City cliché and have a big, dramatic blowup on the sidewalk.

"Sure." Dash held out my tote. "I figured you probably had something important in here."

I reached for it, plunging my hand inside and taking out my key chain, which was shaped like a slice of cake festooned with icing and cherries. "These were in there so yeah, thanks," I said as I let us inside.

My heart was thumping a little faster and harder than the stairs merited when I closed the door to my apartment behind Dash. This was the first time he'd come over to my place, and I couldn't help but take in the studio through fresh eyes—the jumble of paperbacks on the nightstand, the creamsicle-colored duvet, half-buried in clean laundry and shoved to one corner of the unmade bed, the messy tray of earrings on top of the two-burner range, the collection of bras dangling from the standing lamp and every single doorknob . . .

His apartment was warm and comfortable; mine was chaos personified. But then again, so was I. I was Too Much (TM). And even with no one going out of their way to make me feel bad about it, I knew it didn't exactly make me the easiest person to be around.

Not that it mattered anymore, at least where Dash was concerned.

"So," I began, trying not to give in to the urge to cross my arms. That was about as far as I got.

In case it wasn't obvious from the way I'd avoided telling my family the truth about losing my job, I've never really been that good at difficult conversations. With Dash standing in front of me, his forehead all scrunched up and the corners of his mouth turned slightly down, I had no idea how I was going to get the words out.

I shouldn't have been surprised that Dash spoke up first. "I hope it's okay that I came. You seemed pretty upset when you left, and I wanted to make sure that you had gotten home okay. And return your bag and stuff, of course."

I gave him a weird, anxious little nod. "I'm fine."

"And I also wanted to apologize—"

My mouth dropped open. "*Apologize?* You?"

He looked down. "I've been flirting with you pretty aggressively. I wouldn't have done it if I'd thought it was making you uncomfortable, but I realize now that I shouldn't have done it at all, not when we're trying to work together."

"You think I ran away because I didn't want you to kiss me? For fuck's sake, Dash, I've wanted nothing else from the moment we met. I've been flirting back just as hard, you know."

Dash ran his fingers through his hair. "Then what happened?" His lips quirked up into a smile, but I could see the uncertainty lurking in his eyes, and yeah, the knowledge that I had put it there was heartbreaking. "Am I that bad a kisser?"

I snorted. I couldn't help it. "That's not it and you know it. I just . . . got a little overwhelmed, I guess. By how much I like you."

He nodded slowly. "I like you, too, Mariel. A lot. Is there anything I should have done differently? Or could do, in case of a potential second time?"

"You . . . would want there to be a second time?"

"And third and fourth and every number until infinity." He spread his hands. "If that's what you want."

"I do," I said, and took a step closer to him. "And Dash, I'm the one who owes you an apology."

He shook his head. "What, for feeling overwhelmed? You shouldn't have to apologize for that. I just . . . would really appreciate it if you tried talking to me before running off. If you still feel like fleeing after we've had a conversation, then fine."

"You may not have noticed, but I have a hard time being vulnerable with people."

"News to me," Dash said, a smile playing over his lips.

I couldn't help but grin back at him, mostly out of sheer relief. "Right? I hide it so well. The thing is, you weren't that far off the mark when you noticed that I run away whenever things get too emotional. I don't always do it on purpose—most of the time, I'm operating on pure instinct." I forced myself to keep my gaze on him. "When you kissed me, Dash, it felt . . . monumental. Like it wasn't just a kiss, but something bigger. It felt like a beginning."

His eyes were soft. "It did for me, too."

I pressed on. "And the thing is, I haven't been great with beginnings lately, because I've been through so many of them. And the thing about beginnings is that they always come to an end."

He nodded. "And then come the happily ever afters."

"Not everyone gets happily ever afters, Dash." Maybe he did, with his eyes that sparkled like a sprinkle of stars dipped in sunshine.

In need of a beat, I went to hang up my tote on its hook by the door. When I turned back to him, Dash was looking serious.

"It would be too soon for me to promise you all that," he said, resting a hand on my melamine countertop like he wanted to reach out to me, but didn't want to risk scaring me off again. "All I know is that I like you. And look, I know I have a bad habit of getting a little too intense when I really like someone. So if you feel like I'm coming on too hard, or moving too fast, just tell me and I'll stop."

"Maybe if we keep this casual," I suggested, unable to miss the slight flicker behind his eyes, though I didn't quite know how to interpret it. "No beginnings, no endings, and no expectations. Friends who kiss . . . and do other things, maybe. If you want."

Some of the tension in my shoulders evaporated as he broke out into a sudden laugh. "Are you trying to distract me from talking about my feelings?" Despite the laughter, or maybe because of it, there was an edge to his voice. I wasn't sure what it meant—but it couldn't have meant much when he followed it with "Because if you are, it's a better strategy than running away, but you'll never win in the end."

"My evil plan has been foiled," I murmured, with a step forward that put me close enough to Dash to smell a hint of the cinnamon he liked in his coffee. I felt steadier now, like I was on firmer ground. Like we both were. "Note to self: don't kiss people who are more emotionally mature than you are."

"Or," Dash suggested, holding out a hand and threading his fingers through mine, "you could keep on kissing me in spite of my embarrassing lack of emotional damage."

I pretended to sigh. "If I must."

"Would you want to do it again right now?"

I ran my free fingertips over his lips. "I can't believe you still want to kiss me."

"I doubt I would find it possible to stop." He closed his eyes, lowering his forehead to meet mine.

I thought about explaining to Dash that plenty of other people had managed it just fine, but fuck words. Fuck talking. What was the point of all that when Dash's lips were gliding over mine, softly and smoothly and so fleetingly that I had to grab two handfuls of his T-shirt and wrench them toward me to make him understand what I needed.

I must have pulled hard enough to unbalance him because we tumbled backward onto the only piece of furniture in my apartment—my bed. All the laundry piled up in a corner made things kind of awkward, and I ended up on my back with my legs on a pile of folded sundresses and Dash half-sprawled on my chest with one knee on the mattress and another leg safely on the ground.

"Impatient" was his keen observation.

"Like you didn't know that about me," I retorted, plunging my fingers into his hair and pulling him close again.

This time, Dash gave me exactly what I was craving. He kissed me with a need that didn't just echo mine—it merged with it, amplifying it into a single, undeniable roar that rushed over us both. The small, helpless, hungry sound he made when the tip of my tongue touched his bottom lip dove somewhere deep inside my chest and stayed there.

Braced against the mattress, Dash adjusted his stance as I swept my palms over his flexed biceps and twined my arms around his neck to pull him down for one kiss after another.

"So," he said when we resurfaced for a breath or two, "how was that?"

"Still overwhelming, but in the best way possible."

"You feeling up for more, or would you rather take it slow? You know I'm good with whatever you want."

I made myself take a pause to really consider my answer, though a huge percentage of me wanted to drag Dash down again and lose myself in his kisses. I didn't feel too broken at the moment. I wasn't kidding myself that half an hour at a psychic's had cured me of my relationship trauma or even helped me as much as the therapy I was definitely going to sign up for as soon as I had health insurance again, but all the Milo crap that had turned up after leaving Dash's, like earthworms after a rainstorm, had receded enough that I could once again see the shining thread of my attraction for Dash.

I wanted to grab on to it and never let go. I wanted to grab on to *him* and never let go.

"I want to be with you," I told Dash, pushing a lock of hair out of his eyes. "And I'm moderately sure I won't run away again. I think. Are you sure about this, though?"

"I keep going back and forth with myself," he admitted. "I know that the smart thing would be to ignore my feelings and not do anything that would put our work at risk. But honestly . . . I think it's safe to say that whatever hope we had of keeping this platonic has pretty much flown out the window. So if you're up for seeing where this takes us, then so am I. I don't think we were meant to be a slow burn, Mariel."

I squirmed a little, wishing that his biceps would give in so that he would fall on top of me. "What if where I'm hoping this takes us is my bed?"

He ducked his head, but I could still see his grin. "Then I'm glad we're already on it."

"Did you just hair-flip me?"

"Did I just what?" He lifted his head again, looking half startled and half sheepish.

I couldn't resist it—I reached up and caressed the curls above his temple. "Don't you try to deny it, buddy. You know exactly what you're doing when you flip your hair like that. How many people have you made fall to their knees just by doing that?"

"A couple," he admitted, laughing. "I thought you'd be tougher than that, though."

"Not when it comes to you," I told him, tracing the curve of his ear with a fingertip.

And then we were kissing again, his mouth hot and needy on mine. This time, we parted only long enough for me to tug at his T-shirt. Dash straightened to pull it over his head—from my spot on my pillows, I had a great view of the defined contours of his abs, sheened lightly with sweat and gleaming in the pinkish light cast by my palm tree–shaped lamp. When he shifted, his knee nudged me between my spread legs, and I couldn't resist grinding down on his muscled thigh.

"Your thigh is so hard."

"That's not the only thing that's hard," he said, quirking up his eyebrow, and we let out breathless laughs.

He bent down over me again, and I skimmed the front of his chest until I reached the waistband of his shorts. "Do you want me to—"

"No," he said, hunger darkening the honey in his eyes. "Keep going. I want to watch you get off rubbing yourself on me."

I freed the skirt of my dress from where it had gotten trapped beneath his knee and spread my legs a little wider, grateful to the gusset of my panties for providing a muffling layer between his skin and my, uh, throbbing loins.

As good as it felt, though, my gaze kept straying down to the sizable bulge in his shorts. I had a good idea of what was contained within the light gray fabric, and I wanted it.

Dash caught my glance. Raising an eyebrow, he said, "Not yet," and proceeded to scoot away from me, sliding down to his knees in front of the bed. I would have protested, had I not felt his breath on the inside of my thighs a moment later. Each brush of his lips against my overheated skin left trembles in its wake. I tugged up my dress a little to give him access, then let my hand fall on his hair, which was so tousled from the flipping that I didn't feel bad running my fingers through it.

"Don't tell me you already forgot how impatient I can be."

Dash glanced up briefly. "I know what you want, and I fully intend to give it to you. But first . . . I want to make you blush. And sigh. And pant."

"Did you just quote the Duke of Harding?"

He winked at me, and it was a good thing I was lying down because I almost swooned. "I mean, if it worked on his wallflower . . ."

"If wallflowers are your kink, I'm gonna have to get myself a pair of glasses," I said, feeling the hitch in my breath as his tongue delved into the crease of my thigh.

He made an enthusiastic sound at the idea of glasses, but all he said was "Can I take off your panties?"

"You have my permission to do whatever you want with my panties, Dashwood." I let my head fall back, and as he peeled off my underwear and got to work with what I could only call artistry, I took a moment to check in with myself. So far, I didn't seem to be in danger of bolting. The difference between this moment and the one immediately preceding my flail was almost tangible. It wasn't that I liked him any less or that I was less terrified about losing him, or destroying what we were beginning to build. I just knew better than to think I could outrun the fear.

Dash was licking me like he was trying to savor me. Had I really thought earlier that I could lose myself in Dash? I couldn't have been more wrong. This felt like finding myself. Slow, sticky warmth spread over my limbs like syrup on a stack of pancakes, so that I was hyperaware of every square inch of my body. All the places where pleasure pooled, where my skin tingled with awareness. All the nerve endings in my palm as I touched the top of Dash's head and the heated back of his neck.

He took his time, though he must have been uncomfortable with his knees mashed against the hardwood. It wasn't until an orgasm was shuddering through me that he got to his feet.

His hands firmly on my ass, he lifted me clear off the bed and sat down on the spot I had just occupied, keeping me on his lap.

"Nice move," I said approvingly, untwining my arms from around his neck so that I could explore the ridges of his shoulders and biceps.

"A purely selfish one. I get a better view this way," he murmured, giving his hips just enough of a buck so that I could understand what he meant.

I moved off his thighs until I was positioned directly above the heaviness between his legs, my own thighs bracketing his hips like parentheses filled with an exclamation point. Then I lowered myself, slowly, until my bare skin came into contact with the seam in his shorts and we both let out breaths that quickly turned into moans as I began to move against him.

He rewarded me with a cheeky "Attagirl," which almost made me lose my shit right then and there.

And to think I almost hadn't replaced the condom stash in my nightstand.

Gently, he eased the straps of my dress over my shoulders, wriggling down the fabric until my bra was exposed. He removed it as skillfully as he had my panties, and when the faint breeze coming in through the half-open window swept over my nipples, I couldn't help but arch my back—directly toward his mouth.

His lips closed around a nipple, dragging another moan out of me, followed by a breathless, half-strangled "Dashwood."

"I love the way you say my name," he said against my skin. "And the way you taste. Your skin is so sweet."

There was so much I wanted to say to him. I felt like I was crammed with words that were trying to burst out. I held them back, even as my mouth parted to allow entrance to Dash's questing tongue.

Maybe, if I didn't fuck this up like I always did, there would come a day when the words would pour out without the fear that I'd say something to drive him away. Until then, I let the air thicken between us and I kissed him back, and I gave in to the pleasure of his skin.

◆ ◆ ◆

"What are you doing?" Dash asked a few hours later, rolling over in bed.

"Checking our stats," I said, completely unrepentant as I swiped through the Duke of Harding's profiles. "Dash. Dude. Dash." I scrambled into a sitting position, tossing off the cotton blanket clinging to my shoulders. "How is my phone not bursting into flames right now?"

He lifted himself up on one elbow, seemingly more interested in drawing a finger up and down my naked spine than in his views. "We got a few likes, huh?"

"A few? We're going *viral*. Eight hundred thousand likes on Tik-Tok and that's just the teaser video. There's all these followers, and the comments, oh my god, the comments." I gasped out a laugh as I read the first few. "I might have to print some of these out and stick them on my wall. I could *wallpaper* this apartment with the comments."

I could have basked in the sweet, sweet glory of all those views, likes, comments, and shares, but I would've missed out on the best sight of all. I tore my gaze away from the screen to grin at Dash and found him lying on his back, one arm folded behind his head and that bashful little smile tugging at the corner of his lips.

"I feel like Eliza Doolittle at the Embassy Ball," he said. "Or Barbra after Kris Kristofferson got ahold of her."

I gave him my best side-eye, modeled after Yaz's superior one. "That would make me either misogynist Henry Higgins or reckless John Norman Howard—I'm deeply offended."

Flinging my phone on the nest of clean laundry we had pushed to the floor, I rolled over to prop my chin on his chest.

Dash immediately put his arms around me, trapping me against the smooth skin of his chest. "Did you know that the first time you told me about your idea for the Duke of Harding, I thought it might be a ploy to hook up with me?"

"And you still messaged me?"

"I was intrigued. By the idea, but also by your passion. The way you throw yourself so wholeheartedly into everything . . . I mean, you can't even look for something in your bag without running into inanimate objects. I have no doubt that's a huge part of why the videos are doing so well."

"I can think of another huge part," I said, making him squirm as I reached into the sheets.

He grabbed my hand and twined our fingers together. "Don't you try to weasel out of this one. If this is going to work out, you'll have to accept that there are going to be a lot of compliments and a *lot* of mushy moments. I'm going to gaze deeply into your eyes.

I'm going to kiss your hand"—he illustrated his words by brushing his lips over my knuckles—"and most important of all, I'm going to tell you, every single day that we spend together, just how amazing you are."

"You're such a cinnamon roll," I said, grinning.

Dash folded one of his arms behind his head, keeping the other one around my waist. "I fail to see how that's a bad thing, considering your sweet tooth."

"It's not a bad thing. It's a very, very good thing." Purely for the sake of illustrating my point, I traced a delicate line over his collarbone with my tongue. His skin was salty with perspiration, but there was an underlying sweetness that was all him.

"Mmm," I murmured, giving his neck a soft bite. "Just as good as a glazed donut."

Dash's laugh was full and ripe as summer fruit. "What flavor?"

"Lemon blueberry," I said, without having to think about it. "With some sort of unexpected herb, like rosemary or something. Light, sugary, with just a hint of tartness."

He looked at me through his eyelashes. "I'll be a tart for you, if that's what you're into."

My heart may not have stopped, but it definitely skipped a beat or two. "I didn't know I was until this very moment, but yes. Please. But wait—put this on first."

Swinging my legs over the side of the bed, I scrabbled through a heap of shimmery blue fabric until I found the necklace in my dress pocket, all the while praising myself for my foresight.

When I turned back around, Dash was looking at me with light in his eyes, like they were reflecting a starry night. At the sight of it, entire constellations bloomed into life inside me, bursting apart like fireworks.

"Don't get used to this," I warned him as I climbed back in beside him with the necklace clutched in my fist. "I'm too broke and I mess up too often for this to be financially responsible. But I, uh, I got you an apology gift."

I poured the chain into his palm, trying not to look like I was scrutinizing his reaction as he turned it over in his hands.

"H for Harding?" he asked.

"And for handsome." I shrugged. "I saw that you were wearing a necklace in one of your old videos and it looked so amazing on you."

I'm blaming gravity and other irresistible forces for the way I melted into the crook of his arm, in the perfect position for him to trail the cool silver links over the swells of my breasts and my quickly tightening nipples.

"Put it on me?" he asked. "I need to be tarted up, like rock and roll."

I gasped. "Did you just make a *Velvet Goldmine* reference? It's a good thing I'm not wearing any panties, or that would have made me ruin them."

"Are you kidding me? *Velvet Goldmine* was my sexual awakening."

"Hard same," I said.

The clasp was easy enough for even my lightly trembling fingers. When it caught, I ran my fingertip over the beads, right where they kissed Dash's skin. The H nestled between his collarbones, highlighting the paleness of his skin and the round, defined muscles of his shoulders and neck.

I didn't need to verbalize how beautiful I found him, but maybe I didn't have to, because it was more than likely that it was written all over my face. Softly, I touched my thumb to the curled-up corner where his smiles tried to lurk.

"Thank you for the gift," he said, pressing a sideways kiss to my thumb.

"It's an apology," I said. "For running away. And a promise to try my best to not do it again. Unless I'm being chased by like a bear or something, in which case I'd be justified."

It wasn't a deflection, not really, and Dash must have understood because he flipped me over with a growl. "I'll chase you."

My laugh got lost in moans as he devoured the side of my neck, his hands tracing a blazing path up the insides of my thighs.

"I'd chase you to the other end of the world if you wanted me to," he whispered against my skin.

I moaned again, and arched my neck. Words, and the ability to do anything with them, were vanishing from my mind, but I managed a half-panted "I don't think you'll have to go that far."

Later, when I felt myself getting sucked down into sleep, I groped over the bedcovers for his hand. It was warm, and it curled around me as if out of instinct.

I must have been drunk with sleep, because if I had been in my right mind, there's no way I would have whispered into the dark, "Will you still be here when I wake up?"

He turned and pressed his face into the side of my neck. "I'm not going anywhere."

12

At some point during the night, I had swaddled myself in my usual unsexy cocoon of blankets, so it wasn't until sunlight started slicing through that annoying gap in my tasseled curtains and right into my eyes that I even remembered there was a naked Dash on the bed next to me.

Moving out of the glare, I parted my eyelids and glanced across at my guest pillow.

Dash's eyes were still closed, the beam of golden light illuminating his chiseled profile like he was in a goddamn indie film full of honey-voiced vocals and handheld cameras capturing dust motes dancing in shafts of light.

He was still there. He was still there. The words beat a happy tattoo against my rib cage, like the patter of raindrops on a window.

"Would you stop it?" I groaned, giving his shoulder a push.

From the quick way he turned his golden-brown eyes toward me, I knew he hadn't been asleep. "Stop what?"

"Being so fucking handsome. It's offensive to the eyes so early in the morning."

If his head had been lying on anything more beautiful than a faded Urban Outfitters pillowcase I'd bought on sale, I would've had to shove him entirely off the bed.

Laughing, he flipped me around so that he was spooning me, his bare thighs cradling mine. The bristles on his jaw scraped pleasantly on my bare shoulder. "Don't tell me you were watching me sleep."

"I'm not that kind of creep," I said. "But you're so nauseatingly attractive, I might find myself doing something just as—"

"Romantic?" he murmured into my ear.

"Alarming."

A low laugh gusted into the sensitive hollow behind my ear, and I had to fight the urge to squirm.

"You have to admit, watching someone sleep is objectively creepy."

"For the record, I agree," he said.

I wriggled around to face him, even though it meant losing out on the scratch of his stubble against my shoulder.

"What are you doing?" he asked, faintly amused.

"I want to lay on your chest while you do that rumbly thing with your voice."

"What rumbly thing?" he asked, pitching his voice so that I felt the reverberations shiver all the way down my chest and thighs.

I pushed myself up slightly so that he could see how hard my nipples had tightened. "See? *This* is why they call you the talent."

"Oh? I thought it was because I can do this . . ." He trailed his fingertips down my spine, making me shiver. "And this . . ." His hot mouth closed gently around my earlobe. "Not to mention . . . this . . ." And he began to hum, turning the rumble into something deeper, an earthquake shaking my foundations.

His hand dipped lower, following the curve of my hip until his fingertips were delving between my thighs in strong, sure strokes.

I moved against his hand, murmuring something under my breath, not entirely sure of what I was saying but knowing that they were things I needed desperately for him to know. My mouth found his just as my fingers closed around him.

I was awash in pleasure, and I wanted nothing more than to bask in it and let it fill me up.

The light was in my eyes, but it hardly mattered because it was also all around me and I was nothing more than a dust mote floating in the sunshine.

I drifted off into a midmorning nap to the sound of the shower running. When I woke up again, the slice of light had moved up the wall and I expected Dash to be gone. But there he was, cross-legged on the bed in his boxers, a tray with pastries and strawberries and two cups on the mattress before him.

Turning to face him, I propped myself up on my elbow and regarded him silently.

He put down his phone, already smiling down at me even before the screen went black. He didn't dip his head to kiss me, or say anything, or do much but hand me one of the reusable lidded cups I kept by the door.

"Hot chocolate," I said, pleasantly surprised when I caught the sweet, earthy scent.

"Frozen hot chocolate," he corrected. "With whipped cream, caramel swirls, and mini marshmallows. I also got an assortment of pastries, some savory, most of them sweet."

I quirked an eyebrow. "Big spender."

"I'm also very good-looking and *so* refined," he answered, grinning.

The first sip coated my mouth with sweet warmth, making me feel as if fireworks should be going off behind my closed eyelids. "I think frozen hot chocolate might be my love language," I said dreamily—then I froze as I heard the l-word tumble into the space between us.

But Dash didn't look panicked, or like he was purposefully trying to ignore it. He leaned down and swiped his tongue over my lower lip, sucking lightly like he was trying to savor the sweetness. "I'll try to remember that."

More than anything I wanted to believe that Dash was nothing like all the other men I'd dated. Where they were as insubstantial and ephemeral as true ghosts, the man beneath me was solid and warm and *there*.

Not that it made any difference. I tightened my grip around my cup, willing my heart to stop drumming inside my chest. I mean, Milo had seemed as substantial as a brick wall and his ghosting had hit me about as hard. If I knew anything about men and relationships, it was that there were never any guarantees.

I did not have the emotional maturity to deal with this. "Come on, that's too much effort when we're just buddies who bone," I blurted out.

Dash's eyebrows drew up, making him look . . . well, disappointed really. As if he'd been hoping for something more. As if he wanted . . .

Nope—I was not going to read too much into a pair of raised eyebrows. Just because he hadn't ghosted didn't mean that he wanted something serious. We'd all but agreed last night that this was going to be strictly casual. Sex and flirting, no feelings—that was the way to keep things fun.

And safe.

Thrusting the hot chocolate at him, I scrambled out of bed, not panicking. Definitely not panicking. "What are we doing lying around? We have stats to check! Comments to answer! Other creators to boost! Hair to wash!"

He remained in bed, looking at me as I dashed into the bathroom, just barely managing to slam the door shut behind me before I melted into a puddle of cringe.

I know, I know. It wasn't my finest moment. I was a coward and this definitely counted as running away. And after all my big talk over Aria's cards the night before. To be fair, it was far easier to be brave when staring at a painted goblet than when looking into Dash's honey-and-brown-sugar eyes. I turned the hot water tap and squeezed my eyes shut as I stepped into the warming stream. He definitely deserved more than one of my flails.

If the alternative was having another conversation about our feelings, though, I was happy to keep flailing. Even if it did stink a little of self-sabotage. In the clear light of day, away from neon signs and Aria's piercing gaze and, yes, the starriness of Dash's gaze and the desire fizzing all through me, it was hard to believe that I could have let so many things spill out.

It was one thing to confide in a stranger I was probably never going to see again. But to have let Dash see so much of me? To have let him slip even a little bit past the defenses I kept around me?

Anxiety beat at my rib cage, and I had to bite down hard on my lip to keep from groaning out loud as I squeezed out a dollop of shampoo into my palm.

It wasn't that I was any less emotionally immature when I finally emerged out of the shower, it was just that I'd employed my time there wisely. I mean, I'd detangled and washed and conditioned my hair. But I'd also come up with a plan for the day.

"I know that we have a couple of banked videos," I said without preamble as I opened the bathroom door. "But we really need to get started on shooting more content. Do you have plans today?"

Dash was on my bed where I'd left him, looking at his phone. Glancing up, he shook his head. To my relief, he didn't mention my flail. "Not really. Want to go over to my place and get started?"

I barely gave him enough time to pull on his pants—not that I should have deprived my fellow citizens of the sight of Dashwood in a pair of clingy boxers.

When we got downstairs, the sidewalk was egg-frying hot, the humidity so high I could feel my curls tightening into ringlets. As we walked past my pals at the bodega, who were hanging out just outside the door, and the elderly couple who ran the laundromat down the street, I slipped on a pair of sunglasses with flower petals around the rims, to keep my eyeballs from being seared by the bright sunlight reflecting off windows and cars.

Dash gave my fingers a questioning bump with his own, waiting for my answering bump before tangling our fingers together. Big mistake on my part—mine tingled at the contact, so much that I quickly disentangled my hand from his and pretended that I needed to scratch my nose. Buddies who boned didn't hold hands.

We were almost exactly halfway between Dash's block and mine when I saw it again—the basement window with the purple curtains and the neon sign advertising ten-dollar palm readings. I'd been in too much of a haze to give it any conscious thought, but I guess a part of me expected that it wouldn't be there the next time I went by. But there it was, purple curtains shimmering slightly in the daylight.

I was making a mental note to come back later that day with some cupcakes or something to thank Aria for indulging my mini breakdown, when the door at the head of the steps opened and a woman in black shorts and an oversized *The Love Witch* T-shirt came lightly down the steps. My gaze went directly to her shoes, these gold booties with the area where the toes were split into two compartments that made her feet look like hooves.

"Your shoes are amazing," I blurted out a second before my gaze shifted to her face. "Aria! Hi!"

So much for a stranger I was never going to see again. The universe was laughing at me again. Still, I was genuinely happy to see her.

She paused at the bottom of the steps, blinking a little in the sunlight. She was wearing the same sword earrings from last night, and her winged eyeliner was as perfect as it had been then. "Mariel, right?"

Her knowing gaze transferred to Dash.

I introduced him, adding, "Dash, this is Aria, our friendly neighborhood psychic."

Dash was shaking her hand when the door opened again and out came Shy from the bookstore, holding Kitty Marlowe against their chest in what looked like a baby sling made out of a silk scarf patterned with ice cream cones.

Aria's face tilted up in a way that reminded me of a sunflower following the light. "This is my spouse, Shy."

"Oh, we're old friends," I said, smiling at Shy as I gave Kitty Marlowe a cautious pat with the tip of my index finger.

Dash and Shy exchanged greetings, explaining to Aria that they knew each other from the store and laughing over how much of a small town New York City could be sometimes.

"I call it Manhattan magic," Shy said. "Sometimes you can spend a day running from one borough to another and never see a soul you know—and sometimes all it takes to run into everyone you've ever met is a two-block walk."

"I know what you mean." Dash reached for my fingers and gave them a squeeze. "It's like the city knows what you need at any given moment."

This whole moment felt serendipitous to me. We did all live in the same neighborhood, so maybe it wasn't that weird, but how often had the four of us passed each other in the street or hung out in the same coffee shops without knowing how our lives were intertwined?

"What are you guys up to today?" I asked, partially to put off the moment when Dash and I had to be alone together again.

Shy made a face. "It's time to refresh the store windows again—"

"So I'm dragging Shy to brunch and forcing them to sit down and come up with new ideas," Aria put in, looking a little grim. "Even if it kills us both."

"Am I the only one who thinks designing store windows sounds like a good time?" Dash asked with a tilt to his eyebrows that reminded me of when he was desperate for another cup of coffee but had already had three.

I took one look at the naked longing in Dash's face and blurted out, "Dash went to art school. He could help you out."

Mortification burned through me when my brain caught up with my mouth a half second too late, and I glanced over at Dash to apologize for volunteering his services. But he was actually nodding, a hopeful twist to the corners of his mouth.

"I would like to, yeah," he told Shy. "I could put together a few sketches tonight if you wanted me to."

Shy brightened up like a little kid who had just been informed that someone else would be doing their math homework. "I want you to!"

Aria pushed a strand of bright blue hair behind her ear. "No exaggeration, you guys might have just saved our marriage. Why don't you let us buy you dinner tomorrow night? If you don't have any plans already."

"We'd love to," I blurted out again, and Dash confirmed his agreement with a nod and a smile.

As he and Aria exchanged numbers and agreed to go over the details over text, I felt Dash's fingers brush questioningly against mine again. I didn't want to brush him off again, so I hooked my pinkie around his and gave it a friendly tug.

The four of us chatted for another few minutes, then Shy said, "Are both of you coming to burlesque night?"

My heart gave a little squeeze of apprehension at having to make plans ahead of time, and I disentangled my fingers from Dash's. But Dash just nodded, as if it wasn't that big a deal. Maybe it wasn't for someone like him.

"I told Chase I'd be there." He turned to me. "I guess we hadn't talked about it, but I was definitely hoping you'd come with me."

"Sure," I said brightly, avoiding his gaze *and* Aria's. "Sounds like fun! Bring it on!" My manic word shower slowed down enough for my thoughts to catch up. "Actually . . . you know, my cousin Yaz is coming for a visit that week. I'm sure she'll want to come along, too."

"The more, the merrier," Shy said.

They and Aria were going in the opposite direction as Dash and me, so we said our goodbyes and continued on our way. For some reason, I couldn't quite shake the thought of Yaz off my mind, and when I glanced at my phone I realized why.

"That's weird," I said with a frown. "Yaz hasn't texted me since yesterday and she always checks in as soon as she's up for the day. Do you mind if I give her a quick call?"

Dash shook his head. "You need privacy?"

"No, that's fine. It'll be quick." I pulled up my recent calls and tapped on her name, waiting only a few seconds before Yaz picked up. "Hey, girl. Haven't heard from you today."

"Mariel, can I call you back?" Yaz said, sounding harried.

"Everything okay?"

"Yeah, just . . . It's chaotic at work today. Talk soon."

She hung up before I had a chance to say anything. I frowned down at my phone for long enough that Dash had to ask me what was wrong.

"I'm not sure," I said slowly.

I mean, she *was* exasperated that I had refused to follow her advice and instead swerved into another pivot. But that didn't really seem like enough to make her skip out on our daily calls.

I wouldn't have blamed her if she'd decided she'd had more than enough of keeping me on the right track. After twenty-six years, even the most dedicated person was bound to get tired of babysitting someone their own age. Or maybe I was just overthinking it and she *was* just busy?

We reached Dash's building, and as we headed up the stairs, I told myself to get a grip. Yaz was probably fine, just overworked. And probably pissed to be spending yet another weekend morning at the office. She spent so much time on the phone with me during the workweek, sometimes I forgot she was a first-year associate with a whole fiancée to come home to. It was a good thing that she was taking time to deal with her own stuff.

And anyway, I was going to see her in just over a week. Whatever she was going through—if she was even going through something—we'd be able to talk it out in person pretty soon.

◆   ◆   ◆

Dash was so quiet the rest of the way back to his apartment that I was half-afraid that he had only agreed to help Shy with their windows out of politeness. As soon as the door closed behind us, though, he stepped right up to me and gathered me into his arms, pressing a kiss to my forehead.

"Uh, what's going on?" I asked, my voice muffled by his chest.

"Nothing much, except that I've been working up the courage to say something to Shy for *weeks*. The store may be great, but the windows are a mess and I wasn't really sure how to tell Shy without offending them." Dash pulled back just enough for his laugh to curl pleasantly around me. "Thanks."

"This is the first time someone's thanked me for being an impulsive busybody," I remarked.

"Then you should keep hanging out with me, because I happen to really like impulsive busybodies."

"You're really not mad?"

"Mad? I'm *excited* is what I am. I like making things for people to look at. Do you know how many ideas I have for the windows of a romance bookstore?" He cast a longing glance toward his dining table. The remains of last night's interrupted dinner had been cleared away, and his tablet and stylus lay where his plate had been, as if he'd tried to distract himself before going after me. "I'd start sketching right now, if we didn't have content to shoot."

I straightened up the makeshift set while Dash changed into his Duke of Harding costume. He had to take his boxers off to slip into the snug breeches, and I couldn't help casting an admiring glance at the smooth, pale muscles of his thighs, drinking in the light like his body had been made to stand in it.

Dash caught me ogling him and flexed.

"Show off," I said, tossing him his shirt.

He flashed me a grin as he caught it. Pulling it over his shoulders on his way to the mirror, he stopped doing up the buttons to look at his reflection. "Shirt on or off?"

I cocked my head. "Depends on what you're filming first."

"I was thinking maybe the scene we were working on yesterday morning. I finished memorizing it while you were in the shower."

In it, the Duke and his secretly wanton wallflower meet up for a tryst and he gives her—along with the viewer—instructions on how to touch their body. It was one of the most explicit things I'd ever written, and it had helped that he'd been in the Google Doc with me as I wrote it, chiming in with suggestions.

I considered the question for a moment. "Shirt on," I said. "How do you feel about taking off the waistcoat and cravat as you say the lines?"

He gave a slow nod. "A little nineteenth-century striptease? I'm intrigued."

He quickly set up the lighting and adjusted the camera on its tripod, while I moved the vase off the table since we'd forgotten to stop for fresh flowers. Then he sat down, and I went to stand behind the camera as I watched him morph into the Duke.

"There you are," he said, hitting exactly the right mix of warmth and lust as he gazed into the lens. He was sitting back in the pink armchair with his hands resting loosely on its upholstered arms, looking extremely regal and about as fuckable. "I was worried you would change your mind about meeting me—that it would be too scandalous for someone as respectable as you."

He ran a hand through his hair, tilting his head down to give the camera a coy, seductive look. "I haven't been able to stop thinking of all the things I want to do to you. Do you want me to tell you?"

Waiting a beat as if for somebody's answer, he twisted his lips into a little smirk. "I knew you would. You aren't as prim as you'd have everyone believe."

He began loosening his cravat, all the while speaking in a smooth, husky voice that felt like sipping from a glass of really expensive whiskey.

"Will you touch yourself for me? Trail your fingers softly down your neck and show me where you would want me to kiss you." He waited a few moments, letting the desire in his expression spill over into hunger. Standing just behind the camera, I could almost believe that he was looking at me. "You like that, don't you? You like being told what to do. So good, so obedient . . ."

At some point during the previous night, he had figured out just how much of a praise kink I had. Ever since then, he had taken advantage of any minor moment to murmur encouraging things into my ear even if he was just teasing. "You opened that bottle of water so good." It had quickly become a joke between us, except for when it wasn't, and hearing the words fall from his lips unwound something inside me.

Even though thousands of people were going to see this video and put themselves in the wallflower's shoes, I knew the truth—that it was just for me.

Heat was pooling at the juncture of my thighs, and I couldn't help running a hand over the bodice of my sundress as Dash urged his fictional lover to touch their body. Brushing my straps down, I wriggled my dress down over my lavender mesh bra. I circled my tightening nipples with my fingertips, matching each of Dash's words with an action of my own.

He kept going, mirroring my wicked smile as I dragged up my hem and caressed my inner thighs. I paused when I reached my panties, running a finger over the narrow band of lace encircling my thighs. After a charged, anticipatory pause, I hooked my fingers into the waistband and let them drop to my feet, then stepped out of them and went to Dash.

The camera was angled so that it caught his face and most of his chest as he sat in the pink chair, but didn't show me as I knelt in front of him. Surprise flickered in his eyes, but Dash was the consummate professional—even though there was no way we were uploading this one. With barely a pause, he started to improvise on the dialogue we had written to incorporate this new twist, keeping in mind what we'd discussed about keeping things inclusive by never directly referring to the wallflower's gender.

I balled the hem of his shirt in one hand, raising it over his abs, then skimmed the other one over the bulge in his breeches. His head fell back, cushioned against the pink chair's high back, his eyelashes brushing the tops of his high cheekbones as his eyes fluttered closed. Greedily, I followed the line of his throat with my gaze, thinking about how I was going to kiss it when I got off my knees.

Dash was still talking, improvising with surprising ease, but I heard the hitch in his breath when I pressed a little harder on the seam of his breeches on my way to the period-appropriate buttons that held the front closed.

I took my time undoing each button, giving him time to tell me if he'd rather I didn't. Instead, he gave an encouraging buck of his hips and helped me pull down the layers of fabric so that I could touch his warm, bare skin.

Dash was hard in my palm, and velvety soft, and slightly slippery but not slippery enough.

Without missing a beat, he reached for the coconut oil he used for making his abs look sleeker on camera. I waited until he poured a dribble over himself, then I wrapped my hand around him and began moving it up and down in earnest, twisting my wrist on the downward stroke, following his rhythm when he started thrusting into the tight circumference of my grip. He put his own hand over mine, and for a long moment, we were Demi Moore and Patrick Swayze in *Ghost*.

And I . . . I couldn't quite catch my breath. Everything inside me ached. From lust, sure, but also this deep, all-consuming hunger that was almost a yearning. For what, I couldn't tell you. Dash was right there in front of me, thighs parted and eyes half-closed. I could have my fill of him. I *was* having my fill of him.

I was still watching his face, and I saw the exact moment when he went over the edge. And it was a good thing that I was on my knees, because if I'd been standing, my legs would have surely failed me. Because Dash, who could radiate beauty just by standing around, was as dazzling as the sun itself as he gave himself over to his climax.

And knowing that I was the one who'd put that expression on his face . . .

My breathing sped up, even as his slowed. His lips were curled when he opened his eyes and gazed down at our sticky hands, still linked together.

He brushed a light kiss over my knuckles, and even in the soft chill of his air conditioner, my skin felt like it was slowly catching fire. "You have lovely hands. So graceful."

Turning my hand over, he laid another kiss at the base of my palm. He lingered there for a long moment, before reaching for the remote he'd hidden in the chair's cushion and turning off the camera.

And then he was standing up, pulling me up with him and walking me backward until my ass hit his desk.

"You're fucking amazing," he breathed against my neck as he reached between my legs and dipped the tip of his finger into the wetness between my thighs. "Do you want me to go down on you?"

"No," I said, holding his hand in place. "Finger's good. I want to kiss you."

"Tell me how you want it."

It was my turn to give him instructions, which I spoke into his mouth in between gentle flicks of my tongue over his lower lip. For the first time, I understood what it meant when romance novels described their characters as feeling molten with desire—his touch made me hot and liquid, like metal softening at a forge. I had never wanted anyone as much as I wanted Dash in that moment.

His thumb caressed me, mercilessly light. "Does this feel good?" he murmured.

My approval came out in a hum that turned into a groan when the pad of his thumb skimmed me just right.

"I want to make you feel as good as you made me feel."

I moved against his hand, not letting him tease me, wanting only release and the sweet taste of his mouth. I wanted him in me and around me, and I wanted him for more than just a beginning. I wanted him for keeps. For *real*.

My fist clenched on a handful of his shirt. The fabric grazing my palm was smooth and soft, the muscle beneath it as hard as the edge of the desk digging into my ass. I think I let out a whimper. Or maybe I was just trying to say his name through the waves of pleasure shuddering through me.

I came so hard I could feel my ears ringing with the force of it. My knees knocked as I slid against Dash, completely boneless. "That was . . ."

He clasped me to his chest, his soft laugh wafting over me. "Good, I hope."

"Better than good. What was it you said earlier? Fucking amazing."

Still in romance hero mode, he picked me up effortlessly and carried me into his room, where he laid me in bed while he went into the bathroom. I could have sunk down into his excellent mattress and gazed at the ceiling and contemplated life, the universe, and everything, but instead I flipped onto my side to study the contents of his nightstand.

There was a neat stack of paperbacks. A lamp, a sketchbook with a scatter of pens and pencils next to it, the wooden dock for his tablet. It was much cleaner than *my* nightstand, which was usually littered with crumpled food wrappers, empty cups, and discarded earrings.

Dash came back a couple of minutes later with a dampened towel, which he used to wipe off my hands then spread over a chair to dry before getting into bed next to me. He had taken off his costume and wore only a pair of snug-fitting boxers that rode low on his slim hips.

I touched the waistband, not quite ready for a second round but half-afraid of what he would say if I gave him two seconds to think about what had happened in my apartment.

Sure enough, he leaned back against his pillows and looked at me through his eyelashes. "So, we should probably talk about—"

"Talk is cheap," I said quickly, and decided to distract him by wriggling on top of him and clapping my hand over his mouth. "I was thinking. Our set is spectacular, all modesty aside, but I feel like we should vary the background of the videos, at least for the non-spicy ones. What do you say we take this show on the road?"

He raised an eyebrow and tried to speak through the hand I still held over his mouth.

I cocked my head, not releasing him. "Sorry, I didn't get that."

"*Mmmpphhm.*"

"You're gonna have to speak up, Dashwood."

He licked my palm—an advanced move for someone who didn't grow up with siblings or cousins like Yaz—and I yanked my hand away, laughing.

"I said," Dash said, enunciating each syllable with emphasis, "that it sounds like fun. Where were you thinking of filming?"

"Central Park," I said promptly. "There are the carriages and the stables—I have a feeling that the fangirls will go wild for seeing you on horseback."

"And by fangirls you mean you, right?"

If there was one thing I liked about Dash, it was that he couldn't pull off a smirk without looking more sweet than wicked. He brushed his fingertips over my arm and captured the hand that had been pressed against his mouth.

"Your hands really are beautiful, you know." I watched in amusement as he nibbled on my fingertip. On screen, Dash was focused and romantic and seductive. But this, this was Dash at his most genuine—a little slice of his personality that felt like it was just for us. "They make me wish I was more of an artist, so I could draw them and actually do them justice." Noticing my expression, he added, "I did warn you about compliments."

"You certainly did, Dashwood. I just didn't realize they'd be so . . . gallant."

In one fluid, easy move, he flipped me so that I was the one lying on my back. He grinned down at me, eyes crinkling at the corners and curls flopping over his forehead. "Why else would you have picked me to be your duke?"

"Oh, that was mostly 'cause you're cute," I said airily.

"You think I'm cute?"

It would've been bad enough if he'd just hair-flipped me, but he went ahead and added one of his patented brilliant smiles. The combination was almost too much for me. "Bringing out the heavy artillery, huh?" I brushed his hair back and pressed a little kiss to the upturned corner of his mouth. "You're more than cute. You're . . ."

My ace of cups.

Haha, what?

A look of intense wariness came into Dash's face as I sat up, but all I did was grab a handful of blankets, take a deep breath, and force myself to smile. "You're fucking amazing."

13

I was entirely to blame for the fact that Dash and I were almost forty minutes early for dinner with Shy and Aria the next day.

The restaurant that Aria had picked turned out to be this cozy Italian place that, like her shop, was located below sidewalk level in a building at walking distance from my apartment. Garlands of light were strung all around the minuscule front room, bathing the wooden bar in warmth and making the wineglasses gleam. It was the kind of place where a fruity cocktail would have been entirely out of place, so I was very brave and ordered a classic martini even though I hate olives. Holding his own martini, Dash found us a pair of free barstools underneath a high window that looked out onto the street above.

I set my drink down on a wooden ledge before attempting to climb up on the red leather stool. There really was no graceful way for me to get up there, and I resigned myself to clambering up like a kindergartener at a jungle gym.

But there was Dash, holding out his hand, eyes twinkling as he took in my short legs. "Want my help?"

With his hand braced firmly on my waist, I was able to get up on the seat in a single, fluid motion. It felt like flying—though that might just have been the effect Dash's touch still had on me.

"Been polishing your shining armor, huh?" I said, reaching for my drink. "Maybe we should start a side channel and dabble in medieval romance."

Dash's long legs made it enviably easy for him to perch on his own stool. He took a sip of martini just as someone walked past the high window, momentarily obscuring the view.

I lifted my gaze to the glass pane. Up on the sidewalk, someone in a printed maxi skirt and pink ballet flats laced up their ankle had stopped as their tote ripped, scattering tubes of lipstick and colorful pens on the sidewalk. Everyone continued to stride past—except for someone in cutoff shorts and combat boots. She paused, her T-shirt and lavender hair coming into view as she knelt and began to help the other person gather up their scattered items.

Combat Boots picked up a small box and held it up to Ballet Slippers, still kneeling, looking like she'd just proposed. Their fingers touched briefly as Ballet Slippers took the proffered box, and then knelt beside Combat Boots, who dug out a folded reusable bag from her pocket.

I couldn't hear what they were saying through the thick glass, but body language was enough—Ballet Slippers tucked a strand of hair behind her ear as she laughed, and Combat Boots held out her hand once again to help up Ballet Slippers, their hands clasped for a beat too long after they were both on their feet.

When I turned back to Dash, he was still looking at the meet cute.

"You know what people get wrong about Manhattan?" he said. His hair, still damp from his post-workout shower, caught the light and made it look like he was under a spotlight. "They think they have to go up high for the best views of the city. They all want to gaze over the rooftops. But you can see a nice sunset anywhere. This, though. This is a hell of a view."

"If you have a foot fetish," I said, just for the smile that Dash flashed me. "I know what you mean, though. Honestly, I think that's what I've been missing in my screenplay."

I know, I know. I was surprised at myself at hearing the words come out of my mouth. Had sex with Dash made me *introspective*?

"A more intimate knowledge of the city?" he asked.

"A distinct perspective on it. When I first moved here, I made a point of visiting all the places I'd seen in the movies. I learned how to get around, and I even figured out the subway—eventually. But I feel like I haven't gotten to know the soul of the city yet. If there's anything special about it, it's that it's not just one thing. It's something different to every one of the millions of people living in it." I spread my hands. "I haven't figured out what New York is to me. But I'm starting to, I think. Thanks in part to—" *To you*, I had been about to say. "To the Duke of Harding and everything we're doing."

Dash bumped into me, and I couldn't help but be reminded of the way a puppy nudges your hand with his snoot when he wants to be petted. I didn't want to mess up Dash's curls, so instead of a pat, I gave his knee a friendly bump with my own.

"Do you feel like you've found your place in the city yet?" I asked.

"I have," he said softly.

And maybe I was growing more mature, because instead of saying, *Is it inside my pants?* I took a sip from my drink and gave him an encouraging nod.

"I found my people. And maybe that's the same thing." His hand landed on the canvas tote where he was carrying his tablet and a sketchpad, and he gave it a gentle pat. "This is part of it, too. Like, I'm happy for the chance to give back to a person and a place that have made me feel more at home here. But it's a little more selfish than that—I keep thinking about how it'll feel to walk past a window display I helped create and know that there are parts of me that are inextricably linked to someone's commute to work or in the background of an amazing day."

"Like the city is a tapestry and you're intentionally weaving yourself into it," I said.

Dash nodded and leaned forward, his martini forgotten on the ledge as he gripped my thigh just below the hem of my skirt, too focused on what he was saying for me to feel anything other than his urge to communicate exactly what that window would mean to him. "I keep thinking about all the people who will walk past the window, who might not notice its contents or even know that I was responsible for it, but who will be connected to me anyway, if in this tangential, incomprehensible way. I don't know much about what you're trying to do with your screenplay—"

Neither did I, obviously.

"—but whenever you talk about it, I get the sense that that's kind of what you're after. That it's less about leaving a mark on New York than forging a connection to the people in it."

"You're right," I said, and I wasn't sure why I was surprised that he had articulated so well what was in my head. Or that I felt such a sense of recognition in the light brightening Dash's eyes.

Aria and Shy came in just then, though, and whatever else I was going to say was lost in the flurry of getting a table and pretending we hadn't all checked out the menu beforehand and knew exactly what we wanted and ordering appetizers.

Then Dash's foot knocked against mine under the table, and even though all of his attention was focused on Aria as she told us about Kitty Marlowe's latest exploits, the very slight curl on the corner of his lips let me know he'd done it intentionally. As if to point out this one connection we'd already made, this one shining silver thread in the tapestry.

We waited until after dessert to get down to business. Shy, who was wearing a billowing white blouse and a bow tie embroidered with tiny apples, had curated a list of the books they wanted to feature in the window, and Dash had designed a couple of displays based on those. My favorite of the two held the ripeness of a late summer afternoon, vibrant colors poised on the edge of mellowing into autumn shades. It was a profusion of oranges, and paper flowers, and he'd even figured out a way to make tiny little fireflies out of LED lights.

Shy and Aria exchanged a glance in that unspoken language that couples develop when they've been together for a while.

"This'll be good for Second Chance," Aria said, and Shy nodded.

There was a reluctance I didn't quite understand in the gesture, and my heart squeezed inside my chest at the possibility that Dash might not get his window after all.

But then Shy sighed and rubbed a hand over their face. "I guess it's only fair that I explain what's been going on. So . . . you know how used vintage romance paperbacks are incredibly profitable in today's economy?" Their mouth twisted into something that wasn't quite a smile before they said, simply, "The bookstore's not doing well. I might have to close down."

The impact of it shuddered through me. "You *can't*. You can't close."

"I may not have a choice in the matter." Shy let out a breath. "Our rent got hiked up again. I've been playing with the idea of reducing my overhead by working on a bookmobile type situation, but Aria thinks I should fight harder to keep the storefront open."

Aria scowled. "Hell's Kitchen is gentrified enough as it is. The last thing the neighborhood needs is to lose an independent bookstore to gain what? Another Starbucks?"

"Kathleen Kelly would agree," I said. Everyone looked at me blankly. "From *You've Got Mail*? The best of all Nora Ephron's oeuvre? Am I the only one at this table who possesses the slightest shred of culture?" I sighed at their blank stares. "Never mind."

"I'm with Aria," Dash said. "The neighborhood needs Second Chance."

"I don't disagree," Shy said. "I just don't know what else to do. I've been covering most of the shifts myself and trying to hustle on social media. I guess I could host more events, maybe—burlesque nights bring in some money, it's just—"

An idea zinged through me, and I blurted out, "We can help," before my brain had fully finished processing it.

Shy and Aria exchanged another glance.

"In what way?" Aria asked carefully.

"Well, you know what Dash and I are doing, right? With the Duke of Harding?"

Aria and Shy nodded. "I saw the video you posted on Fling," Shy said.

"Well, we have this platform that keeps growing and growing. What's the point of it if we don't use it for the benefit of our friends and the romance community?" The words started coming out without much input from my brain, as usual. But this wasn't just impulse-and-martini-fueled babble. It was an actual plan. One that was making Shy look cautiously optimistic. "We could post about the store, sure, and plenty of people would show up. But why not make it into a game? A treasure hunt that starts over every quarter? We could seed some of our videos with little easter eggs that would lead viewers down two different paths—directly to the bookstore for people who are in the city, and to your website to those outside of it. You do online orders, right?"

Aria leaned forward, her long, pale fingers tightening on her wineglass. "What happens once they get to Shy's?"

"There has to be a pot of gold at the end of that particular rainbow, not just the store. Something related to the Duke of Harding." I frowned, drumming my fingertips on the checkered tablecloth.

"A table featuring the Duke's recommendations?" Shy suggested, leaning forward in their seat. "Among which we could hide little notes written by the Duke himself?"

I pointed at them. "Yes."

"Invitation to a private party with the Duke?" Aria said suddenly. "At the store, of course."

I moved my finger so that it was pointing at her. "Also yes."

We tossed around suggestions, with Dash furiously taking notes on his tablet. By the time we flagged down our server for the bill, Shy was looking a lot more relaxed than they had been an hour before.

The only weird little blip was when our plates were taken away and Dash slung a casual arm around the back of my chair. It was such a couple thing to do that I found it deeply unsettling and also I kind of liked it? Clearly, I'd had too much wine.

The four of us went out for ice cream after. As we strolled down the street with our cones, unable to stop shouting out progressively more unhinged suggestions for things the treasure hunt could lead to, some of which involved Dash wearing part of his costume and a lot of whipped cream, I couldn't help thinking about how much had changed since I'd last strolled through the Upper West Side with an ice cream cone.

My eye caught Aria's, and I got the sense that we were both re-membering the cards she'd drawn for me and the advice that had followed them. *See what life can be when you stop running?*

And yeah, it was pretty good—more than that, actually. It was fucking amazing. This, the four of us together, the lights of the city that glittered just like the stars would if they'd been visible, the runnels of strawberry ice cream that I followed down the cone with the tip of my tongue, sweetness in my mouth and all around me.

And Dash, who knew to tug me to the left to help me avoid a collision with a streetlamp as I focused on the cold bursts of straw-berry on my tongue. And the excitement I could *feel* thrumming in him even as I saw it in his bouncing step and the grin that was slightly wider than normal and the way he teased me about taking so long to savor my ice cream that my hands were sticky with it by the time I'd finished.

We hadn't made a mistake by hooking up. And I definitely wasn't going to spiral again.

I proved it to myself by pulling Dash close after we'd said good-bye to Shy and Aria. Pressed against the stone of somebody's stoop, I brushed my fingers over his curls.

"This is good," I said, looking up at him so intently that I caught the moment when all the excitement that had played over his fea-tures throughout the evening seemed to gather and coalesce into something that made my heart beat a little bit faster.

"What is?"

My hand left Dash's temple to wave in the air in a vague attempt at illustrating what I felt. "This moment. You. Us. You know, every-thing."

His hands on my waist urged me up a step so that I was closer to his height and he did that thing where he was gazing into my eyes, smiling and serious all at the same time.

"This is good," he confirmed, his voice so sure and caramel-smooth that it was impossible not to believe him.

14

Central Park was another part of the city that I had learned about from movies. I would gaze at couples taking winding carriage rides through the trees or dancing around Bethesda Fountain, and dream about someday strolling the paths in a chic coat as golden leaves drifted gently down around me.

It wasn't until I actually got there and wandered around for hours that I gained a real understanding of how vast it truly is. And confusing—I still got lost unless I stuck to the paths along the edges. I'd done my research, though, and at Dash's insistence we'd taken a couple of hours to go over the map and drop pins on the locations we wanted to film in.

The original plan had been for Chase to join us in his first appearance as Lord Loving, since he was back in town for a couple of days before returning to his research trip. We'd had to pivot when he told us that he was in the thick of writing his dissertation and he'd finally been able to schedule a meeting with his advisor, who was apparently as hard to find as a good Adam Sandler romcom. (Don't hate me because I have opinions.) Which meant that Dash and I were flying solo that day.

A couple of days after our dinner with Shy and Aria, he and I met up on the corner of 50th and Ninth and headed up to the park together. It was hot enough that I had eschewed my usual dresses and was instead wearing a crop top and shorts, doing my best to channel Romy and Michele from one of my favorite movies from the nineties, down to the pink resin flower earrings and big orange sunglasses.

The humidity was almost worse than Florida's, though maybe that was just because back home I mostly went from one air-conditioned space to another and I traveled in my car, instead of walking for blocks under the punishing sun.

By the time we reached Columbus Circle, we were both covered in a thin sheen of perspiration. Never fear, though—Dash looked as gorgeous as usual. If anything, the combination of the walk and the sun had put an extra glow on his face.

I wanted to be careful about not getting people in the background of the videos—mostly for their privacy, though obviously I also wanted to avoid breaking the illusion of the Duke as someone who did not exist in our time. There is no such thing as a quiet, empty part of Central Park, which is pretty wild considering how big it is, but we made things work.

One of the cameras in Dash's stash had a tracking feature that kind of followed him around as he moved. It also kept the image steady enough that I was able to get a series of smooth shots as he mounted one of the horses we'd booked ahead of time and promised to take the wallflower on an adventure.

If I'd thought that Dash was athletic while watching him run from a mob of Lady Cerulean-obsessed tourists, it was nothing compared to seeing him on horseback. Not that he could do much more than urge it up and down the bridle path under the supervision of an assigned guide, while I shot clip after clip from the ground.

"How the fuck do you know how to ride like that?" I asked when he paused for a drink of water.

"We had the best riding instructors at the Harding estate, of course," he said, handing back the water bottle with a wink before using his knees to nudge the horse forward at a quick walk.

Somewhere behind us, I heard someone make a whimpering noise.

Before we moved on to the rowboats, I took a few moments to check our stats. I'd gotten used to doing that multiple times an hour, and by now it was second nature. The hit of validation every time I saw our follower count rising made my heart flip. Every comment and like was like someone whispering in my ear, *Maybe you're not such a fuckup after all.*

With every notification, I felt the knots inside me begin to unravel. For so long, it had felt like I was on a boat in the middle of the ocean, paddling furiously and unceasingly and not getting anywhere. And in that moment, it was as if I had just caught a glimpse of shore. It was one thing knowing that our follower count was exploding and our comment section was popping off. This?

This made my heart lift so high it felt like I was soaring over the East River again. Only instead of it just being Dash and me, we'd brought all these other people along on the ride.

I almost drifted instead of walked to the Boathouse.

I wasn't so busy manning the camera that I didn't notice Dash's forearms as he maneuvered us through the water. Sweating for real now, he'd taken off his jacket and cravat and rolled up his sleeves, and I took a moment to shoot a close-up of his forearms before panning back to his face and the thick locks flopping boyishly over his forehead.

"What?" he asked as I looked at him over the camera's lens.

"Nothing, it's just . . . you're so good at what you do. Tilt your head up slightly. A little to the right. It's a pleasure to watch—competence porn."

His face took on a wicked cast. "Oh yeah? Well, I could say the same thing about you." He dropped his voice, giving it the slightest of rasps. "I haven't been able to stop watching you all day. Do you know how hot you look when you're running around, telling me what to do? Or how much it makes me want to press you against a tree trunk and—"

I squeezed my thighs together. "Dashwood. Are you using your leading man voice on me?"

"Is it working?"

"You know damn well it is. Talk about competence porn." I huffed, torn between cracking up at the eagerness in his eyes and disregarding the fact that we were in full view of at least a few dozen people and launching myself across the rowboat. "I swear, you could get me off with just your voice."

Dash opened his mouth again and I pointed at him, saying severely, "Don't you dare."

The corners of his eyes crinkled and he sat back, turning his face to the sun and letting the boat drift. "This reminds me of a game I used to play with myself as a kid."

"Sounds alarming, but continue." I took one last picture, then lowered both the camera and his phone and tucked them into Dash's backpack for safekeeping, lest I do an actual flail and fling them both into the water.

"I called it snapshot moments. It started out as a way of making myself feel better when my parents were arguing too much. The few times when things were actually good, and they were trying to get along for my sake, I would pretend like I was taking a snapshot."

He shrugged, still looking up. I followed his gaze. Afternoon sunlight shone through the leaves and glinted off the icy-blue glass of the skyscrapers peeking above the trees. It was more than cinematic— it was the kind of beautiful that made your heart squeeze inside your chest. Kind of like Dash himself.

"It was really nothing more than looking very attentively around me and trying to remember all the details. I tried to draw these moments a couple of times, but I could never quite capture the *feel* of them."

I knew exactly what he meant.

"This feels like a snapshot moment," he said, lifting his head so that he could look at me. "Being here, with you."

I resisted the effort to turn it into a joke. It took a superhuman effort, but I did it. What I couldn't do was reply in the way that Dash clearly wanted me to. Not yet. Limiting myself to a smile, I brushed my fingers along his outstretched calves, the only part of him I could easily reach.

But Dash wasn't letting me off the hook that easily. "Do you have any snapshot moments?"

And then I did have to shrug. "If I do, they're probably all dirty pictures. Can't you row any faster? We need to get to Belvedere Castle before we lose the light."

Dash looked like he wanted to press back. Like he was more than considering it. He went as far as opening his mouth, but I beat him to it.

"Look, I'm sorry," I said. "But is it okay if we get the filming done first? I really wanna be able to pay my rent next month."

Maybe he could see the genuine anxiety tightening the skin around my eyes, because he nodded and began pulling us toward shore. Of course, I was actually hoping that he'd forget all about it by the time we got all our work done.

It was another couple of hours before I was satisfied with the number of clips we'd gotten and deemed us worthy of a break. As well as content for our socials, we'd laid down the first of the clues for the treasure hunt that would eventually conclude with a party at Second Chance.

As I splashed half the contents of my Hydro Flask on my face, Dash fished a fresh T-shirt out of his backpack. And just like that, he was no longer the Duke of Harding. He was Dash, beautiful and sunny and real.

"I'm starving," I announced, running down my mental list of places I liked getting takeout from. "You want Thai or pizza?"

"Neither." Dash hefted up his backpack. "I packed us a picnic. And I know the perfect spot for it—come on."

Suddenly, he was the one who was all impatience as he led me down a path. He pushed back a leafy branch and I ducked through the opening he'd made, straightening up to find myself at the edge of a large body of water. It wasn't the Turtle Pond, which we'd seen from Belvedere Castle, or even the Reservoir. Turning to ask Dash about it, I was amused to find him spreading a checkered blanket on the ground, complete with a battery-operated candle and a plastic vase with a flower that was miraculously uncrushed after hours in his backpack.

I put my hands on my hips. "Dashwood, did you lure me into a date under false pretenses?"

"Can you really call it luring when you came willingly?" he asked, looking pleased with himself. "And can you call a meal false pretenses?"

I collapsed onto the blanket. "I will if you don't feed me soon."

"Can you try not to die until you've tasted all the stuff I made? I spent all morning slaving over a hot stove for you."

"You what?" I sat up and looked at all the lidded containers he had piled on the blanket. "What the hell, Dashwood? Did you have your valet pack you a hamper?"

He grinned, and began naming the dishes he'd made. Figs in some kind of puff pastry. A farro salad. Heirloom tomato focaccia. Homemade hummus. He'd even made Indonesian cheese cookies *and* chocolate chip ones. It was a literal feast.

"And as long as we're on the subject," he said as he handed me a plate and a fork, "I want to take you out on a date."

I froze. Since when did friends with benefits go out on dates?

I opened my mouth to say something—and immediately snapped it shut when I saw Dash's face.

"A real date," he said. "The kind where we dress up and I pick you up at your door and take you somewhere that has tablecloths and a wine list. And I don't smell like horse." He swept his gaze over me, and I almost shivered in spite of the dense humidity that had gathered in the air. "I'm very good at dates."

"Yeah, like that's impressive. Name one thing you're bad at." Bypassing the Tupperware full of celery and carrot sticks, I stuck an entire finger into the hummus, then brought it to my mouth.

"That is not proper date etiquette," he said, cracking up.

I pointed at him. "There's a snapshot moment, right there."

"Doesn't count," Dash protested as he piled food on both our plates, but his lips were still curled.

"It's been so long since I was on a date, I'm pretty sure I've forgotten what proper date etiquette is. Actually, funny story—the last date I went on took place on that rock over there."

Dash's gaze followed my pointing finger as I swiveled it to indicate one of the large rocks that studded Central Park. "It wasn't with your asshole ex, was it?"

"No, this was a different asshole, a couple of weeks before I met you. It was one of the most epically romantic dates I've ever been on. Or at least it started off that way."

He reached for a fig in a blanket, and I didn't even get the full body shivers when his mouth closed around it. "I sense a storytime."

"Get this. We went for an evening walk and ended up talking on the rock for so long that they closed the gates around us without us noticing. And of course, I couldn't scramble over them because I'm so desperately unathletic, so he had to lift me over. And my foot caught on the wire and I kind of fell onto him and he caught me and pulled me in close for a kiss. I swear, it was like something out of a romcom. The only thing that was missing was the sunset stroll along the Brooklyn Bridge. He even walked me to my street, and we stood in the corner kissing under a streetlamp."

"What happened?"

"He fucking ghosted me, that's what." I laughed at Dash's expression of outrage. "I texted him a few days later and my message never went through. So either he blocked me, or his phone is somewhere at the bottom of the Hudson."

"Definitely an asshole move." Dash forked up some farro salad. "I feel like I should apologize for my whole gender."

I shrugged, reaching for a napkin. "It was incredibly confusing, because I thought the date had gone really well. But at least I got a good story out of it—I'm thinking about using it in my screenplay. You know, when I finally get around to writing it." I paused for a second as it struck me that I hadn't so much as thought about my screenplay in a couple of days. It shouldn't have been surprising, not really. I mean, it wasn't like it was unusual for me to erase something from my mind once I'd pivoted away from it. Why had I ever thought that screenwriting would be different? "If I ever do."

"I feel like you've barely mentioned it," he said carefully, as if he wasn't sure if he should say anything. "I don't even know what it's about."

"That's probably because I don't even know what it's about." I drew my knees up to my chest and wrapped my arms around my folded legs. "It's supposed to be a romcom, but I don't know. This Duke of Harding stuff is so much easier. Do you think we should experiment with other characters for you and Chase? I can totally see you as a cowboy."

"Well, ma'am, I reckon I *could* pass for a cowboy," he drawled, then effortlessly switched into a plummy British accent, "but I believe that we mustn't get too unfocused from our original idea, at least at present. Particularly with this new Georgie Hart program that's about to do a lot of our marketing for us."

"Tell me again why you didn't go into acting?"

Dash shrugged, grinning. "Taking my pants off for fun and profit seemed more appealing."

"How did you get on OnlyFans, anyway? I don't think you ever told me."

"I mean, what else was I going to do with four years' worth of student loans and a degree in visual merchandising?"

"Fair point." I licked a little bit of hummus off my finger, eyeing him. "It's your turn for a storytime."

"I don't know if there's much of a story," he said, setting his plate aside and plucking at the blanket. "It started with my ex. You know, the one I was living with in Crown Heights?"

I nodded.

"She asked me to be in some of her content, for fun, and then people started commenting asking for more and . . ." Dash spread his hands. "I liked it. I *really* liked it. I think it hit kind of how drawing fanart used to—people would ask for stuff that I could easily give them and they would lose their shit over it and that made me feel amazing at first."

I nodded. "It's because you express your love or, um, appreciation for people via acts of service."

"I . . . hadn't thought of it that way," Dash said slowly. "But yeah, I guess that's about right."

"Hence you putting together a picnic for me. And tying my shoe-laces and saving me from the raging mob. The only thing I haven't seen you do is help a little old lady cross the street, and I feel like it's just a matter of time."

"My ex called it a hero complex." For pretty much the first time since I'd met him, I saw the corners of Dash's mouth dipping down-ward, though he quickly tried to drown the expression in a sip of coffee from the flask he'd packed.

A surge of protectiveness rushed over me and I laid a hand on his arm. "I don't know what went down with you and your ex. But I can tell you right now that I really like the way you look after everyone. And how you're always checking in on your grandmothers. In my eyes, all of that makes you a good person, and honestly, that's pretty much what all of us should aspire to be. And truly, fuck anyone who made you feel otherwise."

The storm clouds that were starting to gather on his brow parted to make way for a sunny smile. "Thanks," he said quietly, then dis-solved into laughter as I started licking his arm where I'd patted him. "The hell are you doing?"

"You had a little smear of hummus right there. Just doing you a favor—you know, trying to speak in your love language."

"Next time, get a translator," he said, but he pulled me down for a loud, smacking kiss.

"How serious was your relationship with your ex?" I asked when we separated, putting my palms on his chest to hold him at bay for a few minutes.

"Pretty serious, I guess. We lived together for a year, give or take a month or two. Chase saved my ass by letting me crash on his couch, which is why I was willing to make a fool of myself dancing with him in Times Square. He helped me move into my apartment, too, so I owed him double."

"Wait, so things with you and your ex ended recently?"

"A few months ago," Dash said, confirming my mental math. "I've had enough time—and therapy—to get over it, if that's what's worrying you."

"I wasn't worried," I said. "Just curious. I'm not the first person you've dated since your ex, right?"

He shook his head, and I almost let out a sigh of relief. "There was a hedge fund manager—an older man."

I arched an eyebrow. "Oh yeah? How much older?"

"Around ten years? Maybe a little more. We only went out for a couple of months." He fiddled with a carrot stick. "He was kind of hesitant about introducing me to his friends. Which honestly, I was kind of into because I'd had the opposite problem until then— my ex had this weird thing about wanting everyone to know I was her property. But then he asked me to be his date to a benefit and insinuated that I should lie about what I did for a living."

"So you told him to go to hell, right?" I said, though I already knew the answer.

"I mean, I should have. But I went to the benefit and told everyone I was a model and he . . . he was showing me off to all his friends like I was some kind of . . . I don't know, a trophy or something."

"And *that's* when you told him to go to hell."

Dash shook his head. "I stayed with him for another couple of weeks after that. I wanted a happy ending so badly that I ignored all the red flags. I don't know, I think I maybe pressured him into a relationship he didn't want. I'm not trying to let that happen again," he added quickly, darting a glance up at me.

Knowing that should have been a relief. If anything, it should have loosened the knot in my chest, not tightened it.

His gaze flicked up to meet mine. And I did the only thing I could think of to keep him from looking at me with such probing intensity—I kissed him.

I sucked lightly on his lower lip, parting reluctantly only to say, "I just want to make it clear that there's literally nothing wrong with being a hero."

Dash brushed his lips back and forth against mine. "I'm okay with being a hero as long as it's in one of your stories."

"My leading man."

"The duke to your hellion."

It was just about then that I realized that the darkness rolling over us had more to do with rain clouds than with evening, which was still a good hour away.

A distant clap of thunder had us scrambling to our feet, laughing as we tried to shove the picnic back into Dash's bag. We weren't fast enough. As Dash yanked the zipper shut, the rain started sheeting down, and we were soaked to the skin almost immediately.

"Let's make a run for it," he shouted over the loud clamor of the raindrops.

"And pass up the chance for the perfect cinematic kiss in the rain with the perfect leading man?"

I threw my arm around his neck, and Dash obligingly—and gently—bent me backward.

"A cinematic kiss? You mean something like this?"

He didn't kiss me right away, though. He waited a beat, looking into my eyes. Not gazing soulfully, just looking. It wasn't unpleasant, just . . . slightly uncomfortable. And the rain was getting into my eyes, so I let them fall closed.

And then it *was* a cinematic kiss—the kind of moment that should have been accompanied by a John Williams score. One that started out quiet, with a rising crescendo that built up to something epic.

Dash touched his lips to mine as softly as if he was tasting the raindrops that had gathered there. His wet T-shirt was soft against my palms when I grabbed two handfuls of it and deepened the kiss.

Our tongues met.

And then the kiss shifted again. It was no longer about fooling around in the rain—it was more urgent, there was more need in it, like Dash was trying to make himself heard, or understood. And maybe I was, too. Or maybe I was trying to ask him something, only I didn't know how to, or even if I should.

My hands were full of Dash, and so was my mind. And the thing was, I was starting to suspect that my heart was full of him, too.

15

Screech, rewind.

My heart was full of Dash? No, I wasn't deluded enough to think I was in love with Dash. I'd just gotten caught up in the moment, like I always did. I was the person who cannonballed into pools without judging the depth, who eagerly threw herself headfirst into situations without considering the consequences. I wasn't in love— I was just high on the rush of yet another beginning.

When Dash and I met up a few days later to work over lunch, he couldn't wait to tell me about how he'd spent the past couple of days hanging out at the bookstore with Shy, refining his ideas for the window display.

"I think it might become a seasonal thing," Dash said as we exited the Chinese restaurant where I'd just inhaled half my weight in dumplings. It had rained while we were at lunch, and humidity still hung suspended in the air, adding fuzzy halos to the lights of the city and making everything look diffused. Everything, that was, except for Dash's enthusiasm. "I'd call it a gig, but Shy's not really paying me."

"You sound so excited, I'm pretty sure you'd pay *them* for a chance to decorate their windows."

Dash gave me a sheepish grin. "I wouldn't rule that out. I can't wait for Valentine's Day," he added dreamily, and I froze for a second before realizing that he was talking about decorating. He launched into a long description about how he wanted to put together a display based on Soraya Salcedo's pirate romances. Partly because a pirate theme would be unexpected and would stand out among all the red and pink, but also because of this one detail in her latest book, where the main character steals a ship from her love interest to go searching for a mythical jewel called the Kraken's Heart, which he wanted to make on a friend's 3D printer.

I listened to Dash tell me all about how he could make seaweed out of corrugated cardboard, so caught up in his enthusiasm that I almost didn't flinch when he gave my wrist a questioning graze with one of his fingers before his hand slid over my smaller one.

"This is just so much *fun*. All my favorite things blended together—art, romance novels, and puns," he said, and I couldn't help but hear the slight hitch in his sentence when I moved my hand at the last minute to get a ChapStick.

My backpack was a fuzzy stuffed bear with a zipper so tiny, it kept getting lost in the fur. It took me a few moments to find it as we paused at a crosswalk, and another handful of seconds to locate the small tube rolling around the bear's soft interior.

"I shudder to think what kind of pun you could come up with for a Valentine's display about pirates," I said lightly. "Please don't tell me you're thinking of naming it *Under the Seamen*."

His snort was followed by a brief pause. I glanced up at him as I finished smoothing the ChapStick on my lower lip, and immediately felt the need to duck and cover—he was looking earnest again.

"I feel like I should thank you again for telling Shy I could do the window. I doubt I would've had the courage to say anything."

A small smile was playing over his lips—not his leading man smile, but something a little more crooked, a little more bashful and uncertain. I wanted to surge up on my tiptoes to kiss it. But buddies who bone didn't kiss each other's smiles, and I had to keep reminding myself that was all we were.

"I can't believe you're cool with me putting you on the spot like that," I said instead, tucking the ChapStick away. "Because I know I can be so impulsive and, you know . . ."

Too much.

"Generous? Creative? Cute?" Dash said teasingly, then shook his head. "Honestly, maybe I was a little taken aback in the moment.

But I like the idea of having another creative outlet outside the Duke of Harding and cosplaying in general. And this kind of design isn't just what I chose for my major. It's . . ."

He spent a second or two grasping for words, his fingertips on my elbow guiding me away from a parking meter I hadn't noticed.

"It's its own kind of performance, I guess," he finally said. "Another way of me making stuff for other people to look at."

"Which gets your rocks off," I said.

Dash snorted. "If you want to put it that way. What with the modeling and the cosplaying and all of it, I'd forgotten how much I used to like designing."

"Until the second Shy mentioned the window, and then you were burning with desire. You can't deny it," I teased him, leaning into his grip. "I saw it on your face. You heaved a dreamy sigh and everything."

The hand on my elbow drifted to my waist. "I'm pretty sure I didn't do any sighing. But yeah, I immediately wanted to do it. But I probably wouldn't have said anything, hence me thanking you for being the one to say it." He spread his hands and said, with his voice lowered like he was confessing to something embarrassing, "I have a hard time asking for what I want, sometimes. It can be nice when someone does the asking for me."

I'm not gonna lie—it was a relief to hear that. "Hey, if nothing else, you can always count on me to open my big fat mouth. I'm just happy it worked out for once."

"Yeah, Shy thinks all of this could really make a difference—the window, but also your ideas for a treasure hunt. They're already talking about driving upstate this weekend for an estate sale that'll supposedly have a lot of vintage romances for sale." Dash steered me around a fallen ice cream cone that had melted into a puddle, turning it a cool shade of orange. "And Aria's just happy that she won't have to badger Shy into paying attention to the windows."

We headed up to his apartment to keep working. I claimed a corner of his couch and tucked the skirt of my maxi dress around my thighs, then beckoned to Dash to come sit with me. So we could look at my screen together, not for cuddles, but try telling him that. He took a running start and bounded onto the couch next to me, wriggling until his head was on my lap, butting up against my hand like a golden retriever in desperate need of scritches.

We were nothing if not professional.

"I got you something. Here," he said, using his long arms to reach for a pink gift bag on the floor without moving from my lap. "A scoop of strawberry."

It wasn't ice cream. I pushed aside the tissue paper and found myself staring at a fuzzy pink beret. It took me a second to remember the crack I'd made about looking like a big scoop of vanilla ice cream that day we went thrifting. It had been such an offhand thing, a tiny moment . . . and it was so like Dash to remember it.

Gifts weren't a part of our arrangement. But I admit it—I melted a little. Dash was so *wholesome* and sweet and I always appreciated a good accessory. It didn't have to be any deeper than that.

"Still looking for a matching cape," Dash said, shrugging as if to look casual, but completely unable to hide the pleased flush on his cheeks.

I put the hat on, heroically refraining from making a joke about him licking me up. And then I leaned down to kiss his flushed cheek, my attention suddenly consumed by the devastating curl the kiss had given to his lips. My fingers sank into his thick hair. I grabbed a fistful and tugged until he lifted his head far enough to kiss me. His lips slid against mine, tasting faintly of coffee and sugar, and I wanted so badly to *let* myself be devastated, quietly and thoroughly, by the tenderness in it.

For a couple of minutes. Then I got down to business.

"I emailed Chase the first couple of scripts, and barring a couple of notes, he thinks they're perfect. He says he's ready to start shooting content once he gets back next week. I can make the final adjustments and have it ready by burlesque night so we can go over it before his performance."

Dash nodded.

"Actually, maybe not. Yaz will be there, so it probably won't be the best time to talk business."

I gave a little wiggle, which had the unintended consequence of jostling Dash around. Not that he seemed to mind—he seemed pretty comfortable with his head pillowed on my thighs.

I was still a little apprehensive—read, utterly and completely freaked out—by the way Yaz seemed to have checked out for the past week. But she hadn't canceled her trip, so that was something.

"I can't wait for Yaz to meet you," I blurted out.

There it was again, that weird little blip I had noticed the last time I'd said something about the two of them meeting.

Sitting up, he busied himself putting away the gift bag. "She knows about the spicy videos, right?"

"Yeah, she knows."

"And she's okay with it?"

I studied his face. "What's going on?"

"I just . . . I know how close you two are and how much her approval means to you."

I didn't miss the flicker in his eyes. Or the breath that he drew in, slightly deeper than normal. And I pushed away a thought about how he hadn't said anything about me meeting *his* family, even his grandmothers. And how he left the room whenever he called them. Which was fine, because we were keeping things casual.

So casual that I hadn't even told Yaz about us.

"You have nothing to worry about. If Yaz will disapprove of anyone, it'll be me. For, well, being me."

I was sure I'd hit on the right combination of breezy and self-deprecating, but all my remark did was make Dash frown.

"That's not great either," he said, scraping a hand through his hair, his radiant mood from earlier dimmed and irritation taking over.

"What do you mean?"

"The way you talk about your family. It sounds like they don't appreciate you. Or that they make you think that there's nothing about you to appreciate. Because Mariel, you're so creative and fun and—"

I waved a hand in the air. "Oh, they appreciate me. It's not their fault that I can be a handful sometimes. And by handful I mean an infuriating yet lovable chaos demon who flits from project to project and never actually follows through on anything and then needs to be bailed out of trouble."

Because it wasn't that I didn't have goals. They were just too unwieldy, too large to grasp easily. And it was much easier to give up on them than to keep trying.

"You followed through on the Duke of Harding," Dash pointed out.

"There's hope for me yet, I guess." And Dash had been there alongside me the whole time, keeping me on track and from crashing into poles every time I got distracted. "I love that for me. Dash, you don't have to worry about Yaz. She's not this mean, demanding monster and I'm sorry if I've been making her sound that way. She's a marshmallow, and she's going to love you. I know that for a fact."

"You do, huh?"

Dash's smile didn't look quite as easy as it always did. I buried my face into the crook of his neck, trying to coax the tension out of him. Or to convince him, I guess, that everything was fine and it would stay fine.

"Don't forget, I'm about to be besties with a bona fide psychic. I had Aria read our cards. The stars are all aligned, the universe is on our side, and the cards say . . ."

It was meant to be a brief pause, partly to build anticipation and partly because my brain hadn't yet caught up with my mouth and I hadn't actually asked Aria to read my cards after that one day.

But then Dash pulled back far enough to look me in the eye. "What do the cards say?"

The ace of cups card I had tucked into my mirror frame flashed into my mind's eye. I forced myself to smile. "The cards say, 'Don't worry, be happy.'"

Dash looked mildly disappointed. And it wasn't like I'd been expecting to be hit with a hair flip and eye twinkles and a slowly broadening leading man smile, but his expression went directly to the knot that was forming in center of my chest. "Mariel, I—"

I sat up straight and placed a hand on Dash's arm. "Look, I'll have Aria read your cards, too, if it'll make you feel any better. Though I already know what they'll say."

"Oh yeah?"

I nodded. "You are destined for great things. All you have to do is believe in yourself—and the short, curvy stranger you've already met."

Dash let out a laugh that sounded a little bit like surrender. Or maybe resignation. I didn't really get a chance to find out which it was, because my phone buzzed just then with an emailed query about whether Dash was interested in doing an appearance at a screening of *Kate & Leopold*.

I read it out loud to Dash, who gave me a quizzical glance.

"Dash. *Dash.*" I scrambled up onto my knees so that my head was roughly at the same level as his, and I planted both hands on his shoulders. "*Kate & Leopold*—a.k.a. the movie where Hugh Jackman plays this nineteenth-century guy who gets transported to present-day New York City. Well, present day as in more than twenty years ago, but you know. Close enough. We have to do it, right? Opportunities like this don't come around every day. It'll be good practice for the Georgie Hart ball next month."

He looked at me for a couple of seconds, then shrugged. "Why not?"

"Could you *be* any more enthusiastic?" I said in my best Chandler Bing impression, already starting to tap out a reply.

My fingers were flying over the screen, and I was so focused I barely noticed when Dash got up from the couch and padded over to the fridge for a couple cans of sparkling water.

I took the one he passed me and hugged it to my midsection, enjoying its coolness as I babbled about how I couldn't believe I hadn't thought about doing live appearances and wouldn't that have been a huge missed opportunity? I made a mental note to ask Chase if he wanted to explore the possibility of dancing at bachelorette parties as Lord Loving.

"Also," I added, now on a roll, "how do you feel about doing personalized videos? I think we could charge a good amount for those. Not steamy ones necessarily, but like birthday messages or whatever? Like celebrities do on Cameo."

"Sure." Dash took a swig from his sparkling water.

After all that, we still had comments to reply to and fresh teasers to upload and new scripts to record. Just hearing Dash murmur sweet little nothings into the camera was enough to make every single thought flee my head and leave behind only floating stars and twittering birds, so it wasn't until we ended up in his bed at the end of the day that I remembered that he had been trying to tell me something before we'd gotten interrupted by the email.

I snuggled in closer to him and buried my face in his neck. "Mmm, you smell like a cinnamon brown sugar oat milk latte."

"Shocking, considering I had my evening latte with almond milk."

"Blasphemy," I said, wrinkling my nose.

Dash turned in my arms, his smile almost back to normal. "The almond milk or the fact that I have evening lattes?"

"Both." I kissed the juncture of his neck and shoulder. And look, I would've been happy to leave things there. But try as I might, I couldn't completely ignore the awkwardness from that afternoon. So I took a surreptitious deep breath and asked, "By the way . . . Was there something you were going to tell me earlier?"

A beat went by, then I felt Dash's shoulder rise into a shrug. "Don't worry about it."

And yeah, I did breathe a sigh of relief. It was getting harder and harder to postpone the talk we were more than overdue for—you know, the *where is this going, who are we to each other* talk. But if that day had proved anything, it was that we were on the verge of hitting it big. We'd worked so hard to get here. I couldn't let things go sideways just because one of us was getting a little sentimental.

I gave Dash one last kiss and put my undies back on. And then I walked home, trying to pretend like apprehension wasn't following me the whole way there.

◆ ◆ ◆

INT. THE DUKE'S DRAWING ROOM—NIGHT

A candle burns on the table, next to a discarded pearl necklace, an unfolded cravat, and two wineglasses. The sound of a crackling fire can be heard. The DUKE OF HARDING sprawls in the armchair, wearing only a pair of trousers. His hair is a mess, as if someone has been raking their fingers through it.

                    THE DUKE OF HARDING
              (gazing intently at the camera)
         We shouldn't be here, you know. We
         shouldn't do this again. I shouldn't
         call you my darling, or trail my fingers
         down your neck, or wonder what those
         lips of yours taste like. I know all
         that, and yet I can't help myself. I
         can't help the longing that comes over
         me whenever I catch a glimpse of you in
         another room. Earlier, when we danced at
         Lady Ashdown's ball, I thought I would
         expire on the spot if one more second
         went by without touching your skin. The
         way you gasped when I slid a fingertip

inside the wrist of your glove . . . The
way your cheeks flushed and your rosebud
of a mouth parted . . . Come here, my
darling. Let me touch you. Let me taste
you. Let me make you mine.

16

We'd been at it for a couple of weeks, and money was already starting to roll in. Good money, too. *Quit your job and become a full-time content-creator* type money. Not that I had a job to quit or anything.

Dash seemed to be taking his newfound popularity in stride. I, however, had acquired a newfound habit of losing my shit, oh, at least three times a day.

'Cause here's the thing. If anything, this was proof that I wasn't a *total* fuckup. I mean sure, most of our success was due to Dash's talent and good looks. But this whole thing had been my idea in the first place, and it was my scripts that had the Duke of Harding subreddit more active than a gymfluencer. All of a sudden, there was pressure. And there were stakes.

And we all know how well I deal with those.

I wasn't about to give in to the urge to bolt, though. Not this time. I was going to see this project through, if only because we were finally starting to see some real money from subscriptions, enough that we'd put in our first order for all the merch Dash had designed.

It wasn't all perfume and roses. We'd gotten our share of trolls and a couple of people who kept trying to initiate some Discourse with a capital D. Takes of all temperatures aside, though, the Duke of Harding was proving to be a success in every way that mattered. And I . . .

As sad as it sounds, for the first time in my life, I was starting to feel like I was a success. Like I was finally doing something right. Like things were falling into place.

It wasn't that I didn't notice how long it took Yaz to respond to my texts, or that her daily calls had turned into harried weekly check-ins, it was just that my phone was bursting with so many notifications that I was able to pretend like I didn't feel her absence deep in my bones.

There was so much to do outside my phone now, too. Late nights on the floor of Dash's living room, or his bed, working on Duke of Harding stuff. Dropping off sweet treats at Aria's and hanging around her store and watching people wander in from the bar next door for late-night tarot sessions.

And there was all the stuff we were doing for Second Chance, like the treasure hunt. Dash and I weren't the only ones reaping the benefits from being internet famous. The link we'd added to our profile that led to the page on the Second Chance website where we'd outlined the rules for the scavenger hunt had gotten over half a million hits.

On the morning of the *Kate & Leopold* screening, my phone buzzed with a text from Shy. They'd sent me a video of the store, which was the busiest I'd ever seen it—which wasn't saying much, to be honest. Still, there were a solid half a dozen people looking through paperbacks, which made me smile when I saw that Shy had captioned the picture Getting mobbed.

I think you mean "We're winning at capitalism," I texted back, and set my phone down to attempt a few calming breaths.

It didn't work, but that was probably mostly because Dash was standing two feet away from me, half naked and covered in a thin sheen of sweat that made the muscles on his back gleam in the morning light peeking through the gap in my curtains.

He'd skipped his workout to come over for an early-morning hookup because I had been very careful about avoiding sleepovers after the first night we'd spent together. My thoughts were already too prone to wandering in dangerous directions without subjecting myself to the sight of a sunshine-drenched Dash on the pillow next to mine first thing in the morning.

A girl can only take so much, you know?

"Cream cheese and jelly on your bagel?" Dash asked from the kitchen, which was so close to the bed that I could almost graze his boxers with my fingertips if I stretched.

"How'd you know?"

"It was either that or Nutella, and I don't see any in your cupboard."

"That's because I finished it last week and I haven't had time to grocery shop, what with our demanding production schedule." He didn't need to know that I'd eaten the last of the Nutella by smearing it on a spoon and then dipping said spoon into a box of Cap'n Crunch while watching Meg Ryan be adorably ditzy. "We're recording again today, right?"

"We have a couple of the Central Park videos cued up, but yeah, we should probably start on some new content."

The smell of coffee, admittedly not as unpleasant as its taste, filled the air as it bubbled over into the top portion of the greca I'd forgotten I owned until Dash fished it out from the back of a cabinet. He opened the lid to peer inside, then, satisfied, turned off the stove.

I could have spent hours lying there, watching him navigate my cramped kitchen with the grace of a ballet dancer. Kicking off the sheets, I put on my robe, which was on the short side and printed with pink leopards.

"I kind of wish I had a murder robe," I remarked as I stepped over to the patch of tiles that separated the kitchen from the rest of the apartment.

Dash blinked. "A what?"

"One of those extravagant, silky or gauzy things trimmed with feathers that women in movies wear before they kill their rich husbands." I paused. "Or maybe after. I'm not quite clear on the logistics. They don't seem all that practical to do the actual murdering in, to be honest."

Dash poured his coffee out into my cloud-print mug. His hair, adorably rumpled after the exertion of the past couple of hours, flopped onto his forehead. He flipped it back, raising an eyebrow. "Should I be worried that you want a murder robe?"

"I'm not planning to commit homicide at the moment—and I don't think you're rich enough to warrant being offed by your spouse. Yet, anyway."

"That's something to aspire to, I guess." Without letting go of the steaming cup, Dash hooked his thumb through one of my robe's loops and pulled me closer. "You ready for today?"

"Are *you*? You're the one who's going to be standing in front of millions—okay, like, dozens—of people being sexy and fake British at them."

"It shouldn't be a huge crowd," he said, shrugging. "No pressure."

"Tell that to my galloping heart," I muttered. "Wait, we can do something with that. Let me write it down."

Reaching for my phone, I opened my Notes app and got to tapping. When I glanced back up, Dash was looking down at me with this little frown between his eyebrows.

"Did you stop working on your screenplay?"

I pulled away, reaching for the bagel he'd prepared me. "Where'd *that* come from?"

"I don't know, I just feel like I haven't heard you talk about it in a while."

"You mean, I haven't been complaining about it." The bag of fresh-made bagels he'd brought over earlier was sitting on the counter, smelling warm and yeasty.

Out of the corner of my eye, I could see Dash take a sip of his coffee. "You haven't given up on it, have you?"

I shrugged and licked a smear of cream cheese on the side of the bagel. "So what if I did? It wasn't like it was going anywhere. And anyway, who has the time with Duke of Harding taking off like it is? I might actually pay my rent on time this month."

Dash didn't look disappointed, not exactly. But as he looked down at the inky liquid in his cup, something in his expression made defensiveness swirl up around me.

"Look," I said briskly. "Our fan base is growing. We've got more subscribers than ever—paid ones—and our merch is selling and . . . and we're doing numbers. Why would I waste my time on some kind of New York fantasy where everyone dresses in unrealistic outfits and has wildly implausible careers when we're living in one?"

"You don't have to do anything you think is a waste of time," he replied, "I guess I kind of thought that your screenplay was like my wanting to design store windows. Something you thought of as a pipe dream, not really realizing that it could be real." He ran a hand through his hair and gave me a crooked smile. "I want it to be real for you."

"You know what's real?" I pointed a jelly-sticky finger at him. "Rent money. Grocery money. *I don't have to ask my cousin to help me make my credit card payment this month* money."

He raised a hand. "I hear you. The happiest moment in my life was probably when I told my dad I didn't need his help paying my bills."

"I thought you guys got along," I said.

"We do. It's just that . . ." Dash lifted his bagel to his lips, taking only a nibble from it as he considered what he was about to say. "Asking my parents for anything just feeds their competitiveness, and that gets uncomfortable for anyone involved. Plus my father . . . he means well, but his help, financial or otherwise, comes with a lot of strings. And pretty early in my life, I decided that I didn't want to be tied up. Not in that way," he added as I opened my mouth.

But it turned out that Dash didn't know me as well as he thought, because what actually popped out was "I wish I had strings."

Shit, I hadn't meant to say that out loud.

Dash cocked his head. "What about your family? And your cousin?"

I hadn't brought up the subject of Yaz or her visit again, even though at that point it was less than a handful of days away. Avoidance, thy name is Mariel. And anyway, the truth was that while Yaz and Tía Nena gave me plenty in the way of strings, I hadn't been thinking about them when I'd wished for some.

I mean, I hadn't been thinking at all is the point. Because the last thing I wanted to tell Dash was that my own parents couldn't be bothered with me. And that the thought of parental help, even if it came tangled with strings, sounded kind of nice to someone who wasn't really sure of what her mother's zip code was at any given moment.

I waved a dismissive hand in the air. "Oh, there's more strings there than at a craft store. But I didn't mean to make the conversation about myself. I don't think I've ever actually heard you say much about your father."

"There's not much to say, I guess." Dash took a sip of his coffee. "He's loving and supportive—and he has a lot of opinions and isn't shy about airing them. As far as he was concerned, taking his money meant that he had a say in every decision I made. He was more than happy to buy me a car, but only the one he approved of. He'd pay my tuition, but only if I chose the school he thought had the better art program. Stuff like that. He's mellowed out a lot over the years—especially after my grandmothers bullied him into going into therapy and it helped him realize he was being way too controlling."

"God, your grandmas are my heroes."

"Anyway, the thing is, I get where you're coming from," Dash said with endearing earnestness. "I understand the need to be financially independent—and trust me, I know how good it feels. I just hope the money's not getting in the way of you pursuing your dreams."

He drained the mug and set it on the counter, the corners of his lips turning up and down like a flickering light bulb. "Sorry, it's probably the old hero complex rearing up again."

I couldn't keep myself from brushing back a lock of his hair with my non-sticky hand. "Trust me, I've been avoiding working on my screenplay since before you showed up."

"Because it's safer not to try than risk failure on something you want so badly?" he guessed.

I made a face. "Dash, are you trying to make me be introspective again? Haven't we already established how far and fast I can run to avoid talking about my feelings? I haven't spent all these years building up walls and fortifications and a goddamn moat just to open the door to the first person to knock on it."

He leaned back against the counter, which was all of two feet long. "There's a moat, huh?"

"Of course there's a moat. Don't you underestimate my imaginary fortifications."

"I would never. And I'd never ask you for more than you felt you could give. But if you ever wanted to let down the drawbridge . . ."

I set down the bagel and reached for the waistband of his boxers. "How about I let down my pants instead? Oh, wait, I'm not wearing any. I guess that means I have to let down yours."

Tugging the waistband down slightly, I let my gaze travel over him, slowly, admiringly.

"Like what you see?"

His words were light enough, but the expression in his eyes was molten. If a few words of praise were all it took for desire to start surging through my body, I was pretty sure that being looked at was Dash's kink.

"I like everything about you, Dashwood," I said, matching his light tone even though my gaze was heavy on his body.

"Do you, now?"

The subtle motion he made with his hips was enough to make my fingertips collide with more than his waistband. I let my hand drift down, holding his gaze.

And just like that, another deep, emotional conversation was averted. As I tugged Dash toward my bed, though, I couldn't help thinking that sooner or later, my luck was going to run out. And when it did . . . when Dash finally decided that he'd had enough of me and my shenanigans . . .

Yeah. I probably didn't want to think too hard about what would happen then.

◆ ◆ ◆

"Okay, so it's not a small crowd," Dash said, staring out at the sea of humanity crowded into the rooftop bar where *Kate & Leopold* was being screened.

He and I were behind the screen, mostly out of view of the dozens of people in folding beach chairs. The sun was sinking behind the skyscrapers surrounding us, and lights were coming on all around us, though the lighting in the bar itself was being kept low.

"You got this, though, right?"

The string lights looped above our heads made Dash's eyes sparkle when he looked at me. Or maybe it was just his excitement at being in front of a crowd. I was full of adrenaline, too, only mine was the nervous kind that tightened into knots in my stomach even when Dash answered me with an easy "I got it."

A smile full of confidence and anticipation tugged up the corners of his lips and I found myself smiling back. "You got it, all right," I said, and all the knots in my stomach couldn't extinguish the flirtiness in my tone.

Threading his fingers through mine, he leaned in for a kiss. If I'd been stronger, I would have reacted by placing a hand in front of his face. But I'm not made of stone, okay? He leaned in, and even though I should have known better, so did I.

Or started to, anyway. I didn't get too far before I heard someone clearing their throat right behind us.

Springing back like I was the wallflower who'd been surprised in the middle of an illicit kiss with the duke, I turned to see three girls a few years younger than me clustered by the edge of the screen. Their gazes were darting between us, bright with so much curiosity that I felt myself shrinking back.

"Shut up," one of them said. "The Duke of Harding has a girlfriend?" Her gaze swept over me, taking in my outfit and ending with a nod of approval. "I ship it."

"Assistant," I blurted out, taking a step away from Dash like I'd just been told he was contagious. "I'm his assistant."

The second girl raised an eyebrow. "I'd swap jobs with you anytime, queen. Bet it comes with a ton of employee benefits."

The third one wasn't saying much, mostly because she was looking like she was going to cry as she looked at me.

"It's not like that at all," I started to say.

Without missing a beat, Dash slipped into his Duke of Harding accent. "How may I help such delightful ladies?"

"Would you do a quick video with us for BookTok?" the second girl said. "I have almost a hundred K followers and they all love you."

Dash smiled. "I shall endeavor to do my best, my lady. What would you have me do?"

With the intensity of a Hollywood director the second girl told everyone where to stand. I hung back, taut with anxiousness at the visions of our near kiss going viral on the apps.

The TikTok *was* a quick one, which was a good thing because we only had a few minutes before Dash had to be on stage on the other side of the screen. As they finished recording, the girl that had been silent up till then darted out a hand that she placed on Dash's arm.

She burst out with "Everything you say is just so—so romantic. I've never met a guy who talks like that. It's like you get me. Like you *see* me."

The fingertips on her other hand were toying with her neckline, gliding over her collarbones and hooking on her layered necklaces. From her expression, it wasn't hard to tell that she wished it was Dash touching her.

The knots in my stomach tightened into hard little lumps.

Dash took a subtle step back, ostensibly to sweep into a bow, but I could tell it was his polite way of moving out of touching range. It was a skill he must have honed as a cosplayer at cons. "We endeavor to please," he said easily.

Even with the unsolicited touch, Dash was almost vibrating with excitement when the girls wandered off.

"Sorry for being toxic, but she's not even that pretty," I heard one of them say.

Groaning, I buried my face in my hands, lifting it only long enough to say, "See, this is why we have to be careful when we're out in public."

Dash shrugged. "I didn't realize anyone was looking."

"This is New York, Dashwood. There's an influencer recording stuff in every corner, so remember to keep your pants on."

"I feel like I should point out that I had no intention of removing my pants," Dash said, and flashed me a smile. "As much as I think the fangirls would have appreciated that."

I had a second to imagine the riot it would have caused before Dash accosted me with "Hey, so I was wondering if you wanted me to mention your name while I was up there."

I met his smile with a frown. "Why would I want that?"

"I feel like an asshole taking all the credit for this. I mean, it was your idea in the first place. You do most of the writing."

I gave him my best insouciant shrug, even though the mere mention of giving me credit had made my palms turn clammy. Sliding my hands in the pockets of the sheer dress I had layered over jeans and a tight crop top, I said, "I don't need validation from online strangers. And besides, it'd ruin the illusion."

He raised an eyebrow. "I highly doubt anyone here thinks I'm actually a member of the nineteenth-century aristocracy."

Was he really trying to push the point when there was only a flimsy screen separating us from the hordes of fangirls? Panic fluttered inside me. Maybe a little resentment, too. Things were easy for Dash in a way they weren't for me—it was frustrating how he didn't see something that felt so overwhelmingly obvious.

I wasn't ready to fail in public. Not when all my other failures were still looming over me. Not when I'd barely had a chance to wrap my head around our success.

And yeah, okay, so I did want validation, and I didn't particularly care where it came from. But there was one thing I wanted more than that, and it was to not fall flat on my face in front of the whole world. The way things were right now, if it all went to shit, there would be no harm done. I'd toss the Duke of Harding under the bed along with all the other hobbies I'd abandoned or failed at.

I should have said all that to Dash, I guess. All too aware of the crowd on the other side of the screen, all I did was scowl. "You know what I mean."

And if he didn't, there was no time to explain because the bar's events coordinator was coming toward us.

"Dash and Mariel, right?" he asked, reaching out to shake our hands before removing his black-framed glasses to give them a quick wipe on his T-shirt. "Thanks for coming early, guys. We've never really done this kind of live preshow before movie nights before, so we've all got our fingers crossed the crowd likes it. We should be ready to start in about ten. Does that sound good?"

Dash voiced his agreement, and we spent the next few minutes making sure his hair and his costume were perfect. Then, heart thrumming with anticipation, I went to find a spot where I could watch the whole thing.

We'd put together a little scenario that landed on the sweeter side of the spicy scale, with just enough intensity to keep things interesting. I'd been a little worried that the kind of monologues that did well on social media wouldn't work in real life, but I shouldn't have been. I mean, this was Dash, right? He more than made it work. If I thought Dash was in his element in front of the camera, it was like he came to life when he had a real audience. He commanded the attention of everyone on the rooftop with the same ease that I ate frozen Oreos—and he gave as good as he got, directing comments to this person and hair-flipping at that one and generally making everyone feel included.

I guess I got kind of caught up in the moment, because I recorded a quick video of Dash and sent it to Tía Nena. Who answered a couple of minutes later by saying that she was going to call me later, when she was out of the kitchen and could properly hear me tell her all about it, and then quickly followed up that text with another one.

So proud of you, Chiquita. Have you shown your mom yet?

The urge to pretend that I didn't see the second part of the message was stronger than the applause that met Dash's performance. Tía Nena could be relentless, though, and lately she had been badgering me more than usual about reaching out to my mom, something about how it had been a few months and we had a lot to catch up on. As if the lack of communication wasn't due to my mom's desperate search for her own identity after the eighteen unfortunate years she'd spent being, well, my mom.

"You okay?" Dash asked as he came off the stage and to the table we had set up with some of our brand-new merch.

"Huh? Yeah, fine." The words came automatically, before I had even glanced up to see him peering at me with obvious concern. I shoved my phone back into my pocket. "Just checking our comments. Dash, you were amazing!"

And clearly, I wasn't the only one who thought so. Even though the movie had just begun, a tidal wave of people were approaching, asking for selfies and looking through the pins and stickers Dash had designed for us to sell. Dash immediately switched back into Duke of Harding mode, fielding questions and comments like a pro. I paused for a moment, watching him and coming to a realization— Dash never performed in front of me like he did with everyone else. Like he did with his father, even when it was just a phone call and the stakes were so low they were practically on the floor.

When he was around me, Dash was just . . . himself.

And that was . . . wow. It was . . . not something I needed to analyze just that moment, not with Shy and Aria heading my way and the fangirls shooting curious looks in my direction.

I tried to look as inconspicuous as it was possible to look when my sheer dress was striped with multicolored ribbons, dangly earrings in the shape of stacked flowers hung from my earlobes, and a huge pair of puffy-framed orange sunglasses had been nestled in my curls ever since dusk. Unfortunately, I couldn't quite melt away into the background because I was supposed to be manning the merch table while Dash worked the crowd.

Dressed in ripped denim and a *Lisa Frankenstein* T-shirt over a black mesh top printed with red lips, Aria stepped behind the table and began helping me. Meanwhile, Shy made quick work of neatening the stack of limited edition T-shirts we'd had silk printed with the illustration of the Duke that Dash had made.

"You're weirdly quiet tonight," Aria said during a brief lull, eyeing me. "Shouldn't you be out there signing autographs, too?"

"Like any of these people know who I am."

Even in the dimness of the rooftop bar, her gaze was piercing. "Do you want them to?"

"Nah," I said, and explained how the fangirls would probably get weird if they knew there was a woman in Dash's life. "Even if it's just someone writing scripts."

"I'd say you're a lot more than just someone writing scripts," Shy observed.

"In the sense that I'm a well-rounded person with interests and aspirations and all that junk?" I shot back, determined not to give Shy the opportunity to clarify, because despite all appearances, I did understand that they were referring to me and Dash and our nonexistent relationship. "The whole point of the Duke of Harding is to project an illusion. Putting myself front and center of it kinda ruins it."

"So you're letting a man take the sole credit for your creation?" Aria snapped.

"You guys are worse than Dash," I told them, and repeated the line about not needing validation from internet strangers, which I thought had been pretty good. And fairly truthful. You know, for the most part.

Once the movie was over, Dash ducked into the bathroom to change his clothes, then the four of us made our way back to our neighborhood, squabbling cheerfully over where to stop for dinner.

After wasting almost an hour trying to decide between four different places, we ended up getting an assortment of things delivered to Second Chance, where we hung out until well after midnight.

If I was putting this into a screenplay, I wouldn't have changed a damn thing.

Afterward, Dash and I went back to my place and tumbled into bed for another few hours. We were both tired enough that when I noticed Dash's eyelids drifting closed, I didn't even shake him awake to insist he go home. And I didn't even have the decency to break out in a cold sweat or start spiraling. All I did was snuggle closer.

17

Summer was unspooling like an old-school film reel showing a montage of August highlights. Dash at the screening, making the audience scream out whoops with every hair flip. Going out with Shy and Aria and staying up until daybreak laughing over Aria's newfound obsession with pirate romances. Helping Dash try out recipes for an espresso chocolate chip cake that he swore would make me love the taste of coffee. And through it all, golden hours bright with satisfaction every time I peeked at our socials and saw more comments, more follows, more shares, and more likes.

It took me and Aria issuing daily threats in the group chat we'd started to get Dash and Shy to stop fiddling with the window design and commit to a date when we could all get together to make it happen. The day before burlesque night seemed like the perfect time, with Shy figuring that they could do the grand unveiling just before the event.

The two of them had gone shopping for supplies, and they were all laid out on a long folding table in the garden, alongside snacks and a tub full of ice and assorted beverages. I dropped my contribution—a box of donuts and a box of cookies from that place on 45th and Ninth, which I'd bought without even having to check my bank balance—next to the chips and turned around to survey our workspace.

It was already dark, because we'd waited until the store was closed for the day. As well as the decorative strings of lights hanging from the tree and the balcony, the courtyard was well supplied with the spotlights used for performances. Dash was standing right under one of them as he propped up his tablet against a stack of paperbacks.

I probably wasn't the only person who thought that Dash walked around looking like he was followed by his own personal spotlight—there was a certain kind of magic in the way his eyes caught the sunshine, and the way he'd learned to move so that his features were always artfully illuminated.

And that was on a normal day.

In the deep cobalt of a late summer evening, the spotlight shedding its brightness on his thick curls, the necklace I'd given him peeking out from above the neckline of his navy T-shirt, Dash looked like something I'd conjured from my wildest fantasies.

All of a sudden, I could feel every single one of my nerve endings.

Bumping lightly into his side didn't soothe the bright sting of it—if anything, it only made it worse. You'd think that after weeks of hooking up, my desire for him would have faded at least a little. If anything, though, it seemed to grow stronger by the day.

And it was getting harder and harder to tell myself this was nothing but desire.

"I'm pretty sure this is what the inside of your head looks like," I told Dash as we both gazed down at the drawing on his tablet. "All blooming flowers and shimmering fireflies and romance novels."

"Are you comparing me to a summer's day?" he asked, slinging an arm around my shoulders. "Because I'll have you know, I'm a fall girlie all the way. Sweaters and candles and pumpkin spice and all."

The thought of Dash in another season made my heartbeat speed up. Not just at the thought of him in cuddly knits, cooking something ridiculously complicated like risotto or osso buco, but at the image that flashed through my mind of the two of us wrapped in blankets on his couch, watching the leaves drift by outside the window, the air around us heavily scented with cinnamon and cardamom. It was a maybe sort of thought, the kind that I rarely let myself indulge in.

And I wasn't going to this time, either.

Luckily, someone else coming into the garden chased—if you'll excuse the pun—all those thoughts away. Chase could have been on a catwalk, the way he strutted out the back door and toward where Dash and I were standing.

"If it isn't my favorite screenwriter," he said. "Or should I say smutwriter?"

"Chase! I didn't think you'd be back in town until tomorrow!" I reached out to give him a hug, which he returned by lifting me off the ground and swinging me around. Planning Lord Loving's exploits meant that we'd been in constant touch over text, even though we hadn't seen each other in person since that afternoon we'd celebrated getting away from the Times Square mob with cheap beer and chicken wings and dancing. "What are you doing here?"

"Dash sent out the bat signal and I came running when I heard his big emergency involved doing crafts. I'm great with my hands," he said with a wink, making my gaze go automatically to his hands.

His fingers were full of rings—mostly thick silver ones that flashed in the low light with every movement, but there were a few colorful plastic ones in the mix, including a striped one that reminded me of a candy cane.

I put my own hands on my hips. "You do realize that was basically a challenge for me to add hand stuff to literally every single one of Lord Loving's scripts."

"Better watch out, Chase," Dash said, "she's gonna make you put your money where your mouth is."

Chase smirked back at us. "Doesn't sound sanitary, but I don't kink shame."

I groaned just as Shy and Aria joined us, Kitty Marlowe leading the way. The orange demon wound herself around Dash's ankles, purring lovingly, then glanced at me with a look of extreme disdain before turning her attention to wreaking havoc on the art supplies.

"You couldn't have waited for me to start talking about kinks?" Aria said, dropping a box of craft stuff on the table. "I'm shocked and hurt that you have so little regard for my feelings."

"Don't worry, baby, the evening's just getting started," Chase told her, leaning forward to drop a juicy kiss on her cheek.

It struck me with a small jolt how we'd all found Aria and Shy and Second Chance on our own, only to come together, all intertwined like the tapestry Dash had talked about.

Shy didn't look impressed with our shenanigans. "Anyone else feel like they're gonna need an edible to get through tonight? No? Just me?"

Chase clapped them on the back. "If you're offering . . ."

It took us a while, but eventually we did manage to get our collective asses in gear and start working. The project manager in me had broken everything down, with Dash's input, into small, manageable tasks. Believe it or not, I'd been good at my job once. You know, when I wasn't yelling at clients.

Elaine had once told me that interior design was storytelling. As she'd explained it to me, when you design someone's space, you're helping them tell the story of who they are—or who they think they are, or who they want to be. And even though I hadn't actually been designing, it had been my responsibility to set the designers up for success. Once I'd figured out what Dash was trying to convey, it was easy enough to help him figure out how to do it. Like we'd done when we'd started the Duke of Harding, he and I worked together to set a budget and source materials. Shy put up the money, and Aria and Chase had signed up to help with the labor.

Aria had claimed that she had no useful artistic skills, so she was busy opening package after package of LED fireflies, which Dash wanted strung on nylon thread.

Chase turned out to be as skilled with a needle and thread as he was with his hands, so we'd set him up with two dozen amber-colored beads that Dash wanted sewn to the centers of the flowers he'd already made out of textured paper. Seated next to Chase, I was cutting shapes out of the sheer fabric that would be fixed to the back of the paper flowers to filter the light shining from behind them.

"So you and Dash, huh?" Chase said as he speared a few beads through a large, blunt-tipped needle. "I shoulda seen it coming."

"Because I'm so irresistible that Dash would have never been able to hold out against my many and varied charms?" I guessed.

"Yes, and also because you get him. I can see it in the scripts you write for him." Chase paused for thought, holding the needle aloft. "Most people don't bother looking for anything beyond his surface. They see his looks, and the way he interacts with the world, and they think that's all they need to know about him. You write for him like you've dived into the depths of him and found all the pearls and are bringing them up for everyone to admire."

"Trying so hard to not say anything too dirty about Dash's pearls right now," I remarked, to keep from showing how touched I was.

Chase shot me an amused glance. "You can run but you can't hide, babe. I can tell you like actually like *him*—not the way he looks or how jealous it'd make someone else to have him on your arm. And knowing what I do about his past relationships, I can tell you right now that's not as common as you might imagine."

"Shit," I said softly.

If anyone didn't deserve that, it was Dash, with his earnestness and his hair flips and his smiles that felt like sunshine. Part of me wanted to rage out over all the people who'd made Dash feel anything less than amazing—and yet, another, more self-aware part of me knew that there was a high likelihood I could end up being one of them. Not on purpose, maybe, but it was just a matter of time until I flailed so hard I hurt him.

Chase maneuvered the needle through a cluster of loose beads. "It's probably not my place to speak on it. I worry, though, you know? Dash is good people. I'd hate to see him hurt like that again. Or at all."

A laugh rang out from the other side of the garden, drawing my attention to where Aria was leaning in to feed Shy a bite of donut. Romantic as it looked, the gesture was actually due to the fact that Shy's hands were covered with sawdust, to the detriment of the yellow polish on their nails that matched the fried eggs printed on their shorts.

Dash was standing next to the pair, pretending to be mournful about the fact that no one was feeding *him* donuts. So I went over to the food table, broke off a piece, and pelted Dash with it just to make him laugh.

"Anything to please my man," I said sweetly.

"I take it back!" he yelled through a chuckle, throwing up his hands to avert a second piece of donut and almost smacking Shy, who was using their rudimentary carpentry skills to make a letter R out of plywood.

The letter, which was almost as tall as Dash, was going to be twined with the flowers and the paper vines and the long strings of clementines, and it was going to hold a few short ledges where Shy's selection of summer romances could be propped up on unobtrusive acrylic stands. That was, if Shy and Dash managed to figure out how to begin tackling the general construction of the build.

"That's going well. I'm not even a little scared of being hit on the head with a flying hammer," I remarked brightly as I went back to my spot next to Chase, earning myself a snort from Shy.

Unfazed by my commentary, if not by the task at hand, they got back to work.

"So sorry for the interruption," I told Chase, who was cracking up. "You know how it is when you have hungry mouths to feed. The patriarchy makes monsters of us all."

"No, I get it. Throwing food at your significant other is an underrated avenue of communication."

"It's definitely my love language."

I let the word *love* settle around me, waiting for it to fill the air, expanding until I felt smothered by it. I guess I was a little surprised when it didn't. Not that I had time to dwell on it. Aria had decided that Shy'd had enough to eat and she plunked down at the table, the yowling orange beast in her arms, to ask Chase about his trip.

I tried to focus on what he was saying, but it was kind of hard to pay attention to anything other than the sensation inside my chest.

It was as if my heart had kind of lifted a little. It wasn't like soaring over the East River, exactly—it was steadier than that. And it wasn't just Dash, either. It was . . . all of this. The humid warmth of the evening, the strings of light gleaming against the background of brick and tree leaves. The Lady Cerulean song issuing faintly from Shy's phone, underlaid by the murmur of conversation all around me and punctuated by the occasional burst of hammering.

Being in the city with friends and something to do and finally, *finally* feeling like I was on my way to belonging there.

And—I held on to the thought before it could skitter away—feeling like I belonged with Dash, too. He had set down the hammer and was scraping his hair off his sweaty forehead. It immediately flopped back into place, prompting me to reach into my pocket for the headband I'd stashed there in anticipation of when the humidity got the best of my curls.

I brushed the worst of the sawdust off his dark strands and eased the headband on. "Florals look good on you, Dashwood."

He couldn't hair-flip me with it pulled back, but the sparkle in his eyes and the slow, sweet smile that spread over his lips like Nutella on warm toast was practically lethal. In the sense that I could feel it killing off my ever-present urge to run away screaming.

His kiss connected with the spot just below my ear. "Know what else looks good on me?"

Tingles like champagne bubbles were gathering low in my abdomen, and I squirmed as he nuzzled the side of my neck. "Save it for when we're not in public. And covered in sawdust."

"What was that? Did you just say you wanted to be covered in sawdust?" Dash's arms came around me and he rubbed his body all over mine, making me howl and Chase and Aria burst into hoots and hollers.

"You're dead to me!" I yelped, trying not to laugh as I pushed him away.

"Only happy to oblige my lady's request," Dash said, grinning.

I rolled my eyes, then leaned in close to him again and gave him a kiss. "Just for that, I'm making you do my laundry next time we hit the laundromat."

He caught me by the waist, holding me long enough to whisper in my ear, "If you wanted me to handle your panties, all you had to do was say so."

I cracked up. "Dashwood, I'm *shocked*. What the hell's gotten into you tonight?" Before he could say anything, I jammed my hand against his mouth. "Forget I asked."

Retreating a few paces so that I wouldn't get any more wood dust on me as Dash picked up a piece of sandpaper, I tried to keep the hearts out of my eyes as I watched him smooth down one of the curves in the giant R. "You're in a good mood tonight."

"I like this," Dash said simply. His beautiful mouth turned up at the corners, and somehow the twinkles in his eyes were brighter than the lights strung all around the garden. "And I like you, too."

I was trying to be strong, I really was. But could anyone even blame me for weakening under the full strength of that earnest warmth?

Maybe opening up to Dash didn't have to be such a bad thing. I mean, at this point, I could reasonably trust Dash not to ghost me, right? Maybe—

"Anyone seen a huge roll of duct tape?" Shy called.

"I think it's inside," I said, and went to get it. Not like fast or anything. Or like I was trying to escape. Nothing to see here. Just being helpful.

Sure enough, the tape was where I'd seen it, perched haphazardly atop a towering pile of Harlequin Historicals. I stuck my arm through the heavy roll like a bracelet and was about to turn back when I noticed that one end of the craft paper covering the store's windows had become unstuck from the glass and was hanging down like half-buttoned overalls.

Tearing off a piece of tape, I went to stick it back up to keep anyone from peeking at our masterpiece-in-progress, which at the moment was nothing more than a stepladder and a couple cans of paint placed in the center of the denuded window.

I was reaching for the fallen corner when I became aware that there was someone standing outside, probably reading the poster advertising burlesque night, which Shy had stuck to the outside of the window. The sidewalk was mostly dark, but enough light spilled through the craft paper that the person standing in front of Second Chance was fully illuminated and, once my brain had caught up to my skipping heart, impossible to keep from recognizing.

It was Milo, standing there like a bad omen, or a message from the universe. Or worse—a reminder that however good things appeared to be going, you never knew when you were going to be lied to and ghosted.

◆ ◆ ◆

"Who was that?" Aria asked.

She had followed me inside, Kitty Marlowe screaming bloody murder in her arms, probably in protest at being forcibly removed from the chaos she'd been causing outside.

"Who?" I asked, smoothing my thumb so aggressively over the newly applied tape it was a wonder the window didn't crack under my gentle touch.

She raised her eyebrow at me, clearly unimpressed by my lackluster attempt at nonchalance. "Whoever got you all rattled."

I glanced back at the covered window, as if I'd just realized there had been someone on the other side. "Oh, just a ghost."

"Wanna talk about it?"

I looked into her eyes, made an even more intense blue by the lime green and indigo of her bodysuit, and I hesitated for a beat. Then the door to the garden swung open, and Kitty Marlowe, sensing an opportunity for escape, wriggled out of Aria's arms and streaked outside.

"No time," I told Aria with forced breeziness, pointing at Dash as he came in carrying a carefully balanced tray full of individual LED lights dangling from transparent fishing thread. "We still have to hang all the fireflies."

And look, I'm not proud of it, but I handed her the tape and asked her to take it to Shy so that I could help Dash with the fireflies. I could feel her gaze on me for the rest of the evening, joined at times by Dash, who was perceptive enough to know that something had rattled me, if not exactly what.

The thing was, I couldn't figure out why Milo was continuing to haunt me, not when I no longer had unresolved issues with him. That day at the coffee shop, I'd told him everything I'd been burning to say ever since I'd caught him in his lie. I'd moved on. I was happy with Dash, and with my new friends, and with this life I was building for myself.

And I swear, the only reason I had tears in my eyes was because I had accidentally walked into the Duke of Harding's recommendations table and banged my hip on a sharp corner.

The collision was hard enough that a few of the attractively arranged books came crashing to the floor, along with the vintage flowered teapot holding a spray of silk flowers that Dash and Shy had added for, like, ambiance or something. It was hard not to take it as another bad sign, but I grabbed the broom and a hard seltzer and made a joke out of it and it was fine.

I was fine.

It must have been close to eleven by the time we finished setting up the window and cleaning up the garden. We were all dripping with perspiration and halfway to drunk on canned cocktails that had warmed as the ice in the tub melted under the brightness of the spotlights, and we were the kind of tired that makes you giddy and prone to giggling. We all piled out on the sidewalk in a sweaty mass to admire the lit window.

It was a snapshot moment if there ever was one—the warm glow of the fireflies, swaying lightly, the dark, warm night pressing in around us, our reflections in the glass. Invisible threads connecting us to each other, and to the city, and to our dreams.

Dash's fingers fluttered against mine, and I could tell he wanted to catch my gaze, and hold it, and smile one of his softer, intimate smiles and maybe even lean in to whisper something about snap-shot moments, as if the memory of his upturned face, dappled with sunlight and leaf-shaped shadows, as he told me about his child-hood game wasn't still making my chest tight with emotion that I *didn't* want to feel.

I angled my face away and took a sip from the White Claw I'd brought outside with me.

We could have left then, I guess, and been satisfied with the day's work. But I hooked my phone up to the speakers on the counter and grabbed Shy and twirled them around and made a few not-so-subtle suggestions that we should keep the party going.

It wasn't like I did it on purpose, but Dash and Aria ended up being the ones who went down to the storeroom to get the tequila. When they came back up, I was deep in conversation with Chase—I mean, I couldn't help it if the research he was doing on the history of New York obscenity laws and how they related to burlesque was so fascinating that it took the better part of an hour just to listen to all the stuff he'd uncovered on his trips to the National Archives in DC.

I doubt he'd have run out of things to say about the thesis he was writing, but eventually the others came drifting toward us and the conversation stretched to accommodate them and Dash was next to me with his arm around my waist.

I pulled away slightly, muttering something about the heat. Dash let me go immediately, because that was just the kind of person he was. Unaccountably irritated, I brought the actually-kind-of-lukewarm-by-now can of White Claw to the back of my neck. The glug of tequila I'd added to it hadn't done anything to improve my mood. On the contrary, with every minute that passed I could feel myself coming undone. Or maybe just unglued.

So yeah, I was relieved when Dash glanced down at his phone and excused himself, saying it was his grandmas calling. He wan-dered a few yards away to the swing, scooping up Kitty Marlowe on the way. And I . . . wasn't listening in, not exactly. But the bookstore's garden was small enough that his voice kept filtering back to me, as warm and relaxed as the evening had started out.

The memory of that was only a few hours old, but it felt as distantly removed from me as if it had happened in another lifetime. As inaccessible as something under glass or fossilized in amber.

I turned my back on him and tried to talk to Shy about the scavenger hunt, but then Dash came back over and Chase asked about his grandmas and we all listened while Dash talked about their latest exploits, which involved a heist at a senior buffet that sounded like something out of *Ocean's Eleven*.

His gaze kept straying toward me, and I could sense that he wanted to ask me what was wrong, so when Kitty Marlowe yowled from a tree, doing a convincing impression of being helpless, and Aria, Shy, and Chase went to her rescue, I said the first thing that came to mind. "The Slot Sluts are my idols. I can't wait to meet them." Panic made me buzz for a moment, but I'd had too much to drink to backpedal gracefully out of that one. So instead, I added, "I mean, I'm not fishing for an invitation to meet your family. I know this isn't a real relationship or anything."

"Right," he said after a beat. "We're just buddies who bone."

It wasn't that I didn't hear the tightness in his tone. Or that I didn't care. It was just that there was so much unwanted emotion—not to mention tequila—filling my body like static on an old-fashioned TV, that I couldn't even acknowledge it. And since my brain was already on a merry little *no thoughts, just self-destructive vibes* kick, I went ahead and dug in a little deeper. "I mean, I probably wouldn't put it that way in front of them. I *can* be counted on to muster a little bit of decorum now and then."

Dash had every right to be pissed, but of course he only looked concerned. "What's going on? Did I do something to upset you?"

"Why would you think that?"

He returned my scoff with an eloquent look. "Kind of feels like you were icing me out earlier. And now . . ."

I raised both eyebrows, getting my shit together long enough to say brightly, "Dash, the only ice around here is rattling around in your margarita. Which reminds me, Shy asked me to refill the bucket."

Great, now I was gaslighting him. But I couldn't seem to help it.

Guilt and confusion churning in my stomach, I brushed past him and clattered down to the storeroom, where the ice machine was. And Dash let me go.

I didn't know how to feel about that, but luckily, another round of makeshift margaritas made it so I didn't have to do much feeling. Or thinking. Or anything but let the sweet, sweet tequila course its way through me as I got Chase to teach me a few dance moves.

By then, we'd had enough drinks that we got giddy again as I made everyone write down their most liked and most hated romance tropes on scraps of paper, and then we tried to match each one to whoever had written it. Figuring out Shy's was no challenge, but Dash surprised me by claiming that he had a thing for bodyguard romances because I'd totally had him pegged for the *friends to lovers* type.

Secret baby ended up being the winner of most hated trope. "Unless there's a good reason for the secrecy," Shy added, sparking a debate on what constituted a good reason for neglecting to tell someone they were a parent. Which set us off on a discussion of *The Parent Trap*, which led me and Chase into an impromptu lecture about every film Nancy Meyers had done, by which time it was close to two in the morning and Aria was forcing us all to hydrate in the faint hope of staving off hangovers.

And I didn't exactly forget that I'd told Dash that I'd go over to his place, but with Yaz arriving the next day and me having to be up at an unholy hour to surprise her at the airport, I just figured it would be a better idea to sleep in my apartment. Alone.

It was just common sense, and practicality, and nothing to do with the sickly shakiness that followed me all the way under the covers.

18

Even though Yaz had told me that she would meet me at my apartment, I surprised her at the airport with an embarrassingly large sign on obnoxiously neon-colored paper because of course I did.

I had done it for her, not to distract myself from the snarl of thoughts inside my head when hiding under the covers didn't help. Milo was the snag in the fucking tapestry not just of the city, but of my life, a thread that I wasn't going to pull. Not because I was worried that it would unravel the whole thing—it wasn't that important a thread. It was just a waste of time.

Even though she was dressed in matcha-green cashmere and the dark brown skin of her face was glowing with expensive serum, the Yaz that stepped out into the arrivals lounge at JFK looked so worn around the edges that I felt my sign dip an inch.

She spotted me, and the split second before her face creased into a smile made me hesitant, even though a moment before I'd been about to barrel straight into her for a long-awaited hug.

"How was the flight?" I asked instead, reaching to tug her monogrammed carry-on from her hand.

"Not too bad," she replied.

I'd been so sure that the weirdness that had made me feel the distance between us for the first time since I'd moved to New York would be gone when we were face-to-face. Instead, it seemed to have grown and I didn't know why and I was too scared of the answer to ask her about it as I led her to the subway.

Was it the distance? Stress over her work or her wedding or both? Was it that she was still mad that I had all but dropped my screenplay in favor of the Duke of Harding? Not that we'd been able to talk about it much since our daily check-ins had devolved into weekly texts.

"It smells so good in here," Yaz said when we got to my apartment, not even out of breath after all the stairs.

"That's 'cause this is where I fart," I said. Instead of her usual cackle, Yaz just smiled politely, the way you would respond to an acquaintance who'd made a mild joke. I waved toward the candle warmer in the corner, which I'd turned down to its lowest setting. "I got a creamsicle-scented candle to go with my duvet."

"Don't worry, I didn't actually think your farts smelled like ice cream."

Yaz flopped back onto my bed and stayed there, motionless, for long enough that I couldn't help blurting out, "Hey, is everything okay?"

She sat up slowly. "What do you mean?"

"Just that I've been getting kind of weird vibes from you lately. Are you—"

Reconsidering keeping me in your life given all the time you've wasted trying to help me get my life together?

Honestly, I kind of wish I'd had the courage to say that out loud instead of swallowing back the words and giving Yaz a smile that would have never passed muster under normal circumstances. "Wedding planning getting the better of you? I know I haven't made good on my offer to help . . ."

The way she leaned back on my pillows made it easy for her to avoid my gaze. "It's just this case I'm working on. I can't really share the details."

"Right," I said, and she must have picked up on the awkwardness in my tone because she sat up straight and asked me about my outfit for that night.

Believe it or not, I'd kept it surprisingly simple. Trawling my usual thrift and consignment stores had turned up a short, strapless dress in this brocade fabric that looked simultaneously like the curtains in our Duke of Harding set and like something Cher

Horowitz would have worn on a date with Josh. It was the exact shade of strawberry-ice-cream pink as the beret Dash had given me; adding a pair of silver Mary Janes and a tiny purse completed the whole *Clueless* aesthetic.

Yaz had gone with a polished yet summery cream-colored sundress, which she'd paired with tan espadrilles and understated gold-and-pearl earrings that went with her understated gold-and-pearl necklace. Even the claw clip she was planning on putting her hair up with was cream and gold.

She hung up the dress in my foot-wide excuse for a closet to keep it from getting wrinkles, fussing with one packing crease for long enough that I finally broke down and told her to put her shoes back on because I was taking her out to explore the city.

I treated her to a late lunch in Soho, and we even managed to do some shopping before we had to rush back to get dressed for burlesque night. And yeah, I'll admit it—I was . . . well, not nervous exactly. A little awkward about seeing Dash, now that the tequila had left my system. Even more apprehensive about finally introducing him to Yaz, who would figure out we were hooking up within two seconds of meeting him. I'd wanted so badly for her to see how good I was doing. But after seeing how hard and fast I'd spiraled the night before, I didn't even believe it myself.

Mostly, I was kind of regretting I'd said anything about going to Second Chance. Dash had practically come straight out and told me that he didn't want to meet Yaz. And after what I'd said last night, chances were he'd be even less eager. Don't get me wrong, he'd do it anyway. That was just the kind of person he was. You know, the kind that wouldn't let one measly little spiral get in the way of a commitment.

Dusk was deepening into night when we got to Second Chance. Dash's window was fully lit up—fireflies aglow, their warm light bringing out the translucence of the fabric and the texture of the paper flowers and catching on the beads, while carefully trained spotlights made jewels of the paperbacks being featured and the clementines carefully placed among them.

It was ... art. And Dash had created it, and we'd all helped bring it to life, and even though my stomach had been all twisted up for most of the day, seeing the window he'd poured so much into dissolved most of the knots inside me.

Dash was nothing like Milo. He was honorable and honest and all that stuff. He'd never blindside me. And he'd definitely never peace out without at least attempting to talk me to death about it.

I tried to tell Yaz about the window, but she'd already gone inside.

I'd half expected Dash to be standing by the *Duke of Harding Recommends* table, being charming at someone, but other than the cardboard cutout of the Duke he and Shy had set up, the first person we ran into was Chase.

He had gotten the memo about the evening's theme being candy realness, and he'd changed his look since the night before. His hair, which had been dyed a dark blond when I met him, was now the exact shade of pink as cotton candy, streaked in places with light orange. The combination made his pale brown skin look creamy—lickable, even, if you went by Yaz's expression.

I shot her an amused glance that went thoroughly unnoticed as she took in his whole vibe.

Chase definitely noticed. The smile he gave her was close to a smirk, which made her eyes narrow. Classic Yaz response. Then again, she'd probably just remembered that she had a fiancée and wasn't supposed to be ogling other people. Or maybe ogling was allowed when you were engaged? Clearly, I didn't know anything about relationships.

"Shouldn't you be getting ready?" I asked Chase after I'd kissed his cheeks and introduced him and Yaz.

"I'm not on for another hour," Chase said. The shirt he was wearing was a metallic sequinsplosion in the same colorway as his new hair, shimmering like mermaid scales as he moved, the sparkles echoed by the long earring dangling from his right ear. "And I'm too excited about the lineup to risk missing a single second. Which means getting a good spot—care to join me outside?"

I gave a quick glance around the store. Not that I was looking for Dash or anything. Just noticing that Shy, dressed in a cherry-print button-down, was covering the register with Kitty Marlowe wrapped around their shoulders like an extremely weather-inappropriate fur stole. And that Aria's razor-sharp gaze was trained on the guy she was having a conversation with and not, you know, piercing through me. Which normally would've been Yaz's department, but she was too busy being weird and, well, ogling Chase.

So yeah, we went out to the secret garden, where I flashed our tickets to the Barbie blonde running the event. The place was the most crowded I'd ever seen it, so it took a few minutes for us to snag beers and three spots on the bench that ran all around the garden's back wall.

Chase cupped a hand around his mouth and called out, "Ruby, my love. Please get over here and let me tell you how ravishing you look tonight."

This—yes, ravishing was definitely the word to describe her—redhead came over and saved us all from the indignity of polite chitchat by bubbling at us so enthusiastically that even Zombie Yaz was joining in. Which meant that I could relax a little, at least in the brief moments in between subtly scanning the room in search of Dash.

Or maybe not-so-subtly? Because I returned my gaze to our little group to realize that Ruby had left and Chase and Yaz were looking at me with undisguised curiosity.

"Why so worried, babe?" Chase asked gently.

"Worried? Not me," I forced myself to say. Then, betrayed by my automatic glance down at my phone, which was unhelpfully blank, I was forced to admit, "I thought Dash would be here by now. It's not like him to be late. It's not like him to be anything but scrupulously punctual, actually, which is kind of a pain in my Dominican ass."

"I'm sure he's fine," Yaz said firmly, back on the familiar territory of trying to talk me out of a spiral. "He could have gotten stuck on the subway or something."

"He lives within walking distance. But yeah, I'm sure something came up." I forced myself to smile. "He's probably outside, trying to talk his grandmas out of attempting another casino buffet heist."

Yaz didn't have a reply to that, but maybe it was because Shy was climbing up onto the tiny stage, the cherries on their shirt suddenly revealed by the spotlight shining on them to be covered by a slight layer of glitter. "Welcome to another burlesque night at Second Chance," they said. "As you may already be aware, your ticket entitles you to a ten percent discount on any book from the *Duke of Harding Recommends* table. Don't forget to check out our website for information about how to join His Grace's treasure hunt and for a schedule for this fall's burlesque nights. And since I know you're all eager to get this party started, that'll be all from me. Please help me welcome Ruby Rapture!"

I tried to pay attention. I really did. Ruby was the cutest in her feather boa and her routine was set to a Lady Cerulean song that made you long for a pink cocktail and a karaoke night with your besties. But the whole time she was up on stage—and as she was replaced by each subsequent dancer on the roster—my gaze kept alternating between the door and my still-blank phone. The growing ache in my chest was so distracting that not even the seductive stylings of the future Lord Loving were enough to hold my attention, though the whoops and hollers coming from the audience did manage to pierce through my haze.

And I did what any supportive friend would do, which was climb up on the bench—dragging Yaz along with me—and scream with my hands in the air with every piece of costume that hit the floor.

Before I knew it, two hours had passed and the burlesque portion of burlesque night was over. And not only had Dash not shown up, he also hadn't replied to any of the half a dozen—okay, couple dozen—texts I had sent him over the course of the evening.

Yaz was looking at me when I looked up from one of those texts. She'd woven her straightened hair into a braid that she'd wrapped around her head like a crown, secured with flower-shaped hairpins, and it made her profile look beautifully severe. She was also about five hundred miles less distant than she'd been an hour before, which would've been good if everything had been going according to plan, but of course everything wasn't, because this was me and my life, and it was pretty clear that she'd come back to earth just in time to see me crash and burn. Again.

"How long have the two of you been involved?"

I turned away, preferring to look at the crowd rather than see any potential pity in Yaz's eyes. "Just a few weeks," I said wretchedly. "It wasn't supposed to be anything deep or real. We were just supposed to be friends."

She didn't say anything about how bad of an idea it had been, probably because it was more than obvious.

"Oh, Mariel," she said instead. "I'm sorry."

"It's fine," I replied with a shrug, as if I could shake off my disappointment. "I mean, I'm pretty sure I'm being stood up, but I should be used to that, right?"

Out of my peripheral vision, I could see Yaz leaning forward. "I'm sure he's not standing you up."

A few weeks ago, I'd probably have tried to turn it into a joke, and said something about how Dash was just the newest addition to the graveyard that was my dating life. I had the feeling that it wouldn't roll off my tongue quite so easy now, as I realized just how badly I wanted him to be here tonight.

What else was there to do but to shrug? "Honestly, it was about time that he realized what he'd gotten himself into."

"Mariel." Yaz tugged a lock of my hair. "You're spiraling."

"Am I, though? Or just being realistic? I know I'm not a legal shark, but I know how to read a pattern. This is how it always goes."

Yaz stood up. "Come on. Let's go get another beer. And didn't you have some friends you wanted me to meet?"

We found Shy and Aria, who thankfully didn't ask about Dash. Then we got ourselves another drink. Then Ruby drifted toward us with another one of the dancers in tow and they told us all about this duet they were planning for a Halloween performance at House of Yes.

Through it all, the ache in my chest kept expanding, until it was taking up so much room that I was literally finding it hard to breathe.

This couldn't be happening. Not again.

But time kept passing and Dash kept not being there and it was after midnight and the garden had mostly emptied out and soon Shy would be closing up shop. And I kept thinking about how Dash had looked when I told him that I couldn't wait for Yaz to meet him, and how I'd been so in denial that something was wrong that I didn't even register the sinking in my stomach.

Finally, I just said it out loud. "I don't think he's coming."

"Who? Dash?" This was from Chase, who had put on a pair of sweatpants over his teeny metallic shorts but not bothered to cover up the tassels stuck over his nipples. "He texted me just before I went on to say he wasn't gonna make it."

His words fell into me like a stone into water, sending this crushing heaviness rippling over my limbs.

"Was he okay?" I heard Yaz ask through the ringing in my ears.

"I think so." Chase shot a glance at me. "Mariel, you look—"

"It's fine. I'm fine." I forced myself to smile as I took off my beret and stuffed it into my purse. "Who wants another drink?"

The thing is, I should have seen it. I would have, if I hadn't been so distracted with . . . with all this. Fireflies and tapestries and picnics and scoops of ice cream. I had enough experience to be able to notice the signs.

I'd been so sure that Dash was different, but the truth is, Dash was just like everyone else I'd dated.

I should have known Dash was going to ghost me.

◆ ◆ ◆

I wasn't the kind of person who had happily ever afters. I wasn't even the kind of person who got to have a middle with someone else. As much as I'd tried to delude myself, I'd known from the first kiss that Dash and I would never be anything more than a beginning.

Don't get me wrong—it had been a good beginning. The best one yet.

It was late when Yaz and I got back to my apartment. I wasn't cracking jokes, which was probably scaring Yaz more than if I'd been sobbing. Eyeing me warily, she kicked her shoes off by the door and perched on one end of the bed. I flopped down next to her, breathing as hard as if I'd just run a marathon, and almost let out a yelp when my phone buzzed with a text.

From Dash.

Sorry I couldn't make it. Can we talk tomorrow?

I looked at the message for a long moment, feeling my heart thud uncomfortably inside my chest. Then I deliberately swiped it off my screen.

And flung my phone clear across the room.

"I think you cracked the screen," Yaz said.

I buried my face in my flower pillow. "Who cares. That thing is a fucking cemetery. Full of ghosts," I explained, glancing up briefly.

"He just texted you—that disqualifies him from ghost status," Yaz pointed out. "Look, I get that he disappointed you by not show-ing up tonight. But don't write him off yet—I'm sure he has a good explanation."

I wasn't sure I actually cared about explanations. Not when he'd taken the time to text Chase while not even bothering to let me know that he hadn't been run over by an out-of-control Central Park carriage or, I don't know, some finance bro distraught at having spilled mustard on his Patagonia vest.

Because he knew how much his meeting Yaz had meant to me and he'd gone ahead and blown it off. Which was especially devastating when you thought about how responsible and supportive Dash was, and how coming through for any one of his friends was his idea of a good time. Where was his heroic streak when I needed it?

Yaz fetched my phone and laid it on my nightstand, not forgetting to plug it in so that it wouldn't be dead in the morning, like I would have. Then she perched on my side of the bed. "What can I do to make you feel better?"

"You can't, Yaz. I know you're used to solving all the problems, but you can't make everything better."

"Don't you think I know that?" Yaz asked in this tight voice.

I ignored her, flinging the pillow over the side of the bed and lying back to look morosely at the ceiling. "The truth is, I wouldn't blame you if you ghosted me either."

"Why the hell do you think I'd ever do that?"

I didn't have to be looking at her to know that her eyes were glittering. I sat up.

"Because I *can't* be fixed. Because if you ghosted me, you wouldn't waste so much of your valuable time trying to help me get my shit together. I mean, what's the point of having your own life all figured out when you're constantly having to clean up after someone's messes."

"Got my shit together? Me?" Yaz rubbed a hand over her face. "I don't have anything figured out. You wanna know why I'm really here? Because I quit my job. And Amal—"

She broke off, glancing away. But not before I saw the tears welling up in her eyes. Shit. Shit, shit, shit. Yaz crying? Yaz, who would've faced the apocalypse by rolling up her sleeves and saying, "We can fix it."

"What's going on with Amal?"

Getting up, Yaz went to get the blue-striped pajamas she had laid out earlier. "Nothing. We broke up. It's fine."

"Do you want to talk about it?" I asked, even though it was more than obvious that she didn't.

Yaz shrugged. "Better alone than in bad company."

It wasn't every day that Yaz quoted her mother, and suddenly I could see an echo of Tía Nena's face in Yaz's. Our mothers had always been dysfunctional when it came to love and relationships—each in her own special way—and I guess I hadn't really realized just how much Yaz and I took after them.

Ah, crap. We were both fucked, weren't we?

I folded my arms. "Is Amal actually bad company? Or did something happen?"

"She thinks that my heart isn't in it."

"She what?" I bristled. "You've done nothing but plan that wedding since the day you put rings on each other's fingers."

"Not in the wedding, in the relationship. And she's not wrong," Yaz said, looking down at the toiletries pouch she had grabbed along with her pajamas. And it just went to show how perceptive I was, because there was a simple circlet of gold flowers where her diamond used to be. "We've been together since high school. I have no idea if I truly wanted to get married or if I was just doing what was expected of me. I thought I was settling down, but Amal asked me if I was just settling and I . . . I couldn't answer her. She said that just because it was the next logical step in our relationship, it didn't mean that it was right for us, individually."

"Does your mom know?"

Miserably, Yaz shook her head. "She's been so excited about the wedding, I haven't had the heart to say anything yet. So I've just been avoiding her calls. I'm going to tell her soon," Yaz said, correctly interpreting the expression on my face. "I just needed a minute to process things myself."

"We can tell her together if you want," I offered.

Her smile was wobbly, but there was genuine gratitude in it. Still holding her pajamas and her toiletries, she sat on a corner of the bed, facing me. "The thing is, whenever I do talk to her, I'll have to tell her about my job. And why I quit."

I rescued my flower-shaped pillow from where I had flung it and wrapped my arms around its comforting softness. "Why did you?"

"I've been getting harassed by one of the partners. I thought I could handle it—I *was* handling it. I've always been able to deal with old white men and their boys' club bullshit. But then I was brought under review for what Human Resources claimed was a lackluster performance—meaning that I wasn't working enough to justify my salary, when I'd put in more billable hours than any other first-year in the whole firm." Anger crept into Yaz's tone. "As if anyone would believe it's even possible that a dark-skinned Latina first-year associate would work less hard than anyone else."

"Oh, Yaz," I said softly. "I had no idea."

"Because I didn't want you to know," she said, letting her fingers drift over the fringe on the edge of another pillow. "I know I've been really hard on you about the screenplay. It's just that things were getting rockier at work and I didn't know how long I'd be able to hold out. Mariel, I love being there for you and knowing that you can count on me for anything. You, and my mom. And I was terrified about what would happen if I couldn't be that person. If your savings ran out and Mami's restaurant failed and . . ." Yaz took a deep breath. "I don't want to disappoint her. Or you."

"As if that could even be possible," I scoffed. "Yaz, you know the reason we're all so proud of you? It's not just that shiny law degree or that ring that—well, that used to be on your finger. Or your full scholarship to the Elle Woods School of Attorneydom."

"That's a funny way of spelling Harvard Law," Yaz said.

I held up a hand. "Or your expensive apartment or your perfect eyebrows or the fact that you're ready and willing to bail us out of any financial sinking boats we happen to find ourselves stuck in. We're proud of you because you're *you*."

Yaz's eyes watered again. "You know how you keep saying that you lean too much on me? I've been leaning just as hard on you. I try my best to keep you centered. But I need the way you knock me off course every once in a while."

"All right," I said, rolling out of bed and yanking at her arm. "It's official—we're having midnight cake."

Yaz made a credible attempt at rolling her eyes. "Mariel, we're not nine years old anymore."

"Which is why the cake will come with a side of tequila. Come on."

It was unsurprisingly easy to find a handful of late-night bakeries within walking distance. We brought back the goodies—plus a bagful of snacks from the bodega—and changed into our pajamas. Yaz spread a clean towel on the floor and I teased her about it as I laid out our picnic. And the thing was, that whether she knew it or not, this was Yaz helping me yet again. Because as long as I had to focus on the fact that her life was falling apart, I couldn't begin to think about how mine was on its way there, too.

"On the bright side," Yaz said, delicately balancing a potato chip on top of a forkful of cake, "I did negotiate a very lucrative exit package. Even the assholes in Human Resources couldn't fail to see the optics of the only Afrolatina at the firm being made to quit."

"That, and they were probably trying to keep you from suing their asses for discrimination," I muttered.

"So I'll be okay. We'll all be okay. And I know you don't need my help now that you're an extraordinarily successful writer of romantic online content"—I had no idea how she made that sound like something that should be recognized with an Oscar and a Pulitzer, but God love Yaz, she did—"and you'll probably be supporting all of us soon. You know I'm proud of *you*, right? Even if I don't say it as often as I should. You have more courage than any of us, Mariel. You—Mariel, are you crying?"

"Don't be ridiculous," I sniffled into my alarmingly soggy cake and chips. "The only person who's allowed to make me cry is Nora Ephron."

Yaz threw a Hershey's wrapper at my head. "You'd better add me to that short and highly specific list."

"It says a lot about you that you actually want to be the cause of my tears. Haven't you ever felt the need to prove all those stereotypes about lawyers wrong?"

"Not particularly. All I want, Mariel . . ." Yaz fixed me with one of her sharp looks, which I actually found comforting, given that I hadn't experienced the real deal in such a long time. "All I want is for you to be happy."

"I mean, same. I just wish life or fate or the universe or whatever didn't make that so hard."

"Then help fate out," Yaz replied, lifting her water bottle to her lips. "Are you going to reply to Dash's text? At the very least, give him a chance to explain himself?"

"I don't know," I said, and immediately crammed two forkfuls of soggy cake in my mouth to avoid answering any more difficult questions. Unfortunately, Yaz had plenty of experience in dealing with my avoidance techniques and she waited patiently until I swallowed. "Look, I know I'm hurt and tired and three-quarters of the way to drunk and I shouldn't be making any decisions about, well, anything right know. I know I can't avoid Dash forever. I even know that he probably has a good excuse for not showing up tonight and I'm overreacting and that the only reason it feels like the end of the fucking world is because I've never bothered to deal with my ghosting trauma." I pointed my fork at her. "I may not act like it, but I do have a tiny bit of self-awareness."

"So what does that all mean?"

I sighed, and stuck the fork into the leftover cake. "That I'm probably going to flail like I always do and ruin the one good thing I've got going for me." And by that I definitely meant the Duke of Harding project. Although I also meant Dash a little bit. "Self-awareness can only take me so far."

"But you guys work together. What'll happen with that? What will you do if you're not working on the videos?"

I shrugged. "I just need to pivot again—or maybe even pivot back to project management and start sending out my résumé again. I need to start pulling my weight in this family."

For once, Yaz didn't have anything stern to say about my lack of direction. That, more than anything, was what made the realization crash over my shoulders.

Talk about epic flails—I'd truly fucked up this time.

◆ ◆ ◆

```
INT. THE DUKE'S DRAWING ROOM—DAY

THE DUKE OF HARDING stands gazing out the
window. There are dark circles under his eyes
and his jaw is covered in stubble.

              THE DUKE OF HARDING
         (turning to look at the camera)
    Is it really you? Darling, I've longed
    for the opportunity to beg your
    forgiveness for missing our rendezvous
    at the rose gardens. I was run over by
    a carriage and left grievously injured
    on the side of the road, all my memories
    gone and

    Oh God I think I finally lost it.
```

19

I felt hungover when I woke up late the next morning to an apartment filled with Yaz's soft snores. It was an emotional hangover, as well as an alcohol-induced one, and maybe it was a good thing that I'd always cured both the same way—breakfast banana splits.

Peeling myself off the bed, I brushed my teeth, then stepped over to the kitchen to fix two bowls. I couldn't help peeking at my phone before I dug into my freezer for the coffee-flavored ice cream. No more texts from Dash. Furiously, I blinked the sting out of my eyes. It wasn't like I'd expected a grovel or anything.

You know how sometimes you sleep on something that's bothering you and then the next morning it doesn't seem quite so bad?

Sleeping on what happened last night had left me feeling like I was seeing a nightclub in the harsh, sobering light of morning. A club in the daylight is painfully depressing. But it's also honest. You can see all the scuffs and scratches that are usually hidden by the flashing lights.

And in the bright light of this morning? Dash's and my relationship felt like it had been all flashing red lights warning me to stop before I got too close.

Yaz had slept rolled up into a blanket burrito on one side of the bed even though my window unit was no match for the late August heat. She must have been awake, because as I reached for the coffee-flavored ice cream, she was out of bed and in the kitchen.

Wordlessly, she reached into a cabinet for granola to sprinkle over the whipped cream. I shook my head, and handed her the Froot Loops.

Yaz didn't utter a single word of protest, which was especially staggering considering the midnight cake.

"That bad, huh?" I asked.

She shrugged, and I paused for a moment to squeeze her skinny shoulders.

Without any fruit to finish off the splits, not even banana, I took my bowl of ice cream and cereal and went to sit on top of the rumpled blankets.

"What do you want to do today?" I asked Yaz, forcing myself to be cheerful for her sake. I mean, she was the one who'd broken up with her fiancée. If she could hold it together, then so could I. "I had this whole plan for today, but if you'd rather just chill here or in the park or something—"

"I think you should go talk to Dash." Yaz curled up on the small patch of floor under the window, balancing the bowl of ice cream on her knee.

"*What?*"

"It's pretty clear that you really like him. And seeing as you're working together, you'll need to at least talk through the logistics of keeping your project going or not. And honestly . . . I could use a little alone time to think about next steps." Setting the bowl aside, Yaz hopped up and began to rearrange the tray of bracelets and hair ties on my windowsill, wiping off the city grime with a stray sock. "I . . . don't know if I want to go back to Miami. At least, not yet. I mean, it's not like I have an apartment to go back to. Or a girlfriend. Or a job."

The thought that for once in her twenty-six years, Yaz didn't have her next five to ten years plotted out in a color-coordinated chart complete with timelines and checklists was . . . mind-blowing. And slightly terrifying. I mean, it was bad enough for me to freewheel my way through life. For the both of us to be directionless . . .

Still, maybe that was a good thing. Maybe that was how you found your way.

I had so many questions, but the last thing Yaz needed when she had yet to figure everything out was for me to bug her about what she was going to do next.

"Well, you know half my bed is yours for as long as you need it," I told her, trying to sound like it didn't mean the world to me to finally be able to offer *her* something, as bittersweet as it was that it came at the expense of Yaz's relationship and job and probably her whole identity. "And I won't even make you share with my piles of laundry."

She rolled her eyes and threw the dusty sock at me. "Very generous."

We were both laughing, though. Which was nice, because I certainly wasn't in a laughing place when I met up with Dash a couple of hours later.

I'm not gonna say I'd been looking forward to seeing him, because I had honestly been kind of dreading it. But it was all going to be fine. Because I was going to handle this with maturity and grace.

Yeah, okay, not even I believed that one.

Going over to Dash's apartment was probably a bad idea, but even though Manhattan boasted many things, a wealth of places where two people could have a private conversation wasn't one of them.

I didn't know what to expect when Dash opened the door. Part of me thought he'd be unshaven and red-eyed and full of regret. A smaller part of me wondered if he'd be covered in whipped cream and wielding flowers. For one fleeting moment, I'd even pictured him in his Duke of Harding costume, armed with an apology that he'd deliver in a crisp British accent.

But no. The Dash that opened the door looked . . . normal. White T-shirt under an open button-down, dark blue shorts, hair somewhere between neatly combed and artfully messy. It was hard not to be resentful as me and my slept-on-it-weird curls went into the air-conditioned coolness of his living room.

Where I came to a full and awkward stop as I realized that I didn't actually know how to handle this with maturity and grace.

I automatically crossed my arms, but then I thought it made me look too confrontational, so I dropped them to my sides. But that was awkward, so I recrossed them. The last time I'd stood here, under his grandmothers' portraits, I'd been in knots, too. But back then it had been lust and hope tying up my insides, not . . . whatever this was.

I hated this. I hated this so much. It wasn't just that my stomach was in knots—it felt like *I'd* turned into one giant knot that someone had pulled too tight. And I felt tighter and tenser with every second that went by as Dash raked his fingers through his thick locks and didn't say a word. I had a vague idea that part of handling this situation with maturity and grace meant not impulsively blurting something out, which would have probably been easy for anyone else, but this was me we were talking about and I was more than due for another flail and—

"I owe you an explanation," Dash said.

And now I was glad that my arms were crossed, because the stance went well with my raised eyebrow. Neither of which accurately reflected the knot I had become. "I know you didn't want to meet Yaz. You could have at least texted me back and told me you weren't coming, instead of letting me think you had run away to live with Subway Pizza Rat."

He didn't so much as crack a smile. "I needed to take a beat."

"And I deserve the basic courtesy of a text when you're about to leave me and my cousin hang—"

"Right, the cousin you were *so* eager to introduce me to," he bit out, with so much force that I actually took a step back.

"Yes! I wanted to introduce you to the person I'm closest to in the world. What the hell are you finding wrong with *that*?"

"Look, I know how important that was to you." It was obvious that he was trying hard to keep from losing his hold on his composure. "And I'm sorry for messing up your big plans. But did you ever think that maybe I didn't want to be paraded around in front of your family like some expensive outfit you buy to show everyone how rich and successful you are? Did you ever think I wanted to be treated, I don't know, like a person?"

My mouth opened, then closed, then opened again. "You never told me you felt that way."

"I tried."

But I'd been too caught up in my own excitement to listen. Dash didn't have to say so out loud—I got that and more just from the look in his eyes. A hot wave of embarrassment rushed over me as I suddenly remembered all that stuff he'd told me about his ex, who'd basically used him for views. And the older guy who'd only wanted a hot young man on his arm. And him smiling at me in the thrift shop and telling me that he liked being looked at, but once in a while he just felt like he needed to be seen. And, you know, me just booking it out of his immediate vicinity like he'd tried to set me on fire.

Yeah, I was a deeply shitty person.

If I'd been a better one, I would have said something to reassure him. I would have made it better. Because Dash was everything that was good in the world and he didn't deserve . . . well, me. He didn't deserve me losing my shit all over him yet again. Or living with the expectation that any little thing could set off my internal smoke alarms and make me bolt.

I think Dash saw the exact moment when I realized it, because he softened.

"I know that I have to get better at speaking out. I like you, Mariel—I like you *so* much. And I want something real with you. But every time I try to deepen our conversations just a little, I feel the way you start to shut me out. You won't let me in," he said gently. "And that's okay if all you want is to be buddies who bone, but I don't. I want something real. I *feel* something real. And I guess I need to know if you do, too. Or if you could, at some point in the future."

The trouble was, I could. I could see it with such clarity that it made everything inside me hurt. I wanted to trust him not just with my heart, but with all the small, scared parts of myself that I continually held back from him and from everyone else in my life. Including myself.

But *want* wasn't enough to quell the rising panic in my chest.

I'd trusted Milo, hadn't I? And I'd trusted Aria when she'd told me to stop running. Trust was something I was constantly investing in. It may not have been a finite resource once, but it was quickly running out.

Dash's chest was heaving with one deep breath after another as I took too long to answer him. I gazed back at him. The knots inside me hurt, and the only way I knew to stop things from hurting was to either ignore them or run away from them.

Or cut them out.

I could tell that Dash saw the urge in my face, because his soft, beautiful, articulate mouth flattened into a tight line. His eyebrows knitted together.

"Dash, I—"

That's when my phone started to buzz. And then it did it again and again and again. I won't insult your intelligence by lying and saying that I wasn't happy for an excuse to put the conversation on hold.

"What is it?" he asked, sounding resigned. "Are we going viral or something?"

"Yes," I said, caught between trying to keep any suspicious shininess from my eyes and trying not to hyperventilate as I handed him my phone. "Because Lady Cerulean just posted about you on Instagram."

◆ ◆ ◆

So far, most of our success had come from within the Fling app. Sure, I'd noticed that a few of our videos had been reposted to other platforms and that part of our traffic came from the teasers we posted on TikTok and Instagram, but for the most part, our audience was comprised of Fling users. Until now.

The Duke of Harding had breached containment. And not just

that, we'd landed on the main feed of the world's biggest . . . look, to call Lady C a musician would be to massively understate it. She was a phenomenon. A force of nature.

And one who knew we existed.

I scrolled through the first few comments, growing more and more overwhelmed by the response. Before I could get too far, my phone buzzed again with a text from Chase. I opened it to find a string of exclamation points and a long list of links to different publications that, if the first couple were any indication, were breathlessly reporting on Lady Cerulean's post. And I mean, it must have been a slow news day or the Duke of Harding thing must have been unusual enough that the story was getting picked up by all kinds of outlets.

Another text came in, this one from Tía Nena—a screenshot from the culture section in the fucking *Diario Libre* website. Wordlessly, I turned my phone so that Dash could see the screen. Though he probably couldn't read the text, which was in Spanish, the picture that went along with it was unmistakable.

He let out a breath and ran his hands through his hair. "That's . . .".

"Yeah," I replied.

When I tapped back into Fling, so many notifications were popping up that I felt like the phone should be growing warm in my hands. Carefully, almost gingerly, I set it down on the coffee table. Then I shrieked and jumped into Dash's arms, knocking him backward into the couch. I felt my ruffled top riding up as I straddled him, my hands finding his shoulders so that I could shake him as I screeched.

Dash folded his arms behind his head, his eyes shining. "You do realize . . . this is going to change everything."

"Yeah," I said, quieting down. "Are you ready?"

"I better be." Dash let out a breath. "I just . . . I'm glad I'm doing this with you, you know?"

"Yeah." I looked down at him. "I know."

And look. I was fully aware that we had this whole conversation hanging over our heads. That I didn't, actually, have the grace and maturity to deal with anything real. That I was going to flail and fuck everything up.

Just for a moment, though, I let myself relish how good it felt. How good all of this felt—Dash under me, Lady Cerulean posting about us, our phones about to spontaneously combust.

I could have stayed there forever, my thighs cradling Dash's hard ones and my palm pressed so tightly against his chest that I could feel his heartbeat against my skin. But another sudden barrage of texts had us scrambling to get on Instagram, where Lady C was hosting a livestream.

"Whoa, y'all are really into this guy, huh? Can't blame you. Did y'all check out his OnlyFans yet?" She laughed, and her lash extensions fluttered as she scanned the comments. "Of course you did. You're quick. I don't know, maybe I'll have to reach out, see if he wants to do a collab."

I wasn't hyperventilating—but that was mostly because I seemed to be utterly breathless.

Lady Cerulean smirked. "You like that?" she asked, and for a second I thought she was talking directly to me. Then I saw all the flame emojis in the comments.

"Shouldn't we say something?" Dash asked. His own phone was probably somewhere in the depths of the couch cushions, because for some ungodly reason he didn't feel the need to check our notifications every three point four minutes.

"Yeah. Hold on." I thought for a second, then typed, *I await your invitation with bated breath, my lady.* "That okay?"

Dash nodded, and I hit post.

The comments went so wild that our message was quickly obscured. Lady Cerulean blinked at the screen. "Wait, what just happened?" Her lips, slicked with her signature red lipstick, parted as she read through the comments that were scrolling by at increasingly faster speeds. "The Duke is here? What do you guys say—should I ask him to join the live?"

Another flood of comments and emojis. And then—a notification popped up. A request.

Screeching, I tossed the phone at Dash, who caught it neatly and leapt off the couch to stand in front of the curtains.

"Take off your shirt," I hissed.

His head snapped up. "What?"

"You're not in costume! You'll ruin the illusion! Take off your shirt!"

He hesitated for half a second before ripping off his T-shirt and tossing it toward the couch. And then his chest was bare, bathed in light from the window and framed against the blue backdrop of his curtains.

I didn't pause to stare longingly. I was already scrambling to my feet and racing over to his dining table, where his laptop sat open. Quickly plugging in his bougie noise-canceling headphones, I logged into my personal Instagram account and hopped over to Lady Cerulean's live.

The screen was split, with Lady Cerulean on the bottom, looking gorgeous in a very 1970s caftan. She was curled up on a chaise, surrounded by tropical plants with large, glossy leaves that reflected the purple light from the lamp next to her. The top half of the screen was fully occupied by Dash's face. And his neck and bare shoulders. Even though he wasn't in costume, he had slipped fully into Duke mode, adding a little bit of a smolder to his expression.

And judging by the wicked curl to her red lips, Lady Cerulean was eating it up. Because clearly not even someone with a shelf full of Grammys could resist Dash's rizz.

"Lady Cerulean," Dash was saying in his crisp Duke of Harding accent, "or should I call you Lady Scandal?"

"A hottie like you can call me anything he wants," she replied.

"Then you'd have no objection if I were to refer to you as darling?"

Lady Cerulean fanned herself. "Whew! Did anyone else's panties just flee the state?"

"I'd be more than pleased to offer my assistance in locating them," Dash shot back.

He didn't look the slightest bit nervous. Couldn't be me. I was close to peeing my pants and I was just a spectator.

My hands, pressed to the table on either side of the laptop, felt like they were vibrating. I kept glancing from my screen to Dash's face, and touching my sternum to try to control the fluttering there. Like Lady C with her panties, I had lost my shit so deeply and completely, I wasn't sure I'd ever find it again.

The smoky tinge to Lady Cerulean's voice made something sultry out of her low laugh. "I don't know how'd useful that would be, seeing as you're the one who caused them to vanish in the first place." Her long lashes grazed her cheekbones as she lowered her gaze, looking like she was catching up on comments. Something she saw made her laugh again. "My fans will never forgive me if I don't ask—are you single?"

My heart started pounding.

Dash's gaze remained on the screen. He let his lips soften into a smile that managed to look both bashful and like he had a sinful secret he didn't intend to reveal. "Now, you know that's not fair. A gentleman doesn't kiss and tell—he just takes his breeches off in public." He tossed off the line with a slight shrug of his shoulder and a flirty little wink that turned up the intensity in the comments.

Nobody's panties were a match for Dash at his most charming, and mine weren't exempt. My palm flat against my chest, I made my gaze skip from his and Lady Cerulean's faces to read what everyone was saying.

"And we love you for it," Lady C was saying as she settled back into the pillows of her chaise, somehow managing to keep her phone at a flattering angle. "We stan a man who gives us a little something to work with, if y'all catch my drift."

"I'm honored to help," Dash replied with a hair flip that had her fanning herself again.

Lady Cerulean laughed. "I better go before I self-combust. Your Grace, it was a pleasure making your acquaintance."

"Likewise, Lady Scandal. Dare I hope we meet again soon?"

"I think we just might." Lady Cerulean blew a kiss toward the screen. "I'll catch y'all soon, babies. Behave yourselves—and give the Duke here a follow."

She ended the live, and the laptop screen went dark. Behind it, Dash was lowering my phone, looking a little dazed.

"Holy shit," I breathed, taking off the headphones and setting them on the table next to his laptop. "I can't believe that just happened."

Dash rubbed a hand over his face, but he couldn't hide the grin that was beginning to spread over his lips. "It did," he confirmed. "That just happened. I just chatted with Lady Cerulean."

"And you called her Lady Scandal! That was brilliant!"

"Brilliant? It was terrifying."

"In a good way?"

He collapsed onto the couch and gazed at me from across the room. "It felt pretty good, yeah. I think. I feel like I blacked out for most of it."

"Well, even unconscious, you were really damn good. Everyone was going wild in the comments. I wouldn't be surprised if we got a few thousand followers out of that."

I think it hit us at the same time—Dash was no longer just internet famous. He was the real thing.

For one long moment, we just looked at each other. And it felt like we were suspended in a moment again, insects caught in amber for centuries. Inside that moment, everything might have been fine. We might have been able to brush our argument aside and keep going on our merry way.

Then the moment passed. And the exhilaration moving between us like a live current was replaced with awkwardness—if there'd been an epic film score rising over the past half hour, it would've ended with a sudden and discordant *twang*. Whether Dash knew it or not, this thing between us had always had an expiration date. We were only ever here for a fun time, not a long time. All the hurt feelings just made it clear that it was time to end it.

I closed his laptop and stood up. "So, about earlier."

The elation leeched out of Dash's face, leaving behind a wary line between his eyebrows. He grabbed his discarded T-shirt and started pulling it back on, so that his voice was muffled when he said, "Yeah?"

"Look, I think you need something out of this—" The word *relationship* got stuck in my throat. "Um, this. That I can't give you. I can't be who you want me to be."

"I don't want you to be anyone but yourself."

"And that's someone who can't do serious or real."

"Can't or won't?"

I let the silence speak for me. Dash sucked in a breath, jerking his head into a nod.

"We'll still work on Duke of Harding," I said, like that was any kind of consolation. "Take advantage of all the visibility and stuff."

"Sure." Dash looked away from me, though there was nothing on the wall to capture and hold his attention so intensely. Then he seemed to remember something, and glanced back at me. "What about the ball? For the Georgie Hart premiere? That's next month."

"You should probably count me out," I said. "I doubt you'll have any trouble finding a date, though."

I'd meant it as a joke, I guess. But there was no humor in Dash's eyes—and no twinkles, either—as he looked at me. "I never did."

"Right," I said. "I guess I should be going. I'll, uh, email you the next script as soon as I finish it."

I made it all the way down to the sidewalk before I let the impact of what I'd just done shudder over me.

This was no temporary third act breakup. This was the end of Dash and me.

20

I was so fucking tired of beginnings.

"Where the hell's my third act?" I muttered, staring at the screen of my laptop.

As my screenplay was still unhelpfully refusing to write itself, the only response I got was the blinking of the cursor next to the words *Act Three*. Groaning, I let my head thunk back against my headboard.

Anyone who'd ever met me would have guessed that I'd be as extra about being broken up with Dash as I was about being with him—and they'd be right. I had not only switched to a different laundromat, grocery store, and bodega to minimize the potential of accidental run-ins, I had devised a circuitous route to get to my apartment without having to pass anywhere near Dash's, or past Second Chance. It was so annoying that I ended up staying home more often than not, and though both Aria and Chase had texted me a few times to check in, we hadn't hung out like they'd suggested. I was fully in my hermit era and determined to finish my screenplay if it killed me.

I don't know when exactly I noticed that summer was almost over. It crept in at the edges of my awareness as I huddled in my apartment, writing scripts and answering emails and exchanging scrupulously polite work texts with Dash.

And then one day I forced myself to go out on a mental health walk and realized that a good handful of the trees in Central Park had started to shed their summer green.

Yaz had gone back to Miami to pack up her half of the apartment and tie up some loose ends, after which she'd go visit her mom in

Santo Domingo. Then she was coming back to New York. I'd told her she could stay with me while she figured things out, and even though she had offered to split the rent with me, I was determined to help her out instead.

So even though every fiber in me was straining to give up this whole Duke of Harding thing as yet another hobby I couldn't follow up on, even though I would have liked nothing better than to shove it all under my bed along with all the crap from past flails, I stuck with it.

I stuck with my mental health walks, too, and it wasn't just about procrastination. Even when that walking took up such a good chunk of the day that I was left with precious little time to work on anything but my screenplay and the scripts I was still consistently delivering to Dash.

And it wasn't like anybody asked, but I was technically doing research. In the sense that I was listening to books as I went, but also in the sense that I was developing a comprehensive knowledge of every one of Central Park's nooks and crannies, which was very helpful because that was where a good chunk of my movie was taking place.

I just had to decide if it was a romcom or a horror movie.

Giving up on any decision-making for the day, I flipped my laptop shut and made my way to the park. My head was pretty much buried in my tote as I dug around the layers of junk that had collected in the bottom, trying to find a missing AirPod so that I could finish listening to my *it's-technically-research-okay?* audiobook, when I predictably ended up bumping into someone.

And since I had meandered along a path that had put me perilously close to the Upper East Side, three guesses who that person was.

"Mrs. Greyson," I said with as much dignity and politeness as was possible to muster after having accidentally smacked into a former client who'd seen you unravel. "I'm so sorry."

She looked cool and perfectly put together in a white sheath, beige cardigan, and a handbag that was probably more expensive than my yearly rent. "There was no harm done."

I would have loved nothing more than to flash her a smile and keep going, but common courtesy dictated that I extend my mortification a little longer. "How's the project going?"

"We finished the remodel last week. The house turned out beautifully—Elaine's talent is undeniable."

I made noises that indicated my agreement, desperately wondering how to get out of this. But then Mrs. Greyson said something that made my mind screech to a halt.

"Mariel, I owe you an apology."

"Why?" I blurted out.

Mrs. Greyson's lips twitched up into what looked like a reluctant smile. "When we ran into you in Williamsburg, Elaine explained that she had fired you over our little disagreement. That wasn't my intention at all. As a matter of fact, I wanted you to know that it wasn't me who told her about it. And that I'm deeply grieved that you lost your job over such a small thing—I'd been under the impression that you had been switched to a different project. I know it didn't seem like it at the time, and, well, I know I can be very demanding sometimes . . ." She sighed.

This was the moment where I was supposed to rush in with reassurances that she hadn't been a literal nightmare to work with and that I hadn't felt actual dread every time I opened my eyes in the morning to the realization that I would have to be around her that day. I didn't quite have it in me to go that far, so all I said was "I can understand that you had standards to uphold."

"The fact remains that I was more demanding than usual during this project because—" Was the ice queen melting in the heat or were those actual tears in her eyes? "Because I knew that my marriage was in shambles and I was trying desperately to hold on. It was an unconscious impulse, maybe, wanting to buff away scratches and plaster over cracks, as if by doing so I could remake all that was going wrong in my marriage."

I saw it then, the deep grief that I had failed to recognize while my own was trying to pull me under. It was like one of those *New York Times* word puzzles that Yaz likes, where you look at a jumble of letters and it's impossible to see how they can make up a word, and then someone points out what that word is and your mind is blown over how obvious it was.

"I'm sorry," I blurted out. "Sounds like we were both going through a tough time."

She dipped her head into a nod. "For what it's worth, I do think you are a very good project manager. And I know you'll land on your feet whatever you do next."

"I . . . thank you, Mrs. Greyson."

Her perfectly lined lips moved into a restrained curve. Then, without saying anything further, she started to walk away.

And I guess I should have left it at that, but I called out to her before she could get very far. "Have *you*? Landed on your feet?"

When she turned around, her smile had widened into something more genuine. "I'm getting a divorce."

"Good for you," I told her.

I was still holding the AirPod as we turned back to our respective paths, but the audiobook was the furthest thing from my mind. My entire body was vibrating from the encounter, as if I was a game of Operation and Mrs. Greyson had knocked the tweezers too close to my edges. Because the truth was, I'd been plastering over cracks, too. Only mine were not the fissures of a marriage past repair, but all the little—and not so little—hurts that I had refused to see were causing structural damage in my heart.

Every time a relationship ended—or worse, failed to start. Every time I felt like my family didn't believe in me. Every time I was unable to believe in myself.

I sped up, each slap of my sneakers against the pavement coinciding with another item on the list.

Every word I had deleted from my screenplay. Every time Dash had tried to show me affection.

And it was as if I had shoved all of my hurt into a drawer and kept cramming things in there and all of a sudden, it was so stuffed that it had burst open.

I was not okay.

I was not okay, and I probably hadn't been okay since well before Milo, or else the breakup wouldn't have shattered me so thoroughly.

It was too hot to run and I was definitely not dressed for it. I must have been doing it anyway, because the summer lushness of the park was blurring past and people were jerking strollers out of my way and I had to pull myself sharply to the left to avoid getting tangled up with a dog walker, and I had somehow gotten to the section of Central Park that was directly across from the Museum of Natural History, which was on the exact opposite side from where I'd run into Mrs. Greyson.

But the thing about running is that you can't escape yourself.

Or the fact that what haunted me most was that maybe I was like my mom. And my father, and anyone who had ever left me. That I was as much of a coward as all the people who had ghosted me.

I let my AirPod fall back inside my tote, and grabbed my phone instead. Swiping past dozens of notifications, I went into my contacts and found the string of emojis that signified nothing and simultaneously everything. And I pressed the call button.

My breath caught when I heard a ring. And then another and another, and my fingertips were digging into the hard plastic of my phone case when the sound was replaced by a voice I hadn't heard in months.

"Mami?" I tried to take a deep breath, and felt it snag somewhere deep inside me so that the next thing to come out of my mouth sounded like a sob. "I need you."

◆ ◆ ◆

I couldn't remember the last time when a conversation with my mother hadn't sounded like a terrible mistake. But I guess it was one I was about to make, right there in public, with people milling around me rattling iced coffees and taking selfies and poring over map apps.

Without thinking too hard about it, I turned left on Central Park West and began making my way down the side of the park as I told my mom that no, I hadn't lost any limbs, loved ones, or—before I could think of another word that started with L that wasn't *lizards*, she interrupted me to ask what was wrong.

You already know I tried hard to find any trace of impatience in her voice. All I got was worry, though. Justifiable worry, given that I had called her—like, on the *phone*—out of the blue to tell her that I needed her.

The thing was, I didn't quite know how to answer her. I mean, what was I supposed to say? After years of trying my hardest to push down any emotion related to what were probably some intense—and again, justifiable—abandonment issues, I finally admitted to myself that I was sad because my mommy didn't, I don't know, follow me to college and instead chose to have a life of her own?

"I, um."

I'd never felt the need to give my mother credit for being perceptive, but she seemed to sense that I was not exactly in the best position to answer her.

"I'm glad to hear from you," she said. "I had a missed call from you, from days ago. I tried to call you back, and when I couldn't reach you, I called Yaz."

"And she told you I was on the verge of a meltdown?"

"She told me," Mami said gently, "that it seemed like you needed me. I know I haven't been around a whole lot lately, but that doesn't mean that I don't care about you or that I don't want you to feel like you can lean on me when you're in trouble."

"Good to know." I tried to say it lightly, but my words were dragged down by, oh, a decade of resentment.

Which Mami of course couldn't fail to hear. And I had to give her credit again, this time for not heaving a weary sigh into the phone. "It's on me that you don't know that, Mariel. I guess I need to do better when it comes to saying these things out loud. And acting on them, too."

"I think . . . I guess I could do better about asking for help when I need it."

"Why *do* you need help, Chiquita?"

"Because I . . ." The air was as thick as soup, making it hard to catch my breath. "I tried to straighten my hair this morning and accidentally fried it and now I'm pretty sure I ruined my curls forever."

The newly stiff shanks had managed to remain straight while acquiring the same amount of volume my curls would have, which looked . . . interesting, to say the least. I had wrestled the whole mass into a scrunchie as best as I could, and then spent another half hour trying to jam a hat over it before giving up.

"Boy trouble, huh? Or, well, it's been long enough since we've talked that I guess I should say relationship trouble instead. In case anything's changed."

"Nothing's changed. And you're not fully wrong. It's more like . . . existential crisis trouble?"

"Then you should count yourself lucky you didn't experiment with bangs instead," Mami said. What can I say? I come by my emotion-deflecting tendencies honestly.

I paused at a crosswalk while I waited for the light to change, standing at the edge of a crowd of tourists bickering over where they were going to have dinner. "Considering that instead I experimented with hooking up with my for-all-intents-and-purposes business partner and then flailed my way out of something that could've been really good, maybe bangs would have been better."

You had to give it to my mom—she didn't rush in with empty platitudes. I mean, could she have been a tiny bit reassuring? Sure. Would it have helped? Probably not.

"Nothing is worse than bangs," she said firmly. "But I can see why your existence is in crisis. We Rivera women don't do great when it comes to love, do we?"

"Yaz had it good there for a while. But yeah. We all deeply suck at relationships—and yet, none of us are in therapy."

"Speak for yourself. Nena and I are doing the work. And Yaz was talking about finding someone new when she comes up to New York to stay with you."

"Then I guess it's just me, then. At least until I'm back on some kind of insurance."

The conversation stalled again. Shocking, I know, when health insurance was such a fascinating subject. And such a good excuse to not talk about what was actually on my mind.

Mami had never actually come out and said that I was the worst thing ever to happen to her, but it was implied by the way she'd fucked off the day after I'd turned eighteen. Here's the thing, though— as much as Mami leaving had been this stormy cloud hovering over my head, I had never actually talked to her about it. Or, well, to anyone really, if you didn't count the oblique snarky comments I'd made to Yaz over the years. So like the coward I was, I veered away from it and asked about something else instead.

"We never talk about my father and why he left me."

"Chiquita, your father didn't leave you, he left *me*. And honestly…" Her deep breath rustled into the receiver. "I'm the reason he didn't fight harder to stay in your life."

"Or maybe he's just a bastard who's never thought about me after he ran off," I offered.

"I won't argue with you about the bastard thing. We still have a few mutual friends from back in the day, though, and I know for a fact that not seeing you grow up has weighed on him." I couldn't tell if the sound Mami made was a laugh or a sniffle, or a strange combination of both. "I'm so damn sorry, Mariel. If you want to get in touch with him now, I could—"

"I don't," I said, and I meant it. Whatever space my dad might have left behind had been filled up pretty quickly by Tía Nena and Yaz and even Mami herself. But when Mami left . . . her space was so uniquely shaped that nothing could've filled it. "I've never really been all that curious about him. You're the only parent that I've ever really needed."

That was definitely a sniffle. "Mariel . . ."

I had to say it. "Which is why I've been wondering why *you* left."

There was quiet on the other end of the line. The kind of quiet that pressed in even while I passed a cabbie slamming his horn at a teenager in roller skates and someone blasting music as they whizzed by on a bike, and approximately fifteen million other people carrying on conversations of their own.

Finally, Mami said, "I had a lot of growing up to do. But before I could do that, I had to take some time to be the kid I never got to be."

"Because of me."

"Not only because of you. Nena and I don't talk about it much, but we both had a hard time when our mother died. We were so young. *She* was so young. And even though Nena was older than me, she took Mami's death the hardest. Our father, too." I had faint memories of an older man with a mustache who'd get on the floor and build blocks with me and Yaz. "So I took over. For years, I was the only one in the house who went grocery shopping. Who made sure our school uniforms were clean and ironed. I bullied Nena into doing her homework and applying for college and moved us to Miami. Sneaking out with your father was the only scrap of rebellion that I allowed myself. And then you came along and . . ."

"Ruined your life?" I suggested, trying for funny and ending up somewhere closer to pathetic.

"Made me remember my priorities," she corrected gently. "At the top of which was my family—which now included you. I spent twenty-five years devoted to other people, Chiquita," she said, and I suddenly remembered that she was the one who'd started calling me that. "Nena always said that I'd been forced to grow up too fast, but the truth was that I never really got to grow up at all. I didn't have the time to figure out who I really was or what I wanted out of life. And I was haunted by the idea that I'd get to forty without knowing anything about myself."

I guess it shouldn't have been quite so reassuring to know that she was haunted about stuff, too. But then again, aren't we all? Who among us isn't carting around all the ghosts of who we wanted to become and who we loved or we wanted to love us?

"I like to think that I would've never left if I knew you still needed me. But . . ." There was a brief pause. "I don't know how sure I can be of that."

It wasn't perfect, but it was honest. And that was something I could live with.

"I tried not to need you," I said, and turned left at random, not really heading anyplace in particular. "I'm an adult. What kind of adult needs their mommy?"

"I did," she said. "I need her still. And I miss her still. And I . . . Shit, Mariel, I made you go through the same thing I went through, didn't I? Only with the extra baggage of knowing your mom left on purpose. How much did I screw you up?"

"Oh you know, just enough that I ran away from the first chance I've ever had at having a real relationship with someone amazing."

"No big deal, huh? I guess I should go line up for my Shitty Parent of the Decade award."

"I haven't nominated you yet," I told her. "But only because I don't even have your current zip code. Which honestly makes me a not-so-great daughter myself."

"No, that's on me. I should have called you sooner to tell you the news, but I was waiting until I was settled in before saying anything, in case it didn't stick. You'll be happy to know that I finally have a permanent address."

"I don't know what it says about us that I gotta ask in which country."

Mami laughed. "I'm actually in Vegas. Have been for a couple months now. It's, uh. Kind of a long story."

"It better be a good one."

"I hope so." She blew out a breath. "I'm interviewing for a new job as general manager of a chain of hotels. One that will keep me in one place for a good long while. I already looked at a few places, and I found an apartment with a spare bedroom for you and Yaz and Nena to stay in when you visit me. If you want to, that is."

"I want to."

"Good—we'll make plans as soon as I hear about the job. In the meantime, Nena told me that you were working on this big project?"

I let out a laugh. "So it's called the Duke of Harding."

We must have spoken for another hour, catching each other up on all things, big and small, that we'd missed. I thought I'd feel hungover again when I hung up, but instead there was this lightness spreading over me.

After that, reaching out to Milo didn't seem nearly as impossible as I would've imagined. Because even though I wasn't the one who'd ghosted, I was the one with unfinished business. So I paused, leaning against the warm brick of a building as I opened my personal Instagram account and found his profile.

I didn't deserve being lied to, I typed into a DM. *No matter how loud I was, or how dramatic, or how sure you were that I was going to cause some sort of scene. Not when you knew how much I had started to care for you. I meant what I said about not wanting your apology. I don't want explanations or excuses, either. I just want you to know that you did hurt me. And whether I was too much for you or not enough, I deserved honesty.*

I hit send. And then I really was free.

I'd wandered clear across Manhattan, from the west side back to the east, only this time I was closer to 59th Street than the Upper East Side. And that meant I was close to the Roosevelt Island Tramway.

Acting more on impulse than any semblance of rational thought—you know, for a change—I started walking toward the station. I used my virtual MetroCard to get through the turnstile and waited with a little knot of people for the tram. When it came, I climbed onto the shiny red car and stepped into the corner, where I could look down.

It was the wrong time of day for glittering city lights, but I was in time to catch the beginning of sunset. The shades of pink and orange that looked like melted gelato as they seeped into the blue of the sky were echoed by the river and repeated in the windows of the buildings crowding Midtown Manhattan. I was gazing out toward the snarl of metal and concrete that had somehow, inexplicably, become home in a way it never had been before when an incoming message made my phone buzz in my hand.

I knew even before I looked that it was Milo's reply.

You're not too much, Mariel. And I'm the one who wasn't enough.

21

It was full dark when I got home, armed with a pizza and a few packages of powdered donuts from the bodega. Believe it or not, the first thing I did after locking the door behind me wasn't stuff my face. I found my laptop and pulled up my screenplay.

Because as I'd waited for the crosstown bus to get back to Hell's Kitchen, all the day's emotionally charged conversations swirling around my head, I had realized why I'd been finding it so hard to work on it.

As long as I didn't finish it, I couldn't mess it up.

I'd already made such a mess out of everything else in my life, though. What was one more failure?

I dug out all the discarded Bullet Journal paraphernalia from under my bed and got to work outlining the main beats of my story, using stickers and washi tape and brush-tipped markers to separate the three acts.

If I'd been living in a movie, the rest of the draft would've come pouring out of me then, in a montage set to Lady Cerulean's most bubblegum tones. But real life—not to mention my brain—was slightly slower than that. By the end of the hour, though, I did have a bunch of aggressively decorated pages. And a solid plan for how to get to the end.

Ghosted! was going to be a romcom about this psychic who thought she'd gotten ghosted on a first date, only to find out later that the guy had actually died on his way to meet her. Then his ghost shows up with a request to help him solve his murder, which of course leads her into getting involved with his handsome business partner.

But it was also about me, and trying to fit into this city, and the funnier parts of my incredibly unrewarding dating life, and . . .

And yeah, all the ways in which I'd been too scared to fight for what I wanted.

I'm not gonna lie—I'd gotten so used to Dash's presence as I wrote, whether in the shared doc or by my side, that typing on a fresh, white document and seeing only my cursor was an indescribable kind of lonely. Even without his input, though, the words flowed as they never had before.

Working on scripts for the Duke of Harding, I had learned to write for Dash. I had learned how to structure a sentence to match the cadence of his speech. I knew the words he liked saying, and when he liked to take a pause. As I worked on my screenplay, I learned how to write for myself.

And I did it, going into full goblin mode inside my increasingly messy apartment, fueled by huge amounts of pizza and cookies and other round, flat food. For more than two weeks, I typed until I gave myself carpal tunnel. Then I iced my throbbing wrists and typed some more. I didn't just finish the third act—I went back to the first and the second and dug into the emotional core of the story in a way I hadn't really allowed myself to before. It wasn't easy. In fact, it was hard enough that at least twice a day I thought about shoving my laptop under my bed. I actually did it once, but then I came up with this great line of dialogue and I was forced to fish out my laptop and write it down before I forgot it.

So yeah, I may have struggle-bused my way to the end, but I got there eventually. And when I did, the satisfaction that welled up inside me was so strong that I had to sit there for a few minutes, just . . . existing with the knowledge that this was something I had done. Mariel Rivera, flailer extraordinaire, quitter of everything halfway, had actually finished her screenplay. And I didn't know if it was good or anything, but at least it was done.

After I had basked in relief for a day or two, rereading the whole thing about twenty-eight times, I sucked in a deep breath and emailed Grace Hong, thanking her again for offering to read my screenplay and asking if I could send it to her. And I ended my email by adding a few links and a note that read, Here are a few samples of my work, in case you know anyone who would be interested in more of this kind of thing.

She got back to me way faster than I thought she would. Wait, you're the writer behind that Regency guy who's been going viral?? Those videos are amazing, and not just because he looks like he was made in a factory. Any chance you would want to collaborate on a Regency romcom? Not another Jane Austen adaptation, but something original and ideally featuring people of color. I'm still in L.A. but I should be getting back to the city next month, so if you're interested, it'd be nice to chat over coffee.

My hand went immediately to my phone, and I went so far as to type out a message before realizing that it wasn't Yaz I'd unconsciously tried to reach out to. It was Dash.

It wasn't just that he'd embodied the Duke. He'd embodied every daydream I hadn't let myself have. And now that one of them was coming true, he was the one I wanted to celebrate with.

I didn't know how to reach out to him, though. Or how to make myself text him about something other than work when I didn't know if he'd even want to hear from me. So instead, I did the next best thing—I went to Second Chance.

◆ ◆ ◆

The Barbie blonde from the burlesque event was covering the register, Shy nowhere to be seen. I gave her a wave as I made my way to the garden, holding my breath a little as I pushed open the back door. It wasn't until I stepped out onto the flagstones and my breath gusted out that I realized I'd been expecting . . . something. I don't know. That by some wild, magical coincidence Dash would be there, waiting for me.

As I perched on the swing and twisted myself around, I caught sight of Kitty Marlowe stepping delicately out from behind the tree.

"Well, Kit, looks like it's just you and me."

Giving me a disdainful look, she pushed her way through the cat door.

"Yeah," I said to her retreating tail. "I don't want to be around me either."

There was a slight but very definite chill in the air, making me glad I'd worn jeans and a striped vest over my flowered shirt. As the humidity lessened, so did the size of my hair, which I'd bundled into an oversized scrunchie.

In the movie version of my life, the secret garden would have been in full bloom. Just a total riot of pinks and purples and oranges, and butterflies flitting among the leaves, a long tracking shot moving slowly through all the colors before reaching me on the swing.

In reality, it was late September. Leaves in shades of orange and brown drifted down from the branches above me, dancing lazily over the bare flagstones. Okay, so maybe coming to Second Chance had been a mistake. Maybe I needed to move on and find a new place to hang out in. Not a cafe, that was for sure. Or another bookstore. But there was that bar on Tenth where—

The garden door banged open. And I think the small part of me that did believe in wild, magical coincidences must have expanded out into the universe and sent some kind of signal, because it was Dash coming out into the garden, Kitty Marlowe purring in his arms.

He was in a pair of tapered slacks that I'd never seen. Under his black denim jacket, his shirt left the triangle of skin at the base of his neck bare enough for me to notice, with a lump in my throat, that he wasn't wearing his necklace.

"Oh. Mariel. Hey." With a scratch between the ears, he set the cat down and took a few cautious steps toward the swing. "I thought Shy was back here—we're meeting up to go over designs for the next window."

"I haven't seen them. I was just . . ." I shrugged, changing tacks before I finished the sentence. "I finished my screenplay."

"Hey, that's great! Congrats," he offered. "I knew you would."

I tugged at one of my curls, destroying the shape as I pulled it taut and released it. "That makes one of us, because I was sure that I would abandon it like I do everything else—and pretend I never wanted it in the first place."

"But you didn't," Dash said, a slight flick of his eyebrows betraying his surprise at hearing me talk about my feelings so candidly.

"I stuck with it, believe it or not. All the way to the end. Even though it was hard, and even though it turns out that crafting an emotionally honest story involves, you know, being honest with your emotions. And feeling them, and thinking about them, and all the things I told you weren't worth doing. Which, spoiler alert, were absolutely worth it. And not just for the sake of the screenplay."

Dash leaned against the trunk of the tree. "Did your story turn out to have a happily ever after?"

"It did, actually." I wanted so badly to ask if *we* had a happily ever after, but instead, all I did was dig my phone out of my pocket. "Also, I made a couple changes to our Duke of Harding bio. I hope it's okay."

I tapped my way into our Fling profile and held up the screen so that he could see the words I'd added earlier that day: *Created by Mariel Rivera and Dashwood Bennet.*

He studied it quietly for a while before saying, "I thought you didn't want to ruin the illusion."

"About that . . ." I tucked my phone away. "It was less about ruining the illusion than being scared to fail out loud. I guess I figured that if the project flopped, no one would really know it was me, so it wouldn't really count as a failure. Or something. There wasn't exactly a lot of thought involved in the process."

Another pause, this one shorter. "I thought you were ashamed of me," Dash admitted. "That you didn't mind doing this for the money or whatever, but that you didn't want your name associated with it."

I shook my head. "I'm so proud of everything we've done. And

I'm sorry I didn't make that clearer to you, especially after you told me about that asshole finance guy you dated."

"I guess I should have been a little more up front about my feelings, too," Dash said.

I snorted. "As if I would've let you. Never mind running, I'd probably have hopped on a plane to get away from *that* conversation."

He offered me something that wasn't quite a smile, not really, but it had the potential to become one. "Are you open to hearing a little more about my feelings now?"

I straightened up, nodding. "Try me."

He paused for a second, like he was trying to gather his thoughts. When he finally began speaking, his voice was slow and measured and almost thoughtful. "I feel like I'm always performing. For the fangirls, sure, but also for my parents, to keep them from realizing how much their competitiveness gets to me. I even do it for random people in the street who take one glance at me and immediately start spinning into daydreams of who they think I am. Spending time with you, it was like I could finally be . . . just myself."

"I noticed that," I said softly.

"Then your cousin's visit was coming up and I was feeling this pressure to . . . well, to perform again." The rest of his words came out in a tidal wave of emotion that would probably have drowned me a month or two before. "And it brought me back to where I was last year. I told you that I started doing OnlyFans with my ex. I didn't tell you that we were only posting on her profile, at first. It took me an embarrassingly long time to realize that she didn't want to be with me anymore and was just using me for content. And then I stayed anyway, because she was in a tough spot and she really did need the money. Hence her accusing me of having a hero complex." Dash raked a hand through his hair. "The thing is, though, I mostly stayed because I wanted to be in a relationship so badly. Then the same thing happened with the older guy. Then you. I keep turning the past few weeks over and over again in my mind, and I can't help feeling like I was trying to pressure you into something you weren't ready for—or something you didn't want in the first place . . ."

My hand tightened on the swing's chain as I blurted out, "Dash, my mom left me."

He stilled, like someone trying not to scare off a skittish animal.

"My father, too. He left us, like, five minutes after I was born. He and my mom were all of eighteen when they had me. She did her best when I was little, but . . . well, there's a lot of backstory there. The point is that she grew up too fast, without any time to herself that wasn't spent caring for someone else. The moment I was old enough to fend for myself, she left. And she's been gone ever since."

He let my words settle into the air between us. "I did always wonder why you never talked about your parents. Why didn't you tell me?"

I let out a breath before admitting, "It makes me feel like there's something wrong with me that even my own parents couldn't be bothered to stick around for me. Like, why would anyone else? Then Milo left, too, and it felt like I didn't just lose him. I lost this image I was starting to get of myself, as a person who deserved someone who stayed."

"I'd have stayed for you, Mariel," Dash said softly, and the past tense slayed me.

"I know." I lifted my gaze to his. "I think that's maybe what scared me so much. Dash, my parents peaced out on me. Everyone I've dated has ended up ghosting. I used to think that if they only got to know me, they'd stick around. But then Milo"—I waved my hands—"*happened*, and it convinced me that everyone left me because they had gotten to know me. And I think that on some level, I would've always been waiting for it to happen with you. And the longer you stayed, the worse it would hurt when you did finally leave. So no—you didn't pressure me into anything I didn't already want and was too scared to reach for."

There was an entire book's worth of unspoken thoughts behind his eyes when he met my gaze. "Are you still too scared?"

We'd come too far for me not to be honest with him. "I don't know. Maybe I am. Maybe I always will be."

A beat went by, then he nodded. "I think I can understand that."

The heartbreaking thing was that he probably did. He understood all my limitations, accepted them even—but it didn't mean that he was willing to continue wasting his time with me.

I sat in the knowledge of it for what felt like a full minute, just breathing in. I wasn't going to see Dash in the fall, or surprise him with seasonal candles, or wrap my arms around him from behind as he stirred something warm and hearty at the stove.

I was going to have to unpick most of the strings we'd woven together, even though I was sure that most of them wouldn't survive it. But I would. I'd be okay. Who knew, I might even thrive.

That was that, then.

I hopped off the swing to stand in front of him, as earnest and open as I knew how to be. "For what it's worth, Dash, I've never felt as safe with anyone as I did with you."

"That's good to hear," he said softly.

"You're an amazing person. You deserve to be with someone who can give you everything you need. Who isn't constantly holding back or thinking about how to use you to make themselves look better. And you know what? You're going to find them. You're going to get your happily ever after."

Even if it wasn't with me.

Something flickered in his eyes—a moment later, though, it was gone.

There weren't any cinematic kisses or grand gestures, but as I walked out of Second Chance and turned toward home, I felt the deep sense of closure of one movie ending so that another one could begin.

22

A full week of exchanging emails with Grace went by before she suggested me coming out to Los Angeles instead of waiting for her to return to New York. I'd had a virtual meeting with her agent, who was interested in representing me, another one with Grace's producer friend, and who knew? Maybe L.A. was where I needed to be right now. Not a pivot, but a clean slate. A fresh start away from New York and all its ghosts.

My share of the Duke of Harding proceeds was enough that I could afford the plane ticket and a week's stay and also pay my rent. The steady stream of viewers and subscribers had become a deluge after Lady Cerulean's livestream and even though Dash and I hadn't seen each other in person after meeting in Second Chance, we were back to collaborating on multiple scripts per week, enough to update Fling and OnlyFans with new videos every couple of days. Even though the Google Docs were sadly devoid of flirtatious comments these days, things were going surprisingly well. We had a publicist now, and partnerships with brands, and a producer of romantic audio had reached out to ask us to pitch him a new project.

Best of all, we had a fandom. Like, for real. The self-named Hardies were going hard (heh), writing fan fiction about the Duke and making fan art and edits and tagging us in requests to do a meet and greet at Fling's annual romance con. We'd even gotten duetted by other creators in Regency costumes. Being the inspiration behind such a thriving community was more than I'd ever even dared to hope for and not being able to squeal over it with Dash did feel kinda like a thorn in a bouquet of roses.

A crisp breeze was coming in through my open window as I

finished zipping up my suitcase and rolled it to the door. With only three and a half hours until my flight, I should have probably started heading out. Instead, I leaned against my counter and thought about how Dash was probably on his way to the premiere of the Georgie Hart series, in the fancy new Duke of Harding evening wear we'd ordered when we thought we'd be going together. My own dress had arrived a couple of days before, and I hadn't even opened the package before shoving it deep under the mess in my closet.

I must have had some kind of masochistic streak, because I opened up my Fling app and checked the updates Dash was posting on the Duke of Harding account. He *was* at the ball—with Lady Cerulean on his arm.

Something like bittersweetness kindled inside my chest as I scrolled through Dash's clips and pictures and thought of how incomprehensibly spectacular it was that in the course of three months, we had gone from me being chased by people wanting to believe I was Lady Cerulean to Dash attending the premiere of a streaming series with the real deal as his guest.

He was handsome in dark blue, as at ease in the spotlight when it involved dozens of cameras pointed at him as when it was just the two of us in his spare room. Lady Cerulean was also in blue, her Regency costume embellished with what looked like tiny feathers and beads.

I went into the premiere's hashtag, telling myself I just wanted to see a detail shot of her star-shaped necklace. There were more clips of the two of them than of the show's actual cast—understandable, seeing as how the two of them shimmered and sparkled with a light all their own.

The bright sting of tears prickled at my eyes. They were proud tears, I guess, if not entirely happy ones. Dash and I had come so far. We'd flown so high. And against all odds, instead of plummeting back down to earth, we were both still soaring.

My intercom chose that moment to make a rude noise. I'd have ignored it, seeing as I wasn't expecting anyone, but the intercom went off again with a series of buzzes in quick succession that had me lunging for the receiver.

"I didn't order anything," I said irritably.

"Mariel, it's Aria. Shy and I are downstairs and if you don't buzz us up right now, I swear to all that is good in the universe that I will—*fmphh!*"

"As much as I really like being fmphed—" I started to say before another voice cut me off.

"Sorry, Mariel," Shy said over Aria's muffled protests. "Would you please let us up? We came to bring you ice cream and books, not to issue threats against your person."

"I have serious doubts about that," I said, but I pressed the button.

"We've been worried about you," Aria said as she came inside, her Doc Martens making her look like she was stomping. Well, okay, and also the fact that she *was* stomping a little bit.

Shy glided in with a little less force, wearing a short-sleeved shirt in a shade of deep blue that matched the blueberries on their tote, and cradling a brown paper bag that did, in fact, contain All The Ice Cream. They busied themself lining up the cartons on my counter— then realized my counter was way too short and started stacking them instead—and setting out the cone-shaped bowls and colored plastic spoons they'd also brought.

As for Aria, she had dropped a load of paperbacks on my bed, shoved aside the ever-present bundle of clean laundry, and was sitting there with her arms crossed, glaring at me.

Between the two of them, the parent energy was so strong that I was half-afraid they would pick up and leave.

"Where the hell have you been?" Aria asked as Shy dished out the ice cream and toppings. "And why the hell did you go radio silent on us?"

"I replied to your texts," I said defensively.

"Lol idk is not a reply. Especially not when someone's asking how you are."

I took the ice cream Shy offered me and sat cross-legged on the sliver of floor in front of the bed. "I'm sorry I haven't been better about keeping in touch."

"We were worried about you," Shy said, passing Aria a bowl and joining me on the floor. At the collar of their shirt was a pin shaped like a stack of pancakes smothered in syrup. "Dash told us that the two of you decided to keep things strictly professional?"

They said it with a question mark, as if they weren't sure they'd heard right.

"Yeah," I said, picking at a toasted coconut flake. "We should have never gotten involved in the first place."

The noise Aria made conveyed exactly how incorrect she thought my statement was.

I pushed back a stray curl. "Look, it's just too complicated to date someone when you're working on a project together. Which is actually doing really well. It'd be silly for us to jeopardize everything we've been working toward just for—"

"For the sake of true, everlasting love?" Aria snapped. "Yeah, seems silly."

I didn't bother correcting her, and not just because I knew she'd argue back. But because the word *love* had snagged against something inside me, like when your sweater gets caught in someone else's bracelet and you're momentarily brought short. And I remembered feeling it before, when we'd been working on the window display and I'd been so full of this sense of possibility and connection and I hadn't flailed my way out of . . . everything I'd ever wanted.

"Well anyway, it's too late."

Aria looked thoroughly unconvinced by my shrug, but she did soften a little, much like the untouched ice cream in my bowl. "Do you know why Shy named the store Second Chance?"

"Because it's their favorite romance trope?"

Shy shook their head. "It didn't used to be. Not until Aria and I got back together after being apart for six years."

"You broke up for *six* years?"

Aria nodded. "And they were pretty good years for both of us. We dated some amazing people, got head starts in our careers, we figured out what we really wanted from our lives . . . and more importantly, we grew as people. So when we came across each other again, we were better equipped to be part of a mature relationship."

"Are you trying to tell me that I should stay away from Dash for another few years?"

"No, you bonehead," Aria said, rolling her eyes. "I'm trying to tell you that it's never too late."

Shy set their ice cream down. "Obviously," they said, shooting a look at Aria, "no one can tell what's going on in any given relationship except for the people in it. From the outside, though, it looks like you and Dash make each other happy. If that's not the case, then maybe you made the right decision."

"But given your tendency to run when you get scared," Aria put in, "I'd say there were some deep, unresolved issues at play."

"I've been working on resolving them," I admitted. "But I'm still scared. Not of Dash hurting me, really, not anymore. But what if I do run again? What if I hurt *him*?"

"Then we really will issue threats against your person," Shy said, making me crack a smile.

Aria gestured with her spoon. "I don't know, Mariel. People hurt each other all the time—over big stuff and little stuff. And it's always easier to leave than to stay. But remember the new beginnings we talked about? And the ace of cups?"

I'd taken the card out of my mirror frame when I was cleaning up the apartment for Yaz's visit, half-afraid she'd comment on it and I'd be forced to disclose yet another flail. Which yeah, felt a little silly, given everything that had happened. The card was still buried under several layers of socks and underwear, where I didn't have to look at it every day and know that I had undone the tiny bit of progress Aria had managed to wring out of me.

"I'm trying not to avoid feeling my feelings anymore," I said.

"And?" Aria prompted.

"And I hadn't realized how scared I was to fight for the things and the people I wanted. And I guess I'm still scared. But I'm also . . . I'm supposed to be leaving for L.A. tonight." I checked the time on my phone. "Shit, I'm late. I'm going to have to race to the airport and there won't even be a declaration of love at the end of it."

"So that's it?" Aria demanded, setting her bowl down. "You're just gonna run away again? You're not gonna try to win Dash back?"

"Not tonight," I told her. "I can't miss my flight. And anyway, he's at this event with Lady freaking Cerulean, who is now apparently his new bestie. Or his date. Maybe they're the ones who are going to overcome the odds and have a beautiful happily ever after."

And it said a lot about Shy and Aria's ability to distract me that I'd managed to forget the image of Dash and Lady C being gorgeous and perfect and historically accurate together. A few weeks ago, that would have sent me into a spiral. All I did now, though, was stick a spoonful of cake batter ice cream into my mouth and calmly tell myself that whatever I felt for him, Dash and I were just not meant to be.

Only Aria was rolling her eyes. "Yes. Dash is madly in love with a Grammy award–winning pop star. That's exactly why he stopped by Second Chance earlier and wistfully said he wished he was going with you."

"He *did*?" I flicked a coconut flake at Aria. "You could have *said* something."

Not one to back down from a fight, she picked up a paperback from the stack she and Shy had brought and sent it sailing toward me. "Well, I'm saying something now—you better stop letting your fear get the better of you and fight for your happiness."

"It's okay if Dash isn't your happiness," Shy put in. "If there's a chance he could be part of it, though . . ."

I picked up the paperback, a Georgie Hart from a decade ago with a couple embracing in a garden and a Kitty Marlowe look-alike perched atop a stone wall. I smoothed out its creased pages, then dragged a fingertip over the spine.

Maybe my relationship with Dash—what was left of it—was like a cracked spine. You know, permanently damaged. Try as you might to unbend it, the crease is always there.

Aria opened her mouth as if to say something else, but Shy laid an arresting hand on her arm and she subsided, though from her glower it was clear that she still had a lot to say.

Exchanging the paperback for my phone, I opened Fling again to look at the latest picture Dash had posted. And that was when I saw it—nestled just below the silk cravat we'd picked out together was the necklace I'd given him.

The thing about a cracked spine is that it doesn't prevent you from actually reading a book. And maybe the cracks of Dash and me didn't have to be scars—maybe they could be laugh lines.

◆　◆　◆

So yeah, I dug out the costume from the back of my closet and let my self-proclaimed fairy godparents help me get all glammed up to go to the ball, figuring I could always reschedule my flight to Cali if tonight didn't go according to plan.

My empire-waist gown was white. In a departure from the inspiration pictures we'd pored over, the dressmaker and I had chosen to embellish the gauzy overlay with dozens of multicolored beads that looked like sprinkles. Which was particularly appropriate, seeing as the bodice of the gown was so well constructed that it made my boobs look like two scoops of ice cream.

There were more beads on my white satin shoes, as well as on the clips I'd gotten for my hair, which Shy was attempting to wrangle into a braid along the crown of my head.

"I gotta say, when you commit to a theme, you don't exactly hold back," remarked Aria, who was giving me a glazed donut manicure—and inadvertently revealing just how much time she spent on Hailey Bieber's Instagram.

"My spirit, much like my hair, cannot be contained," I replied.

If I'd been writing this moment into a screenplay, I would've been tempted to turn it into a montage, set to some fun bop. For once, though, I was glad this was real life and that I could soak in every second of Aria and Shy squabbling amicably as they helped me turn into my best Regency self.

They came down with me when my Lyft arrived, waiting on the sidewalk like they were going to whip out handkerchiefs to wave in the air as my carriage rolled away. I looked at them, desperately grateful for everything that had happened over the summer to lead me to the two of them.

"Guys," I called out to them, hanging on to the Lyft's open door. "I just—You know how much I appreciate you both, right?"

Shy blew me a kiss.

All Aria did, though, was scowl. "Save it for Dash," she told me, coming up to me. "And get in the car already. You remember the chariot you pulled that night, right? I'm pretty sure it was less about running away and more about this moment. Not just moving on, but moving forward. So what are you waiting for? Fly, you fool."

Missing my flight to pull off some kind of grand gesture was pretty much the opposite of all the romcoms I loved. I'd always enjoyed a good subversion, though. As the rideshare sped toward Lincoln Center and I looked out the window at the city flashing past me in streaks of light and color, I examined myself for any shreds of doubt.

I had plenty of those crowding inside me—fears, too. The belief that I was easy to leave had been at the center of everything I'd done for years. Even after talking to my mom, and getting that scrap of validation from Milo, I wasn't sure I had fully released its grip on me. I'd always be just a little hesitant in relationships. Just a little anxious. Just a little too eager to notice any red flags so I could do the leaving first.

The only thing that had changed was that I was finally admitting to myself that I didn't want any more fresh starts. I wanted Dash. He was everything I'd always wanted but told myself was impossible. The one who woke me up with a cup of hot cocoa and flirted with me over Google Docs and held my hand as we soared over the East River and shared my awe and wonder over this city that had brought us together.

Most of all, he was someone who I could count on to stay, if I ever gave him the chance.

My heart was hammering inside my chest when the car pulled up down the block from Lincoln Center.

"I can't get any closer than this," the driver said, indicating the barriers that were diverting cars away.

Wishing that the platform on my white satin shoes wasn't so high, I grabbed two handfuls of skirt and made my way past the paparazzi and a horde of phone-wielding fans, to where metal barriers and a handful of uniformed policemen and people discreetly dressed in black blazers restricted access to the area around the fountain. A few members of the show's cast were still lingering outside, signing autographs and taking selfies with their fans, but neither Dash nor Lady Cerulean was anywhere to be seen.

I didn't even make it close to the crowd jostling against the barriers before a wave of defeat swept over me. I didn't have my own invitation—I'd only been Dash's plus one. There was no way they were letting me inside.

Which was fine, because this wasn't a movie, and the big moment where I declared my feelings for Dash didn't have to happen while in formal wear, in front of a crowd. I'd just . . . go home and text him tomorrow.

I turned away to find someone in breeches and a top hat getting out of a yellow cab. Her short, dark hair was slicked back and tucked behind her ears. I placed her checkered backpack a moment before I recognized her face.

"Oh, hey," I blurted out. "We met at Prince Street Pizza, right?"

"You're the one who was hanging out with the Duke, right?" she asked, and nodded to the crowd outside Lincoln Center. "Were you going in there?"

"Not without an invitation, I'm not," I admitted. "I was supposed to be somebody's plus one, but he came with someone else. And I was in such a hurry to rush over here and blurt out every single feeling I've ever had for him that I completely forgot about it."

Checkered Backpack looked at me for a moment. Surprisingly, not as if she was wondering why a near stranger was spilling her guts all over her and the sidewalk. But as if she was considering helping me. Which she did. She said, "Come on," to me and, "She's with me," to the clipboard-wielding lady at a side door a few yards away from the madness, and just . . . led me inside.

The lobby of the theater was all flashing lights, more crowded and chaotic than it had been outside. Backdrops the size of billboards with the name of the series in scrolling letters over pictures of an English manor house lined the room. In front of them, celebrities in Empire-waist gowns and extravagantly folded cravats were being interviewed by people holding mics and cameras. Even the lush, raspberry-colored carpet underfoot was stamped with the series logo, a silhouette of a horse and carriage.

In front of a green wall blooming with cascading flowers was Georgie Hart herself. Her dress was a long column of sparkling silver, but her long gloves and the cropped fur stole around her shoulders were the same bright shade of pink as her hair. Give or take a few decades, she looked almost exactly like Shirley MacLaine at the end of *What a Way to Go!* when she goes to the movie premiere with Pinky Benson in his equally pink car.

As I gawked at her, too overwhelmed to even pretend I wasn't fangirling, she parted her fur stole to reveal that the bodice of her silver gown was a bright red heart.

"Holy crap, this is unreal," I said, turning to grin at Checkered Backpack. "And you're amazing."

She held out her hand. "Actually, I'm Indira."

"Nice to meet you, Indira. I'm Mariel. I'm so grateful for your help." I smoothed my skirt down with my hands, glancing around the room again as I blurted out, "And nervous. I'm about to pull the ultimate romcom move and tell someone I love him. You know, if I can even find him in this crowd."

"The Duke, right? He's over there," Indira said, pointing out the exact center of the room, where Dash and Lady Cerulean were posing for flashing cameras.

I'd been right, that day in Times Square. Lady Cerulean looked *nothing* like me—she was taller and slimmer. And while her hair *was* a cascade of curls, they were sleek and well behaved, pulled back into an intricate bun and decorated with fuzzy pink feathers.

"Oh," I said. "Thanks. That's—" My gaze swiveled to Lady Cerulean again. "Wait. That was *her* that night at Prince Street Pizza? With the fuzzy pink barrettes?"

Indira nodded, her eyes crinkling with amusement. "We were watching *Clueless* and she got the munchies. You'd think some fake freckles and a couple of hair accessories wouldn't be enough to hide her identity, but . . ."

"People only see what they want to see," I said automatically. "Are the two of you—" My mind, which was still spinning, caught up with my mouth. "Sorry. I don't mean to pry."

"No, it's okay. Yeah, we're together, but we try to keep it as close to the vest as possible. It's not easy being with someone in the spotlight, you know? For me or for her."

I looked at Dash. Really looked at him, as I hadn't for a while. He was still as beautiful and charismatic as ever. He was doing a hair flip as I watched, and turning the full potency of his smile on the cameras pointed at him.

"No," I said. "It's not easy."

I won't lie and say I wasn't tempted to back down and back away and just , . . hide under the covers, I guess.

I'm not sure I know how to explain why I didn't. All I know is, one moment I was looking at Dash just as I'd always looked at him. And the next, I was *looking* at him. Like a romance heroine is supposed to look at the hero when she first meets him. A little dazed, like the world had slowed its spinning, or maybe sped up.

And I *knew*.

We'd been weaving a tapestry all along, he and I, bright silvery threads and warm gold ones, and it wasn't just the city we were making connections to, it was each other.

23

I don't know how much of that showed in my face. Something must have, because when Dash turned and saw me through the crowd, his lips parted.

And I think we started to drift toward each other, but I wanted him to stay in the center of it all because I'd come to say something and I wanted everyone to hear it. Because I'd been trying so hard to avoid failing in public, and if I failed at this, too, if I failed at telling Dash I loved him, I wanted the world to know it.

Not to make this premiere all about me or anything.

I reached him when he was only a few steps away from Lady Cerulean. And I guess I should have prepared a speech or something, but this is me we're talking about. Forever winging it. Though who knows—maybe telling someone you love them is the kind of thing you shouldn't rehearse or prepare for.

None of that was what came out of my mouth, because of course it didn't. I stopped in front of him, and I said, "I figured it was about time that I reenacted your favorite trope."

His expression was unreadable, his brown eyes reflecting only the photographers' lights. "I've never needed a grand gesture."

"How about a grovel, then?" I took a deep breath. "Dash, I came here to tell you that I want to do the work. For myself mostly, but also for you. Because you're worth feeling for."

My very public declaration was becoming even more so as the ball attendees held up their phones and cameras, maybe thinking this was part of the proceedings—a skit or some other performance. I focused on Dash, letting everything else fade into the background as I took another step that put me a handful of inches closer to him.

"I love how earnest and sweet you are. I love how watching you work is almost literal competence porn. I even love your horrifying coffee addiction. I . . . I could stand here and list all the things I love about you and they would number more than ten. Because the truth is, Dash, you've always been more than a buddy and more than the person I occasionally bone—you're the one who makes me feel like I can fly."

He looked at me, perfectly still.

"And Dash," I said, swallowing. "Dash, I love *you*."

It was subtle, but I noticed it—the slight shift in the set of his shoulders. The way he eased not out of character, but out of the Dash that was forever performing for everyone around him. The way he became the Dash who existed mostly for himself.

And maybe, a little bit for me, too.

My mouth was so dry that I had to swallow again before I was able to ask, lowering my voice so that only he could hear, "You know how you told me you always have trouble asking for what you want? I need to know, Dash. What do you want?"

The smile that always seemed to lurk at the corner of his lips burst across his entire face.

"You," he said, and his eyes were shining. "Just you."

This time, I was the one who held out my hand. When our fingers met, it was like fireworks going off inside me. Like morning dew glittering in the day's first rays of sunshine. Like picnic blankets and fireflies and watching movies under the stars and three-dollar beers and running through Times Square in the dead heat of summer.

He used his grip on my fingers to pull me closer. And then we were kissing. And it was wild how his touch could still make me feel like I'd been sprinkled in fairy dust, as shimmery and floaty as when we first met and every glancing touch made my body spin into an overreaction. Underneath all that, though, there was a new sensation. Or maybe it wasn't new, maybe I'd just been trying my hardest to avoid noticing it. Because when Dash and I kissed, it didn't just feel like flying—it was like I had run so far that I had reached home.

All around us, people were clapping. It was as cinematic a moment as a moment could get. But it was also real, and true.

And scary, because there was still so much more I had to tell Dash.

Just not at that exact moment—a tinkling of lights and a change in the music indicated that the screening of the series premiere was about to start, after which the ball would begin in earnest. As people in black blazers gently began herding the crowd into the next room, Dash glanced around as if remembering where he was.

And who he'd come with.

Raking a hand through his hair, he looked at Lady Cerulean, still standing a few steps away. "Milly," he said. *Milly?!* "I should . . ."

Lady Cerulean laughed at his obvious reluctance. "I'll be okay, Your Highness," she said with a subtle glance toward Indira. "You go with your girl."

Taking one glance at the crowd still waiting outside, Dash and I ducked behind a life-sized cardboard cutout of the show's main characters and found the door Indira and I had come in through. And then we were walking out into a surprisingly warm night that felt like the end of summer and the beginning of a new season, our fingers threaded together and our costumes drawing the occasional glance.

"I guess this is where I ask you if you want to stay and figure things out with me. And maybe try to see if we could work as a couple—a real one." I came to a stop, swiveling to look into Dash's face. Or so that he could look into mine, I guess, and see how much I meant what I was saying. "I know things won't be perfect, and I know I'm as liable to hurt you as you are to hurt me. But if I do, I promise I'll stick around long enough to work it out. No more running, Dash. Not unless you're running with me."

"That's probably the most romantic thing you've ever said to me," Dash teased.

"Oh, yeah? Then how's this?" I came to a stop right there on the sidewalk behind Lincoln Center and said it again. "I'm so in love with you."

"You finally figured it out, huh?" he said. "Took you long enough."

The pad of his thumb grazed my jaw, and I drew in a sharp breath at the contact. And then another when I saw that his composure had slipped. That he was choosing, as he had before, to show me the parts of him that he kept from everyone else—including the naked longing that made his lashes flutter when he said, "I guess it's pretty obvious by now that I have feelings for you."

"What feelings?" I demanded, reaching for his crisp white shirt-front and holding on, not caring if I wrinkled it because the Dash I loved wasn't the perfect, polished, charismatic Dash he presented to the camera and everyone else.

The Dash I loved was the one who let all the layers of who he was to everyone else fall away until it was just him, standing in front of me.

He smiled. "All of them."

It would have been the perfect moment for another kiss. Instead of lowering his face to mine, though, Dash reached into his pocket and pulled something out. "So, the real reason I talked myself out of going to burlesque night is that I had this whole plan to give you this."

I narrowed my eyes at him. "I swear to God, Dashwood, if that's an engagement ring—"

"It's strings," he said, with this bashful curl to his lips as he opened his hand and showed me what he was holding. "You said you wanted some, remember?"

My throat felt tight as I picked up the threads he'd carefully wound together into a bracelet. "You unbearable sap," I said softly.

"A sap, huh? You know what you are?" Dash asked me.

"I have a good idea, but I think I'll like your version better."

"You're like finding the pot of gold at the end of a rainbow. Only you're made out of rainbow, too, all color and light and glistening raindrops." He wrapped his arms around my waist and pulled me even closer, his lips brushing my earlobe when he said, "I love you, too, you know."

Liquid warmth trickled through me. For the longest time, hope had felt like building a home on quicksand. Watching Dash smile down at me, I felt the ground firming up beneath me.

It was a while before we pulled apart. When we did, Dash linked our fingers together again and began pulling me down the street. "Come on."

"Where are we going?"

"To celebrate you finishing your screenplay—with a real scoop of strawberry ice cream. With syrup and sprinkles and cereal and everything you want loaded on it."

I grinned at him. "Plus make-up sex?"

"Plus make-up sex." Dash flipped his hair and paused to give me the kind of foot-popping kiss that would make Mia Thermopolis weak in the knees. "And maybe a happily ever after of our own?"

I stroked Dash's shoulder blade, right where the words *Happy endings, they never bored me* were tattooed into his skin. And I found myself confessing something I'd never told anyone, not even Yaz. "I want it so badly," I murmured. "A happily ever after. I feel like I've been chasing it for as long as I've been alive."

"You're not the only one." Dash lifted my hand to his lips to brush a kiss over my knuckles. "I was scared that maybe mine had passed me by."

"The universe isn't that cruel, Dash. You were always going to get your happy ending."

And now, maybe, so was I.

EPILOGUE

```
INT. THE DUKE'S DRAWING ROOM—DAY

In the FOREGROUND, THE DUKE OF HARDING stands
by the window. At the sound of footsteps, he
turns around.


    THE DUKE OF HARDING (smiling softly)
   I've been waiting for you, darling. Have
   you come to
```

D: I made pancakes.

M: I love you.

D: Yes, that's an extremely appropriate reaction to pancakes.

M: No, I mean. *I love you.*

D: By which you mean you want me to bring them to you in bed.

M: However did you guess? See, Dashwood, this is why you're the perfect man for me. You always know what I'm

"The Slot Sluts are going to be here in three hours. We better hurry up and get to the laundromat if we're going to be on time for lunch," Dash said as he came into his room, bearing a plate of pancakes and two forks.

The buttery, syrupy smell reached me where I was still ensconced under his duvet, not ready yet to exchange its warmth for the chilly October air.

"Don't even worry about it," I told him as he claimed his spot on the mattress. "I only have a few loads to do. Plus, you'll notice that I'm all packed up."

He glanced at the corner of his bedroom where I had deposited my suitcases when I'd come over the day before. "You sure you're only going to Los Angeles for a week? Because it looks like you packed for two months. At least."

"Nah—one of those is for all the accessories I'll be buying at estate sales. And books. Shy gave me a whole list of paperbacks I'm supposed to track down for them."

Grace and I had been working on another project of our own that was similar in vibes—if not in content—to the Duke of Harding, and our agent had gotten us a meeting with a studio.

While I was gone, Dash was going to start on his next window for Second Chance. I'd already seen the sketches—a big swath of canvas painted to look like the night sky, tiny pinpricks made in it to make the store's lights look like stars shining through. Two figures painted on the glass of the window itself would look like they were stargazing. Dash was still trying to work out how to suspend books from the ceiling like he'd done the LED lights.

I held up a corner of the duvet so that Dash and the pancakes could join me under it. He pressed in close to me, handing me a fork.

It wasn't that I wasn't still scared of how full my ace of cups was. Here, though, in Dash's bed, with the scent of pancakes in the air, I could almost believe that all the good things in it would never spill out.

ACKNOWLEDGMENTS

This book wouldn't be in your hands if it weren't for my eternally encouraging and supportive agent, Sarah E. Younger. I'm so grateful to her for believing in me and my stories and for calmly listening every time I go on and on about a new plotbunny (usually when I'm supposed to be working on something else).

Many, many thanks to my enthusiastic and insightful editor at Primero Sueño Press, Norma Perez-Hernandez. I'm so thankful for all the effort she devoted to helping me polish this manuscript into something that leaves me all shimmery and floaty inside, and I'm so excited that we get to keep working together.

Everyone at Primero Sueño Press and Nancy Yost Literary Agency get my eternal appreciation for all their work in making this dream of mine a reality.

I owe all the gratitude to Lory Wendy for playing along when I burst into WhatsApp one day to procrastinate on a deadline with a random conversation about Regency-themed spice. (Don't ask!) She deserves all the donuts and sugary drinks for her unflagging patience and sense of humor in the face of my chaos—and for that day in Orlando when she broke out the plotting Post-its to keep me from hyperventilating because I had no idea how to get to the end of this book.

A huge thank-you to Lorena Zimmerman for giving me Mariel's name when we were coworking and I thought I was writing a fun little short story. Little did we know that Mariel was too much to be contained in five thousand words!

Many, many thanks (and frozen passion fruit juice!) to Priscilla Hamilton, whose brain is as big as her heart, for guiding me through potential reasons for Yaz's corporate law woes. I know literally nothing about that world, so any mistakes or wild inaccuracies are definitely on me.

My brilliant sister gets credit for helping me name Fling and for taking me to Prince Street Pizza, even if all my lactose intolerant self could do was steal the pepperonis from her slice. Don't worry, we already made plans to find some dairy-free pizza the next time we're in the city together.

I wrote most of this book with two good little boys sitting at my feet. Goro is currently living his best life in Germany with his parents. Sadly, Kalam is no longer with us, but he lives forever in the pages of this book. Thank you for the company and the distractions, gorditos. I miss you both!

And finally, thank you to New York City for being a second home whenever I've most needed one. I've bawled in the subway, soared starry-eyed over the East River, strolled from Manhattan to Brooklyn and back again, always dreaming.

ABOUT THE AUTHOR

Lydia San Andres lives and writes in the tropics, where she can be found reading, sipping coffee, and making excuses to stay out of the sun. As much as she enjoys air-conditioning, she can sometimes be lured outside with the promise of cookies and picnics. Find her on Instagram, Threads, Bluesky, and TikTok, @lydiaallthetime and on her website lydiasanandres.com.